Has Anybody Seen My Earl?

The Hellion Club, Book Ten

by Chasity Bowlin

ARE YOU SIGNED UP FOR DRAGONBLADE'S BLOG?

You'll get the latest news and information on exclusive giveaways, exclusive excerpts, coming releases, sales, free books, cover reveals and more.

Check out our complete list of authors, too!

No spam, no junk. That's a promise!

Sign Up Here

www.dragonbladepublishing.com

Dearest Reader;

Thank you for your support of a small press. At Dragonblade Publishing, we strive to bring you the highest quality Historical Romance from some of the best authors in the business. Without your support, there is no 'us', so we sincerely hope you adore these stories and find some new favorite authors along the way.

Happy Reading!

CEO, Dragonblade Publishing

Additional Dragonblade books by
Author Chasity Bowlin

The Hellion Club Series
A Rogue to Remember (Book 1)
Barefoot in Hyde Park (Book 2)
What Happens in Piccadilly (Book 3)
Sleepless in Southampton (Book 4)
When an Earl Loves a Governess (Book 5)
The Duke's Magnificent Obsession (Book 6)
The Governess Diaries (Book 7)
A Dangerous Passion (Book 8)
The Lady Confesses (Book 9)
Has Anybody Seen My Earl? (Book 10)
Making Spirits Bright (Novella)
All I Want for Christmas (Novella)
The Boys of Summer (Novella)
When The Night Closes In (Novella)
The Lady in White (Novella)

The Lost Lords Series
The Lost Lord of Castle Black (Book 1)
The Vanishing of Lord Vale (Book 2)
The Missing Marquess of Althorn (Book 3)
The Resurrection of Lady Ramsleigh (Book 4)
The Mystery of Miss Mason (Book 5)
The Awakening of Lord Ambrose (Book 6)
Hyacinth (Book 7)
A Midnight Clear (Novella)

The Lyon's Den Series
Fall of the Lyon
Tamed by the Lyon
Lady Luck and the Lyon

The Lyon, the Liar and the Scandalous Wardrobe

Pirates of Britannia Series
The Pirate's Bluestocking

Also from Chasity Bowlin
Into the Night (Novella)

Part One

Chapter One

The Conversation

London, May 17, 1840

MARINA ASHTON WAS not the belle of the ball though the Farringtons were hardly renowned for hosting the event of the Season. Though the event was technically in her honor—well, in Stanford's honor—she was content to remain in the background at the small gathering. In fact, that suited her perfectly. The Season she had so looked forward to was not really what she had imagined. It wasn't vanity to say that she was beautiful. In truth, beauty was a bit of a nuisance. She'd quickly come to realize that her appearance was a commodity to some and a source of contention to others. Then, of course, there was the fortune.

An indiscreet comment made by a clerk in the office of her uncle's solicitor had disclosed to one and all amongst the *ton* that she was a very wealthy young woman, despite her somewhat scandalous beginnings. Subsequently, whomever married her would be incredibly wealthy.

Between her appearance and those unfortunately truthful rumors abounding regarding the fortune her Uncle Devil had set aside for her, she'd discovered the very double-edged sword of being sought after to such a dizzying degree. And in all, she'd been terribly disheartened and disillusioned. Gentlemen who had not even bothered to dance with her prior were suddenly writing odes to her beauty and dancing attendance upon her.

All the gossip had brought far too much of the wrong sort of attention. But Stanford had been there all along, courting her, being quietly attentive and respectful at all times. The perfect gentleman, she thought, long before her financial status had been disclosed to one and all. In truth, that lack of foreknowledge about her future means had seemed such a reassuring fact early on. But like so many things in her life, she found herself doubtful. It was grossly unfair of her. He'd given no indication that his motives were anything but pure. He was always a perfect gentleman, never even trying to steal a kiss. He'd insisted to take such liberties would be a dishonor to them both. And so she was two days away from her wedding and had not yet been kissed. *Which did nothing to reassure her that he was marrying her for the right reasons.*

Marina clenched her fists at her side. And inside her glove, she felt the small, folded note she'd tucked securely away earlier. The corner of it bit into her flesh.

It had arrived only that morning and with it had come the sinking feeling that perhaps Stanford's reticence to take liberties had less to do with honor and more to do with the fact that his heart was engaged elsewhere. How she'd wanted the words on that small, nondescript bit of stationery to be false—to be something she could share with Stanford and together they would laugh about it. But she hadn't shown it to him. Indeed, she hadn't shown it to anyone. She'd hidden it away and not spoken of it to a soul. But she'd read it. Again and again throughout the day, she'd pored over it, looking for some indication of the anonymous sender's identity. Alas, she could only trust their signature at the bottom of the page. *"A Concerned Acquaintance."*

Slipping the note from inside her glove, Marina scoured it once more. She didn't worry about being observed. Even at such a small gathering, where everyone present knew that she was very firmly off the marriage mart, no one paid her the least bit of mind. She could disappear a bit, blend into the background.

Initially, when she'd noticed the effect, it had been a relief. It was as if a weight had been lifted from her. Now it was a necessity. And this would be her last opportunity to act with any sort of subversiveness. The next time everyone present would be assembled would be on her wedding day. Her cloak of invisibility would vanish then, once she was dressed in all her bridal finery and walking down the aisle. All eyes would be on her once more. It had been an exciting prospect before.

Before the note. And after the note. How could one tiny slip of paper alter her life so completely that it should be demarcated as before and after its arrival?

Perhaps it was the proximity of her leap from being a girl to being someone's wife which had her feeling so out of sorts. Her wedding, much anticipated by everyone in her family and most of society, as well, was scheduled for only two days hence. Two days until she was to become Mrs. Stanford Williams. Two days until her uncle would escort her to the altar and "give" her to a man that she was beginning to wonder if she even knew at all… and with the entirety of the *ton* watching. Her stomach tightened and the room seemed to spin a bit. A couple waltzed past her—so close the young woman's skirts whipped at her own. Watching them spin about intensified the nausea that assailed her. Even then, she had a moment of envy. Staring at that young woman, so obviously enamored of her partner, she appeared so carefree and so very full of life. And free of doubt.

The weight of the betrothal ring on her hand was a tangible reminder of why such things no longer mattered. Mentally, Marina ticked off all the many reasons her current position was so enviable. She had secured an excellent match for herself—while he wasn't a titled gentleman, he was most definitely a gentleman and one of significant fortune. He was handsome and articulate and kind, if a bit reserved at times. Always perfectly proper, he never put a foot wrong in society—a boon given her somewhat scandalous background. In short, Stanford was everything she could have dreamed of. Even her uncle, exacting as he had been in considering any suitor who had dared come to call, had been unable to find fault.

And until that morning she hadn't the slightest qualms about marrying him. But all that had changed with the letter that arrived in its nondescript glory.

She might have ignored it altogether but for one thing. Every event that had been hinted at in that letter had come to pass. He'd declined to accompany them, instead insisting upon meeting them there. No sooner had they arrived, than he'd greeted them and immediately departed to the card room. And now, only ten minutes later, she'd watched him taking a circuitous route around the ballroom and down the corridor farthest from the card room on the pretext of needing to speak to a business acquaintance. It wouldn't have been suspicious, note aside, as he rarely danced attendance upon her at such events. Stanford was always circumspect. He'd been a consistent suitor if not an ardent one.

Now, watching him take that circuitous route around the ballroom, her heart sank. He was heading for the corridor where the retiring rooms were. *Along with other rooms that she knew were often utilized for secret trysts.*

That clandestine exit not only deepened her suspicions but also her resolve to discern the truth of it all. The other accusations in the letter swarmed in her mind like bees. *Fortune hunter. Unfaithful. Lying. Scheming. Never loved her.* And all of those thoughts were only punctuated by one entirely of her own making. *He's never even kissed me.*

Thinking of the last time she'd asked him to kiss her, all but pleaded with him in truth, and his very pat answer about propriety and honor, she burned with the humiliation of it. Never mind that every betrothed couple skated along the lines of impropriety a bit. Never mind that it was common knowledge that most betrothed couples, at least in private, would display such affection for one another. Kissing, for a betrothed couple, was not considered scandalous at all unless one did it in full view of everyone. The letter called into question his motivation for denying her such reassurance of his affection and desire for her. Perhaps it had nothing at all to do with altruistic reasons and far more to do with the fact that she was simply not the one he desired.

"Forgive me, Aunt Willa. I must excuse myself to the ladies' withdrawing room." She hadn't even realized she'd made a decision until the words escaped her.

Willa looked at her with concern. "Are you well, Marina?"

"Quite," Marina lied. "My head aches a bit, but the quiet will help with that I think." That part at least was true.

"Should I accompany you?"

Marina looked past her to her Aunt Lillian. "No, not at all. Aunt Lillian has only just returned to town. Enjoy catching up with her, and I will rejoin you shortly."

Leaving them talking amongst themselves, she skirted the ballroom and headed down the corridor to where the withdrawing rooms were. But she sailed past the door to the withdrawing room and made for the terrace doors at the end of the corridor. Doors that were still slightly ajar. As she neared them, she slowed her steps, all but tiptoeing as she moved as surreptitiously as possible into position, concealing herself within the folds of the draperies.

Beyond the glass panes, she could hear voices. Hushed whispers that sounded impossibly intimate. She recognized Stanford's voice, but he spoke to the person on that terrace with him in a way he'd never spoken to her. *Like a lover.*

"Stanford, I can't bear it!" the unknown woman said.

"If there were any other way, my love, you know that I would be with you! Marrying so far beneath me, given the truly indecent circumstances of her birth and the scandalous way her uncle carried on—marrying his niece's very own governess—but, alas, I have no choice. Even now, I am hovering on the brink of ruin. What I have is only the illusion of wealth… and no illusion can be maintained indefinitely. If I were to follow my heart and the two of us could wed… Alas, it would never work. You are not free to marry where you please and neither am I. One can weather a scandal if flush enough to bear up under it. I am not. When the truth comes out about my debts, I will be ruined, and you will be ruined with me. You cannot risk it, my love."

"I can't simply watch you marry that wretched girl! Not when she will never be worthy of you," the unknown woman all but shouted. "Why didn't you ask for my hand years ago?"

"Shush, my darling. Your family would never have permitted you to marry me given the state of my finances and the fact they were only too well aware of them. Your own father held the mortgage, after all... and now your brother."

"Perhaps, if all the obstacles in our path were cleared away, and we were to marry, then he might forgive the debt if you asked."

"I cannot, my darling. You know that. I would never be able to forgive myself for taking such charity from anyone. This is the only way. I must marry her, though there is no doubt I will spend each day wishing she were you."

"What about me? Am I to be trapped in a loveless marriage forever? I will wither away into a wretched old crone while waiting for you to be free!"

He sighed heavily. It might have been sadness, but in all likelihood, it was exasperation. The melodramatic and pleading tone of his companion was enough to grate on anyone's nerves, Marina thought with no small degree of bitterness.

"I would never ask that of you," he said. "I am not in a position to ever be your husband and while it will pain me to say it, I cannot envision a way in which you would ever be permitted to be my wife. But just because we are not wed, we need not part. There is no reason that we cannot simply go on as we have for so long already."

"Be your mistress? Warm your bed and fulfill your needs while you parade the daughter of a harlot all about town?"

"*It's the only way. Think before you speak rashly, my love. I beg of you.*"

The terrace doors opened, and Marina made herself as small as possible, shrinking back into heavy velvet drapes which were not so different in color from her own gown. From her hiding place, she could now see the identity of the woman. *Lady Crowden.*

"Don't leave me like this… Can't you slip away with me for a bit?"

He looked back at her and Marina did her best to stand as still as possible lest she alert either of them to her presence. "Not now. We've both been gone from the ballroom for far too long already. But later… after supper. I'll slip—ostensibly to the card room—you'll plead a headache and make for our little bower in Bloomsbury."

Stanford walked away, leaving the other woman standing there in the hall, dejected. Still Marina did not move or make a sound. A confrontation with Lady Crowden was the last thing she wished to have when she was already so off balance by everything that had transpired.

Marina had heard enough. More than enough. Lady Crowden made her way along the corridor and as quietly as possible, Marina slipped from her hiding place. This time she did go to the ladies' retiring room. Ducking behind one of the many screens that had been placed about the room for privacy to repair hems and torn flounces or to see to more personal needs, she focused all her efforts on simply taking in one gulping breath after another without retching.

Why on earth should it matter to Lady Crowden if Stanford were to wed when she was already married to another? Never mind that she was a good ten years Stanford's senior and her marriage to Lord Crowden had failed to produce a child, though he had several daughters from his previous wife. Stanford would never marry her even if she were free because she could not give him what he needed, what he insisted was so important to him— an heir. Though now it became clear there was nothing to inherit. Those thoughts raced through Marina's mind, but on their heels came others that were even more distressing.

He'd told her he loved her. He'd painted such a sweet picture for her of what their life would be like together. Was he lying to her? Or was he lying to his now-embittered lover? And ultimately, did that even matter? If he was capable of such a grand deception, he was clearly not the man she had thought him to be. But their wedding was only two days hence.

Two days!

If she broke things off now the scandal would be horrendous. It would destroy her socially. It would wreak havoc upon her family. How could she not go through with it when the choices she made could mar her cousins' reputations for life? Isabella would be making her debut in ten years. And ten years was not enough time to make the whispers vanish. Marina knew that from personal experience. Even now, a decade and a half had passed since her mother's untimely death, and she was still reviled. If Marina walked into a room full of people, her trans-gressions were still whispered about. And from Stanford's own lips, she would forever be tainted by them.

Chapter Two

The Wedding

May 19, 1840

WILLA KEPT HER smile firmly in place as she stared out over the gathered crowd occupying the pews of St. George's Church in Hanover Square. Half of them were not their friends or even people they cared to know. And most of them had been invited by Mr. Williams. But the other half—her smile shifted to one of genuine happiness. Effie was there along with her handsome duke. Lillian and Valentine were as well. Other girls whom she had grown up with at the Darrow School and who had become like family to her were in attendance—some still unmarried and working as governesses or companions and others who had married exceptionally well and moved from one of society's lower tiers into far grander positions. Though that had certainly never been the motivation for any of them.

Despite the pleasant prospect of having a moment to see and catch up with her old friends during the wedding breakfast, Willa could not stop the feeling that something truly awful was about to happen. She tried, with all her might, to simply dismiss it as nerves, but she couldn't.

She felt the approach more than she saw it, and when she glanced to her left, Effie had exited her pew and made a beeline for her.

"What is the matter?"

Willa sighed. "Am I so obvious?"

Effie shook her head. "Certainly not to anyone else. But I know that you are worried. She will be fine. It's a good match, isn't it?"

"On the face of it… yes," Willa answered.

Effie arched one eyebrow. "And beneath the face of it?"

Willa's expression tightened as she met Effie's worried gaze. "I wish I knew. I simply cannot stop thinking that something horrible is about to happen."

"If it does, then we will address it," Effie offered with her normal pragmatism. "Worrying about such will not prevent it from happening and there is little point in anticipating how to solve a problem that has not yet occurred… and may never occur for all that. But should something happen, you know that Marina will always have our full support. As will you."

The organist hit a note from the massive instrument positioned in the gallery above them. It was their cue. Guests hurried to their seats and the loud buzz of conversation receded to a quiet hum.

Effie squeezed her arm once more, a swift gesture of reassurance and then retreated to her seat. Willa did the same, taking her place in the pew nearest the altar, her gaze fixed on the door where Marina would enter on Devil's arm. Isabella would be behind them, along with Lillian's daughter, Deirdre, who was a few years younger, acting as her bridesmaids. They were being entrusted with the task of keeping Marina's veil from getting snagged on anything as she walked down the aisle.

Was that the source of her anxiety? Praying that the little girls could manage the task and Marina's gown or veil would not be ripped or that she might trip and fall? Those were certainly terrible options but not catastrophic. How she hoped that was all!

The doors opened and Devil stood there, handsome as ever. Tall and straight, with his hair combed back from his forehead, it nearly took her breath away. The man truly was ridiculously handsome. Seventeen years together and still he took her breath away. But it was not the time to be distracted by him. Forcing her gaze to her niece, Willa's heart stuttered in her chest.

Marina did not appear to be a happy bride. Her face was pale, her steps slow and hesitant. But there was a tension in her that she had never seen before. As if the weight of the world was pressing down on her, she thought. Was it simply nerves?

As they walked in, the notes of the pipe organ ringing out, and Devil caught her eye. It wasn't simply her, Willa realized. He too was concerned. Had Marina said something to him? Was she having second thoughts about the marriage? Had Stanford Williams done something to make her regret consenting to his proposal?

The minister began the service, his monotonous drone filling the near silence of the church with his somewhat nasally speech. She had attended services presided over by him countless times and never before, Willa thought, had she found him so terribly annoying. But her gaze stayed firmly on Marina. And on Devil who continued to stand at the front of the congregation as he waited on the minister to ask that very pointed question of who was giving Marina away. She almost hoped he would refuse. Something was terribly wrong. Her poor girl looked as though she were going to the gallows rather than the altar.

"Into which holy estate these two persons present: come now to be joined. Therefore, if any man can show any just cause why they may not lawfully be joined so together: Let him now speak, or else hereafter forever hold his peace," the minister intoned and then paused, waiting for someone to speak up.

Willa had to bite her tongue.

When no one stood up and shouted down the match as the travesty that it now appeared to be, the minister continued, "I require and charge you (as you will answer at the dread full day of judgment, when the secrets of all hearts shall be disclosed) that if either of you do know any impediment, why ye may not be lawfully joined together in matrimony, that ye confess it. For be ye well assured, that so many as be coupled together otherwise than God's word doth allow: are not joined of God, neither is their matrimony lawful."

Neither of them spoke, Marina and Mr. Williams facing the cleric with stoic expressions.

"Stanford Carlisle Williams, wilt thou have this woman to be thy wedded wife, to live together after God's ordinance in the holy estate of matrimony? Wilt thou love her, comfort her, honor, and keep her in sickness and in health? And forsaking all others keep thee only to her, so long as you both shall live?"

Stanford cleared his throat. "I will."

The myopic little man turned to Marina, blinking as he took in her deathly pale appearance. But still he spoke, "Marina Elizabeth Ashton, wilt thou have this man to be thy wedded husband, to live together after God's ordinance, in the holy estate of matrimony? Wilt thou obey him, and serve him, love, honor, and keep him in sickness and in health? And forsaking all others keep thee only to him, so long as you both shall live?"

Silence stretched interminably. So much so that the sound of a pin dropping would have been akin to cannon fire. Finally, the minister cleared his throat and asked, "And forsaking all others keep thee only to him, so long as you both shall live?"

Marina opened her mouth to reply, but no sound emerged. And as Willa stared on in horror, the bride simply sank to the floor in a dead faint.

DEVIL DIDN'T HESITATE, nor did he feel the need to offer any explanation. Instead, he simply scooped Marina up into his arms and carried her out of the church. He'd known. The entire way over in the carriage. He. Had. Known.

Something was wrong. He'd even questioned her if she really wanted to go through with it. Her answer both puzzled and worried him.

What else would I do?

There had been no protestations of her love for Stanford Williams or even any indication that she wished to become his wife. Instead, she had appeared resolute. Resolute and terribly unhappy.

So now, as he carried her out of the cathedral and to the waiting carriage, he didn't bother to offer explanations to anyone. Those who loved her and cared for her would seek them at home. And those who didn't could just hang.

Loading her into the waiting carriage, he looked back just as Willa emerged from the church, racing toward them. He helped her in, climbed in after, and then rapped sharply on the roof. "Home!"

"What is happening?" Willa asked him. "Until two days ago, the night of the Farringtons' ball, she could not have been happier to marry him… I thought."

"I don't know either," Devil said. "But I vowed she would never be forced to marry where she did not love. And if she has misgivings about Williams then we will support her in that. Whatever the cost."

Tears glinted on Willa's lashes. "You truly are the best of men. You've no notion, even now all these years later, how good you really are."

"I protect those I love. Because I know how great the cost is for doing anything else. I will not see her succumb to the same fate that her poor mother did. I will not fail a second time."

"It was never your failure."

"It wasn't only mine," he conceded. "I will grant that, but I cannot absolve myself completely when my sister is no longer here. All I can do is as I have done already and devote myself to seeing Marina happy and safe."

"There will be scandal," Willa said.

Marina stirred on the seat. Devil nodded. "Then so be it."

Willa nodded in agreement. "Indeed. So be it."

Chapter Three

The Rejected Groom

S TANFORD WILLIAMS STOOD at the altar listening to the buzz of whispers that slowly grew to a deafening roar. What had happened? What the devil had just happened?

"Sir, will the young lady be returning?" the minister asked.

"I've no notion what she'll do," Stanford snapped. "And she's no lady. Clearly. No lady of breeding would have dared behave so poorly."

"Perhaps she is ill," the minister suggested. "Young lad—women have such delicate constitutions and are quite prone to hysteria. I'm certain things can be corrected."

They couldn't. Because he couldn't marry her now. Not after such an embarrassing incident. That sort of scandal was the very last thing he could have. His only hope was to turn it all around on her. To make her the villain.

"No. This insult will not be forgiven," he said. "I have stead-fastly stood by her, ignoring all the whispers and rumors of her fast behavior. I longed to give her the benefit of my trust and to deny that she was indeed her mother's daughter. Alas, I can no longer."

There was a shift then in the tone of the whispers that filled the church. There was certainly still shock and no amount of enthusiasm for the drama that was unfolding, but there were also whispers of assent. Whispers of misdeeds long past but never forgotten.

With his head high, Stanford left the church, walking past the stunned guests as he made his way to the street. His carriage was waiting there. And as he glanced across the street, he saw her. Astrid, Lady Crowden. She wore an expression that could only be described as gleeful. Stupid woman, he thought, with no small amount of bitterness. She'd been useful to him. But she longed to be loved and adored. She craved adoration the ways one craved food, water, or even opium. The need for it was an affliction of unparalleled strength. And he'd used that. But now, there was bitterness. After all, she had been the one to suggest that he pay court to Marina Ashton, the one who had told him in the strictest of confidence about the ridiculously generous marriage portion her uncle had settled upon her. In short, Astrid, his lover and partner in the Machiavellian scheme, had failed him.

Without acknowledging her presence, he simply placed one foot in front of the other and strode away in the opposite direction. There were other wealthy women he could woo and wed. Women who would be far more malleable than Marina Ashton ever would have. He'd get himself one of those. They wouldn't have the same degree of social currency. After all, bastard or no, Marina was the niece of a powerful lord and was doted on by numerous powerful and well-regarded family connections. Marrying her would have given him the sort of power and social cachet that he'd been scrabbling to attain throughout his life. It had been within his grasp and slipped through his fingers as ephemeral as smoke.

It wasn't simply anger or even wounded pride that kept his blood hot in those moments. It was a sense of being wronged, of being denied the very things he was entitled to by virtue of having been willing to sully himself with one born so low. He'd followed her around like some callow youth, making a fool of himself, only to be rejected in the most public of fashions. That was an affront he would not forgive. And once he'd paid his own debts, he'd extract his pound of flesh from those who had wronged him. Astrid and Marina, as well.

Part Two

Chapter Four

The Reluctant Earl

January 14, 1842

CALEB HALLIWELL HAD come to London for one reason alone. He was in dire need of a wife. The magnitude of the fortune he would forfeit if he chose not to pursue wedded bliss was beyond considering. The very idea of sacrificing so much for the sake of bachelorhood, which in all honesty had not been nearly so much fun as he'd been led to believe, was nothing short of foolishness.

His very recently departed great-uncle had left him both a title and a hefty inheritance if—and *only* if—he got himself married to a society miss. A London society miss, at that. She had to be at least loosely connected to someone with a title. There was only one great obstacle to his quest. He deplored society. He found it awkward and trivial and terribly dull. Not to mention, he would have the devil of a time finding a wife of his own when so much of his time and energy was now being devoted to fending off the already married women of the *ton*. They'd scented him like predators in the wild.

He wasn't so vain as to mistake, or overestimate, his own appeal. Handsome enough if far from the patrician prettiness of the aristocracy, he was taller by a head than most men with the raw-boned frame of a man who'd done hard labor. In short, he was something of a novelty to them. Because he'd worked with his hands. Because he'd dug in the mines himself, gotten dirty, and was rough enough around the edges to show it. The same reason they all turned their noses up at him was the very same reason many of them were turning back their covers and inviting him into their beds.

"Is it really so dire? You're an earl for heaven's sake! One would think you'd be sought after by most of the ladies. Surely there is something in your current situation to be enjoyed?"

Caleb turned to Jacob Danvers, his oldest friend and his companion in the current madness. They'd gone to University together, though Jacob's father had only been a clerk in the mining company Caleb's grandfather had owned. Jacob had been put through school with the understanding that he would come to work for the mines in the same capacity that his father had done, but as time wore on, it became quite clear that work was a concept Jacob deplored merely on principle. He certainly had no practical experience with it.

It had never seemed an insurmountable gap in their stations—he the heir to the mine's founder and his friend the son of an employee—not until recently at any rate. Not until every time someone addressed Caleb as "my lord" or called him the Earl of St. Aiden. Then there was something in Jacob's expression which would shift, a hardness entering his gaze and a sudden bite to his words. Jealousy was both an ugly emotion and a dangerous one. Friendships had been destroyed for much less than a title.

"I have no desire to be pursued to such degree by the masses or their very eager and terrifying mothers. I need one woman. One suitable, tolerable woman," Caleb groused. "That is all. This entire mess is not of my choosing—neither the title nor the hunt for a wife."

"What the devil does that mean? Suitable and tolerable?"

Caleb shrugged. It was simple enough to his mind. "I want only to meet a young lady whom I can get on reasonably well with, pretty enough that marriage to her will not feel like a chore and who can, I pray, hold a conversation about something other than fashion or gossip. Is it so wrong to hope that, despite the rather bloodless impetus put upon me to marry quickly, I should still hope to marry at least contentedly?"

Jacob shrugged. "I know of no man content in a married state. It seems unnatural. One woman for the rest of one's life—well, if one buys into all that rot. You should hope to find a woman of a practical enough nature to appreciate a husband who won't be forever demanding she bear the fruitful burden of his attentions."

"No such woman exists," Caleb said dismissively. And in truth, he had no desire to meet or marry a woman who'd meet that description.

"And that is why the state of matrimony is not for one such as me. No, thank you. I'll continue my carefree carousing like a tom cat until I cock up my toes."

Caleb said nothing. Jacob's carousing was a source of consternation for him. The small bequest his grandfather had left to Jacob's father had already been frittered away along with everything else he might have passed down to his son. Lost to brothels and hells, the money that should have secured his friend's future had been squandered on momentary pleasures.

In that moment, Caleb was suddenly distracted from any concerns he might have over his friend's poor behavior and poorer decisions. It was like being struck by lightning. Like the clouds parting for the sun, he could now see precisely what—and who—he wanted. Whatever sun idioms came to mind, she was definitely a creature far more inclined to moonlight. Pale skin, eyes of midnight blue, and a cascade of black curls that were darker than a raven's wing—she was simply stunning beyond words. And she seemed to be both in the crowd and well above it at the same time. They milled about her, but she paid them not the least bit of mind. Self-contained, he thought. And that appealed to him greatly.

"Who is she?" Caleb asked, almost whispering the question to himself.

"The dark one?"

Caleb couldn't actually speak to respond, so he simply nodded.

"I have no idea. Perhaps you should beg our hostess for an introduction... once she's done with you, of course." Jacob offered the last with a teasing note.

Caleb grimaced. He would have done just that, asking for the introduction that was. But he knew Lady Crowden would likely demand he service her like a stud in exchange for the favor and he was not inclined to do so. Given that they'd met because she'd cornered him on a darkened path at Cremorne Gardens and kissed him, quite soundly, before he'd even recognized who she was—well, that was the only reason he'd been invited at all that night. She wanted much more from him than a mere kiss. And while he was not inclined to give it to her, it would be a mistake to offend her. She was a powerful hostess in society. Putting himself outside of her good graces would result in a dearth of invitations, making his search for a bride inherently more difficult. "No. I'll find out on my own."

Jacob shook his head, clucking his tongue. "You cannot simply introduce yourself to the young woman, Caleb. She isn't a miner in the fields to be approached with a hearty handshake! Society misses such as that rare beauty require introductions. Then they require calls. And letters. Posies and chocolates and carting them about in Hyde Park—let them parade you around like a dog on a leash."

Caleb turned to Jacob with one brow lifted skeptically. "Have you always been so jaded?"

"Have you always been so naive? You'll have to toady to the girl for weeks before you'll even get to know her well enough to discover whether you like something other than her pretty face," Jacob answered with a sneer. "And then, if you don't, you'll be starting all over again with the next one, won't you?"

It had become a familiar refrain. Whenever Caleb had seen any woman who had piqued his interest, though none had done so with such immediacy as the woman before him, Jacob had been the naysayer. The voice of doom. The obstacle in his path. Not for the first time, Caleb wondered why his friend seemed so determined to keep him from making a match. "I will find a way to speak with her, Jacob. Perhaps you'd have more fun at one of the clubs on St. James Street? These ballrooms full of young misses apparently bore you to tears." It was true enough; Jacob was yawning through Caleb's reply.

"And miss seeing you make a fool of yourself? I think not."

"I'm going to speak to some other acquaintances present and see if perhaps anyone—other than Lady Crowden—can manage an introduction." With that, Caleb walked away, leaving Jacob to stare after him. It sent an icy frisson down his spine to present his back to a man he would have, not so very long ago, trusted with his funds, his secrets, and even his life.

MISS MARINA ASHTON smiled politely at the aging man she had just danced with. Dance partners were not so plentiful for her now that she could afford to turn one down. Despite the age spots on his hands, his balding pate and pudgy middle, it had been a pleasant dance. He'd been a perfect gentleman—simply not the gentleman for her. She had begun to believe no such gentleman existed. After all, in her first Season, she'd been courted by some of the most eligible bachelors amongst the *ton*. And she'd scorned them all in favor of Stanford. Recalling what it had once been like, to be so sought after, even if for the wrong reasons, her current predicament was almost laughable.

After she'd returned to society, two years following the debacle at the altar, she'd been hopeful, if only briefly, that her life might take on some semblance of how it had been before. But those hopes had been quickly dashed and had now been replaced with the kind of ennui that made every society event seem a chore. And every man who looked at her now, who paid her the least bit of attention, was suspect, at least to her mind. In fact, Marina had become so convinced that there was no one for her, that she'd all but given up on the idea of marriage, though for the sake of appearances, she still had to maintain the illusion that she was on the hunt. After all, any young woman professing to have no interest in marriage was an object of curiosity. She'd drawn enough attention to herself already.

Her dance card was empty for the next set, which was something of a relief actually. The hem of her pale-pink silk ball gown had been trodden upon several times already. It was an unfortunate byproduct of being relegated to dancing with less eligible men. From belle of the ball to the purgatory of not quite a wallflower. Of course, she was believed to be a jilt, a tease, a fickle miss who didn't know her own mind. And Stanford's pettiness in retelling the tale of it countless times in the wake of their failed wedding had done nothing to mitigate that sort of gossip.

Neither had it helped that she'd refused so many suitors in her first Season. And with good reason, after all, since they had only bothered to court her after discovering that becoming her husband would obtain a fortune for them. Was it any wonder she'd turned them down? It was grossly unfair to be thought of as fickle and inconstant when, in fact, she'd refused so many offers of marriage precisely because she did know her own mind. Of course, not even the promise of a fortune could tempt most men to court the kind of humiliation that Stanford insisted he had suffered due to her collapse at the altar. There had been only one offer of courtship during her second Season and none so far in her third. Though to be fair, there was a gentleman who would offer, but she dodged him at every turn. Refusing him outright would only further cement public opinion of her.

Still, all of it stung a bit. Because doors had been closed to her through no fault of her own. After all, she'd have happily married Stanford had she not discovered he was a liar and a fortune hunter—yet it was her reputation which had suffered. Her reputation which now meant the men who danced with her were more often than not refused by their first choices. And then, of course, it was quite obvious to most people that many of the men who asked her to dance never had any intention of courting her, much less marrying her.

Realizing that she was being as hard on others as she was on herself with her mental castigation, Marina took a calming breath. No, it wasn't entirely their fault, just as it wasn't entirely her own. She had, albeit inadvertently, called off an engagement as the wedding itself was in the offing. And in the eyes of the world, Stanford was the wronged party. In truth, even if his perfidy was disclosed, her sin of publicly humiliating him would still be viewed as far greater than his—after all, who didn't marry for money? And how many men were truly expected to be faithful? But just because she didn't necessarily want to marry, she still wanted a degree of romance in her life. She wanted to at least feel that she wasn't a pariah. So she clung to the thought that eventually some other scandal would come along and she would be largely forgotten about—hopefully before she was too firmly on the shelf.

As she was making her way across the ballroom, Marina was beset by the sudden sensation of being stared at. It wasn't unusual and typically meant those staring were whispering about her. But this felt different. Turning her head just slightly, she saw a far-too-handsome gentleman standing near the edge of the dance floor. Dark haired and curiously rugged in the midst of so many gentlemen who looked as if a stiff wind might bowl them over, he stood out in the crowd. She did not know him. They had never been introduced, which meant he was likely new in town. Looking away for just a moment, she glanced back at him and still he was staring. This time, he offered her a smile and a slight nod. It was most decidedly not her imagination. He was not only staring, now he was flirting. Well, not flirting perhaps, but certainly not hiding the fact that he had indeed been staring at her.

Uncertain what to do as no truly eligible gentleman had flirted with or even displayed the slightest interest in her in some time, Marina simply continued on her way. Perhaps he would follow? Perhaps he would ask for an introduction from Lady Crowden. Though thinking of that woman, Marina couldn't stop a shudder. She still recalled that fateful night when she'd overheard her with Stanford. But she'd made peace with it of a sort, because he'd been lying to her also. He'd married another very quickly, almost as if he'd had an alternate in mind all along.

Another glance back, but she couldn't see him through the throng of guests now. She was rather curiously disappointed by that. If he were the sort of gentleman worth considering that is what he would do—ask for an introduction. Would Lady Crowden warn him off as so many others had been warned away by her? If so, there was naught she could do about it. And as she didn't want to have her hopes dashed, it was best not to entertain them at all.

Across the room, she could see her Aunt Willa watching with concern. On this, one of the few truly grand events she'd been invited to for her third Season, Marina was forced to admit that her aunt's concern was valid. Even the hefty dowry that her Uncle Devil had settled upon her was not an enticing enough inducement for most men to make such a scandalous match. Her own choosiness in her first Season had marked her as "difficult." Others said she was too high in the instep. More still said she was destined for the same fate as her mother—to run off with an entirely unsuitable man. Another thought entered her mind then, one too scandalous to ever utter aloud. *Perhaps she would, one day, as the suitable men were becoming fewer and farther between.* Those who would consider her as a prospective bride were either too old, too greedy for her wealth, or simply a terrible match for reasons her Uncle Devil would not divulge. And if he wouldn't tell her, that meant only one thing. They were wicked and likely not in a way that might be enticing.

Although, if some of the things she'd heard about her Uncle Devil's reputation were to be believed, he'd been quite wicked himself. And he'd made a marvelous husband to her Aunt Willa. In truth, Marina could hardly recall the rough start she'd had in life. That thought brought a pang of sadness with it, as well. For that also meant that she had no truly clear memories of her mother. They were faint, mere shadows in her mind. It was like a tune that one caught oneself humming without knowing where they'd heard it or how to finish it beyond a few simple bars.

"You're frowning. You'll never catch a husband that way." The words were uttered in a conspiratorial whisper.

Marina looked over at her dearest friend, Charlotte Hamilton, who was just as scandalous as she herself was. Through no fault of her own, of course. Like Marina, Charlotte was very much tarnished by the sins of her parents, though Charlotte hadn't left a man practically at the altar, so at least there was that.

"Apparently, my difficulty isn't in catching a husband so much as not throwing him back. Besides, I'm not looking for a husband, so I may frown all I like," Marina answered with a grin.

Charlotte's lips primped as she tried not to laugh. "You are quite wicked sometimes, but I do love you for it."

Surreptitiously glancing over her shoulder, she caught a glimpse of the dark-haired man. He was still watching her. "Charlotte, do you know that gentleman?"

Charlotte, never one for subtlety, simply turned about and stared directly at him.

"For goodness' sake, Charlotte! You might as well be shouting like a fishwife that we're talking about him," Marina hissed at her friend. "Turn back around."

Charlotte did so with a sigh. "I do not understand why, if we like the look of a gentleman, we cannot simply ask for his name. It's senseless—all this proper introduction business… But alas, I do not know him. Though he is remarkably handsome! Don't you think?"

Marina was saved from admitting how handsome she found

him to be by the disruptive cacophony of an all too familiar and grating laugh. The sound had originated nearby. Glancing in the other direction, Marina fervently wished that she knew more curse words. Miss Elizabeth Whitmore. Vicious gossip. Evil incarnate. Arch nemesis. But she was disarmingly beautiful. It was her third Season out, as well. And she'd have been long married off if only she weren't such a terrible person. She was feared more than liked courtesy of her viperous nature. And if anyone did make the mistake of thinking her cold exterior hid a heart of gold, they certainly didn't think so for long. If there was one truly safe wager to make, turning one's back on Elizabeth was like presenting one's back to a venomous snake. You might not see it coming, but the strike would occur regardless. She could not be trusted. Marina had learned that the hard way.

At the beginning of her first Season, she'd struck up a friendship, of sorts, with Elizabeth. Until Stanford. Marina hadn't known that Elizabeth had any feelings for him. They'd never discussed it, never spoken of him. It was only when he'd made his intentions known, that he intended to court her and pursue an understanding, that Elizabeth had disclosed that she had a tendre for him. She'd accused Marina of betraying their friendship and had turned on her very quickly. Funnily enough, in retrospect, she'd done Elizabeth a favor without meaning to.

"Oh, how I detest her!" Charlotte fumed. "Look at her. Smug. Self-righteous. Superior. And all the while she's just a viper in pink silk."

Picturing a snake wrapped in pink silk, the image prompted a giggle from Marina. It bubbled out of her so quickly she had no chance to stifle it. And the moment it erupted, Elizabeth's cold gaze landed on her. There was no question how it looked or that repayment for the perceived insult would be harsh and swift. They were caught staring at her and giggling, after all, and she would be quite right in presuming that it had been at her expense. It was an offense that would not be overlooked or forgiven. In truth, Marina was well aware that there would be veritable hell to pay.

"Oh, we've done it now," Charlotte said.

Marina tried to appear calm and unruffled. "It isn't as if she can hate us more than she already does. She would be hard pressed to be more unpleasant, at any rate."

Charlotte smothered a laugh behind her hand. "Let's take a turn about the room before we get ourselves into any more trouble. I have only danced with a few gentlemen tonight, but it feels as if an entire army has trod upon my toes and abused my good nature." Charlotte cut her gaze to the left and in a lower voice added, "Also, unless we make a hasty escape, you're going to find yourself fending off yet another request from Mr. Nutter for a private audience."

Marina suppressed a shudder of distaste. A more aptly named fellow she had yet to encounter. He was, perhaps not ready for the asylum, but certainly very, very odd. Linking arms with Charlotte, they crossed the ballroom and disappeared down the hall, heading for the small room that had been designated for ladies to refresh themselves, make use of the necessary, and repair trod upon hems. It was also, thankfully, a very convenient place to hide from unpleasant gentlemen.

Chapter Five

The Hunter is the Hunted

CALEB WATCHED THE dark-haired beauty as she walked through the ballroom, her petite blonde-haired companion at her side. They'd been giggling as only young women can and, with no small amount of curiosity, he wondered what had prompted their mirth. The level of interest she had stirred within him with a mere glance was unprecedented.

He was in something of a quandary. Having spoken to the few people in attendance whom he knew, he now had her name—Miss Marina Ashton—but no one could claim, or possibly would claim, acquaintance enough with the young woman to provide the much-needed introduction. It placed him firmly at square one. He was entirely dependent upon the generosity of his hostess, Lady Crowden. Generosity that he felt would surely be lacking, given their current situation. He could hardly beg an introduction to his mystery woman from her. With his intent to disabuse Lady Crowden of any notion of a romantic entanglement between the two of them, to immediately ask her to introduce him to another woman would truly be adding insult to injury. And she hardly seemed to be the magnanimous sort.

Thinking of the night at Cremorne Gardens, he frowned. The kiss had taken him by surprise and his reaction had been unfortunately delayed. He'd had just enough brandy that his wits had been dulled ever so slightly, preventing him from disengaging himself from her in as timely a manner as he should have. He could understand how that could be misconstrued. Accepting her invitation for the evening's ball had only further cemented that version of events for her, but he was only there to inform her, as gently as possibly, that he had no wish in furthering a romantic entanglement with her.

Thinking of all the scheming and machinations, the clandestine power plays as everyone jockeyed for social position—he had to bite back a curse. It was all a bloody mess. It was at just such times, he wished he'd stayed in Yorkshire. Of course, that would have violated the terms of his great-uncle's will. He had to marry a young woman, who had never been wed to another, who was part of the *ton*. He might have gotten by without inheriting the funds as well as the burdensome title, but for one thing. *Death taxes were the very devil.* They would eat away at the fortune his grandfather had amassed. The upkeep on the estates would drain it as well, and that would result in unnecessary strain on his other business enterprises. There was no way, barring completion of the terms of his great-uncle's will, that he would not be either bankrupt, or robbing Peter to pay Paul for the rest of his days.

Casting his eyes over the ballroom once more, his gaze fell on the beautiful girl with coal-black hair and sapphire eyes as she disappeared from view. If he'd stayed in Yorkshire then he would never have laid eyes upon her, and that wasn't something he was willing to forfeit for any reason. Not when, at first glance, he'd decided she was his best prospect. And it wasn't just that she was beautiful, though that certainly was enough given the degree to which that statement was true. She seemed somehow apart from all of it. As if the nonsense of society was nothing to her but the ineffectual and slightly irritating buzzing of an insect.

Seeing an opportunity, Caleb positioned himself in the path that she and her friend would likely take as they navigated the periphery of the crowded ballroom. It wouldn't be an introduction, but he could at least be certain that they had some interaction.

As he neared them, he caught her glancing surreptitiously at him from the corner of her eye. Oh, yes. She was as aware of him as he was of her. It boded well.

Watching the two of them whisper together, he saw her friend reach over, take the dance card from her wrist, and immediately drop it to the floor. His black-haired beauty stared at her companion in horror. It was an incredibly obvious method, but he was grateful for it.

Retrieving the delicate silver case, he stepped closer to the pair of them. "Your pardon, miss. I believe that this must be yours?"

She turned toward him then. At their present distance, her blue eyes were beyond piercing. He found himself utterly captivated by her beauty. And yet, he was cautious. Because the *ton* was full of women who were merely beautiful. He wanted a woman who could capture his mind and not simply his gaze. In short, he was afraid to hope for too much lest he find himself terribly disappointed.

"How humiliatingly clumsy of me, sir. Thank you."

"I fear we have not been introduced," he said. "But if I may be so bold, I am Lord Caleb Halliwell, Earl of St. Aiden."

"Miss Marina Ashton," she replied smoothly, "And my friend Miss Charlotte Hamilton."

"This hardly counts as a formal introduction, my lord," Miss Hamilton informed him primly, though her eyes twinkled with delight as she said it. "Though your gallantry does do you credit."

Seeing as it was her scheming that had resulted in his gallantry, she very well ought to think so, he thought somewhat bemused. As he watched Miss Ashton less than subtly drive her elbow into Miss Hamilton's ribs, he had to suppress a laugh. "Indeed, there is no substitute for a proper introduction. Perhaps if we compare a list of acquaintances in attendance tonight then we might happen upon a mutual one who could do the honors."

"Our hostess, Lady Crowden, perhaps?" Miss Hamilton suggested.

A shadow passed over Miss Ashton's face at the mention of their hostess. He found himself suddenly very glad that he would not have to count on Lady Crowden for that honor as it seemed to disturb Miss Ashton greatly. "Alas, I am not very well acquainted with her. I believe I was invited merely out of curiosity as I am so new both to the title and town," he explained. It wasn't technically a lie. It simply wasn't the truth in its entirety.

"Uncle Valentine knows everyone," Miss Ashton supplied. "Viscount Seaburn?"

A feeling of relief settled over him, as if a burden he hadn't realized he'd been holding had suddenly lifted. Her uncle was a viscount. The criteria set forth in his great-uncle's will began to tick steadily in his mind, like the striking of a clock. One, she was a society miss. Two, based on the pale color of her evening gown, it was safe to assume she had never been married. Three, she was a London girl born and bred. In short, she appeared to be everything that the old wretch had demanded. And more importantly, she appeared to be everything he wanted, as well. "We are acquainted enough," Caleb replied. They'd met at their club only days earlier. "Should we seek him out before the next set, Miss Ashton? It is a dance I mean to claim if no one else has done so."

"He is in the card room, sir. Perhaps if you seek him out, he will be inclined to grant your request," Miss Hamilton said, but her gaze was on a point past his shoulder.

He wanted to ask who it was that had caused such an expression of alarm for her, but Caleb was halted from doing so by the appearance of a footman who appeared quite anxious. "Beg pardon, my lord. I have a message for you," the young man said, appearing for all the world as if he expected to be kicked for his troubles.

Caleb offered what he hoped was a reassuring smile to the footman who stood so nervously beside him, a glass of champagne on his tray and next to it a folded missive sealed with wax. Taking both, Caleb broke the seal and read the note.

No, it wasn't a note at all. It was a summons. Lady Crowden beckoned and expected him to comply. She was bound for a terrible disappointment. Even had he been inclined to indulge in a tawdry affair with a married woman, all of his attentions were now captured by a young woman whose name he had but just learned.

"Forgive me, Miss Ashton, Miss Hamilton. I will have to postpone importuning your uncle for that introduction. Please, if you'd be so kind, reserve space for me on your dance card."

She inclined her head, but it wasn't agreement. It was acknowledgment of his request only. That, Caleb determined, would change.

Chapter Six

Baiting the Trap

"T HAT MAN IS terrifyingly handsome. And, in truth, just terrifying," Charlotte whispered as they ducked into an alcove to avoid being spotted by Mr. Nutter.

"If he's so terrifying why in heaven's name did you throw my dance card at his feet?" Marina demanded, her tone perhaps a bit sharper than it ought to have been. The man unsettled her. Although that was a bit like saying the night was dark. He more than unsettled her. Much more. It had been in the way he looked at her, yes, but also in the way her breath had caught when she looked at him. It was all very peculiar.

"His handsomeness overshadowed how terrifying he was for just a moment… and he's not terrifying for you, but for me. You have always been the more bold of us," Charlotte explained. "Do you deny that you find him intriguing?"

Marina remained silent. If she'd said no, it would have been an outright lie. But not even Charlotte knew why it was that she'd removed herself so firmly from the marriage mart. She'd never disclosed to anyone the horrible things she'd heard Stanford say to his unknown paramour. It was too humiliating to admit that she'd been so easily duped by him. It was also too humiliating to admit that she no longer trusted her own judgment. Her ability to determine whether or not a gentleman had honorable intentions for her was something she could not accurately predict and the cost of being wrong was simply far too great.

"I am not looking for a husband, Charlotte," she finally said. "I am quite content to settle into spinsterhood without a backward glance."

"I do not understand it! You have refused more offers of marriage than most young women will ever receive!"

Marina rolled her eyes. "I've accepted one then changed my mind. I've refused two others outright, though those were before Stanford. Still, that's hardly an enormous number."

"And how many men have you discouraged so that they would not ask?" her friend challenged.

"Not as many as you might think," Marina said softly. They had not been legitimate offers. They had been men who only wanted her fortune or a connection to her illustrious family. None of it had been about her.

As if summoned by her thoughts, she heard a familiar and quite grating voice. It wasn't that the timbre of his voice was displeasing but rather everything he said simply preyed upon her already limited patience with the man. Mr. Roger Nutter was a plague upon her, and he was far too close for her peace of mind. "Let's go… quickly. While we can still play convincingly that we have not seen him!"

Charlotte needed no further prompting. Emerging from the alcove, they moved quickly to the exit and hurried from the ballroom. They didn't slow down so they reached the corridor to the ladies' retiring room in record time.

Once inside the retiring room, Marina breathed a sigh of relief. It wasn't that she disliked Mr. Nutter, so much, or that there was anything truly objectionable about him beyond his dogged determination to woo her. It was rather that she did not wish for him to have hopes where no good outcome could be had. She had elected, after her first disappointment, never to marry at all. If she were ever tempted to take such a step, it surely would not come about solely out of desperation to shed her spinster status without any love or feelings of fondness. So many people told her that she was being a hopeless and silly romantic, a foolish young woman with schoolgirl dreams. Others told her still that she read too many romantic novels. But they didn't know the truth and she couldn't share it. Nor would she. That was her shameful secret to keep and keep it she would even in the face of their concern for her marital state. The final bit of wisdom, offered up by everyone, was that with one broken engagement behind her, and with multiple proposals refused or prevented entirely, forthcoming offers would be scarce. The implication being that Mr. Nutter's offer, should she ever be unable to evade him, would be her last and final chance. Perhaps it was that which encouraged him to continue tilting at that particular windmill.

"Miss Ashton and Miss Hamilton… keeping one another company as you sit out yet another dance?"

Marina did not quite succeed in biting back the groan. Of course, Elizabeth had followed them. Naturally. How else could the evening get worse?

Turning, she acknowledged the other woman coolly. "Miss Whitmore. I don't believe I've seen you wearing out your dancing slippers tonight."

"I suppose," Elizabeth continued, ignoring the rather pointed barb that Marina had landed, "that when you are too scandalous to catch husbands, the company of friends is the best one can hope for. No gentleman of note will risk the inevitable rejection by paying court to you. And now that Mr. Stanford Williams has returned to town—fresh out of mourning for his departed wife—I imagine speculation will run rampant about the possibility of you two reigniting that old flame."

The words hit her like a physical blow. And the implications of all that had been said and unsaid swarmed her. *Fresh out of mourning. Had he murdered his bride? Had she, by not being forthcoming, been complicit in the young woman's death?*

Elizabeth's grating laugh filled the room. "Oh, dear! You hadn't heard, had you? I suppose that effectively squashes any hope of a reconciliation, doesn't it? Obviously, if he'd intended to repair your broken relationship, you'd have been the first person he contacted upon his return."

"Miss Whitmore, is there some purpose in all of this?" Charlotte asked. "You did feel compelled to follow us here, after all. I cannot image that, even for you, leaving behind the gaiety of the ball just to trade barbs with us would have been an irresistible temptation!"

"You'd hardly know anything of irresistible temptations, Miss Hamilton. At least Miss Ashton has had proposals."

Feeling Charlotte stiffen at her side, knowing that Elizabeth's verbal arrow had found its very sensitive mark, Marina managed to shake off the gloomy thoughts that had claimed her attention so fully. "Ignore her, Charlotte. She's simply a malcontent—always miserable and looking to make others share in it with her."

Elizabeth's eyes flashed with barely controlled fury. "Such a pity you squandered all those proposals. Dowdy, poor relation that she is, at least Miss Hamilton is a true companion to you." Then she smirked. "Perhaps you can use whatever annuity your relations choose to settle on you and share a small cottage by the sea... Just two crones growing older and uglier together every single day. Though I daresay that won't matter in Miss Hamilton's case."

Marina bristled at that. It was one thing for Elizabeth to take aim at her. It was quite another for her to start in on Charlotte, who was not at all a poor relation. She and Charlotte were in the same boat, being raised by doting aunts and uncles who were impossibly generous. But Marina felt much more secure in her station than Charlotte did, or at the very least she could don that facade. And Elizabeth knew that. She'd taken aim where it would cut the deepest.

In defense of her friend, Marina's tone was sharp. "I haven't exactly noted any prospective suitors beating a hasty path to your side, Elizabeth. Indeed, I think your dance card far more empty than mine or my dear friend's here. As for Charlotte, she is neither dowdy nor a poor relation to anyone. Your nasty and covetous nature will give you wrinkles from all the scowling you do."

Elizabeth merely smirked in response. "I'm not the one frowning at every man who dares to flirt with me. Like that new fellow in town… the Earl of St. Aiden. I saw you speaking with him after Miss Hamilton's ham-fisted attempt to incite a flirtation between the two of you. Heaven knows it failed miserably. Why the man couldn't get away from you fast enough!"

That hadn't been the way of it at all, Marina thought. He'd expressed interest. She'd even consented to an introduction presuming that Valentine would be willing to facilitate it. Not that she held out much hope of anything coming of it. "You speak of things you know nothing of, Miss Whitmore. Though I daresay that is quite the habit with you. The earl was quite attentive and very complimentary. Not that it should concern you in the least."

"It might be for the best if you simply retreated to the countryside," Elizabeth continued. "Perhaps when your cousins marry and have families of their own, they'll take you on as a governess… unless, of course, you've decided to put yourself back into the marriage mart fully?"

Marina didn't answer. She wouldn't give her the satisfaction. So Elizabeth continued.

"I'll make a wager with you, Miss Ashton, unless of course you are too afraid to do so?"

"What sort of wager?" The question popped out before Marina even recognized she was speaking. Elizabeth Whitmore goaded her like no one else.

Elizabeth smiled like a cat who'd gotten the canary. "Whichever of us does not marry before the Season is out will owe the other a public mea culpa, indeed, one of utter humility and obsequiousness. Every nasty thing said about one by the other should be owned up to as a falsehood. Maybe such a painful prospect will finally propel you to the altar!" Her chin lifted as her eyes swept up and down Marina, as if finding her lacking in some way. "Unless, of course, that you are so certain of your poor outcome that you are afraid to accept such a wager."

"I accept." Even as the words escaped her, Marina wanted to call them back. She'd allowed Elizabeth to goad her into making a wager she had absolutely no hope of winning. Not unless she wished to throw herself upon the questionable mercy of Mr. Nutter. In addition, it was a wager she didn't truly want to win! She did not wish to marry. Except that if Stanford Williams truly had returned, was he a danger to her? Would the presence of a betrothed gentleman deter any schemes he might be hatching?

Elizabeth's smirk spread into a full-blown smile. She beamed with evil intent, if such were possible. "Excellent. And Miss Hamilton may serve as our witness. She has so little to recommend her beyond her honesty, after all."

As their nemesis breezily sailed out of the retiring room, the two of them were left alone. Marina wanted to scream in frustration. Charlotte was ever more practical. "You must beg off this wager, Marina," her friend insisted. "You have no reasonable prospects. The public humiliation of dancing attendance on that odious creature will be your undoing!"

Marina's stomach churned. "I cannot beg off! Not yet at any rate. I would never hear the end of it... and there are other considerations, as well. Besides, Elizabeth will tell everyone about the wager and if I renege, she will crow far and wide about how I was so uncertain of my own ability to carry through with an engagement or simply so certain of my impending spinsterhood that I refused to rise to the challenge. I cannot publicly kowtow to that awful woman... But to find a suitable gentleman and get myself betrothed in the length of time allotted? Oh, Charlotte. This is dreadful. Just dreadful."

"What will you do?"

Marina shook her head. "I do not know. For now, my nerves are too jangled to even contemplate returning to the ballroom. And no doubt Mr. Nutter has not yet given up the chase. I would just as soon avoid him lest Elizabeth Whitmore assume that I am capitulating to his suit out of desperation."

"Would it be worse to marry him or to publicly shower her with false praise and admissions of guilt where none exists?"

Marina shuddered with distaste. "They are both equally abhorrent. Go back to the ballroom and tell Aunt Willa I have a megrim. Ask her to have the carriage fetched. I'll go home and try to discern some way out of this awful tangle I've allowed myself to be backed into."

Charlotte nodded and quickly departed the room. Marina was left alone with her own anxious thoughts and a tight ball of nerves twisting in her stomach.

Chapter Seven

A woman scorned...

"I REGRET TO inform you, Lady Crowden, that you are laboring under a misapprehension. I did not attend this ball in order to further our acquaintance, but simply to clear up a misunderstanding that occurred during our first meeting," Caleb said firmly, even as he removed the woman's arms from about his neck and set her away from him. The very moment he'd entered the library she'd launched herself at him.

Dismayed, Lady Crowden stepped back. "A misunderstanding? How can you be so cold to me after the incredible intimacy we shared?"

"We did not share any intimacies, madam. You stumbled into me while walking at night in the pleasure gardens and then kissed me because, in the darkness, you mistook me for your most recent paramour," he corrected her.

"But wasn't it a truly magical kiss? Surely you felt something for me to have kissed me back so ardently!"

He hadn't. Not at all. But she'd imbibed quite freely of champagne that evening and her memory seemed to be impacted by it. "Regardless of your perceptions of that kiss, it shall not be repeated. I am not in town to embark on an affair with another man's wife. I am here to seek a wife of my own."

And that was when she began to weep. Loudly and copiously.

Caleb stared at the woman before him utterly perplexed. Never in his life had he found it more confoundingly difficult to sever a romantic relationship that hadn't actually begun. The entirety of it existed solely in the mind of one party. Added, the woman in question was also quite thoroughly married and that their romance consisted of one drunken grope in a garden—which she had initiated—it was simply beyond reason that she should carry on as though they were some tragically doomed love match.

"How could you do this to me, Caleb? How could you humiliate me this way? I've never suffered such cruel rejection."

He'd never actually given her leave to call him by his given name, but as her grasp on reality appeared questionable at best, pointing it out was likely not the most advantageous course of action. "We shared one kiss, madam. Only one. And I was not even aware of your identity until after the deed was done. I certainly was not aware of your marital state or I should never have participated at all."

"Married!" She scoffed, her tears having dried up quite quickly. So quickly that he had to question whether or not they'd been genuine at all.

"What has that got to do with anything?" she continued. "It's the way of society, Caleb. Once heirs are produced, then husbands and wives may live separately and do as they please... with whom they please. Indeed, husbands may do so all along."

He wasn't so naive that the bloodless and often miserable marriages of society were unknown to him. But while others may have entered into their nuptials with an eye toward future infidelity, that was hardly how he wished to begin. Shaking his head, he denied, "When I marry, it will certainly not be that way. No wife of mine will stray, nor will I. I may be new to society, but I do not mean to conform to the immorality that is apparently rampant within it."

She blinked at him rather owlishly, as if he were something

she'd never encountered before. Caleb was well aware that he sounded like a prig, but so be it. His very middle class–bourgeois upbringing was still a part of him, however much the upper classes might disdain such a thing.

Then Lady Crowden began to laugh, a bit madly and more than a bit meanly. When she spoke, her voice dripped with condescension. "For such a rough and tumble looking fellow, Caleb, you are adorably naive. Such a belief is based on the notion that marriages are initiated for love rather than position and wealth. Something that the middle class has the luxury of doing. Now that you are a titled gentleman, that will change."

"No," he denied quickly. "It will not."

"You will have to marry someone who has something to offer you financially... and sadly those matches rarely produce tender feelings. You will find yourself seeking affection and passion outside the bonds of matrimony far sooner than you could ever imagine."

"Your union might be happier and might produce more tender feelings if you cultivated it to the same degree you cultivate your affairs." His tone was not unkind as he offered that observation. But she was in no mood to see reason and he was in no mood to continue arguing with her.

She shook her head, clucking her tongue like he was a misbehaving child. "You are so quick to judge and so quick to condemn. I think you haven't the ability to understand how trying it can be to spend your days with someone you do not even like, much less desire. If you did, then surely you would not begrudge me a few hours of happiness. A few hours, Caleb, of exquisite passion... and it would be exquisite," she promised.

Caleb didn't care for her opinion of him one way or another. As for her assertion of how exquisite it would or would not be, that wasn't something he could or would permit to matter. He had hoped to disentangle himself from the matter with minimal fuss. He understood her value as an ally, especially as the first woman who had caught his eye was one of her guests. But he wasn't about to sell his soul or his body for the benefits her acquaintance would afford him. It wasn't in his nature to be cruel and hurtful but there were people in the world who understood nothing else. Lady Crowden appeared to be of that ilk as she continued to act as if he'd wounded her in some way by refusing to be a party to adultery with her.

Of course, it wasn't as if he'd broken her heart. Caleb was well aware that what he was dealing with was her vanity. Her feelings weren't truly involved, at all. It was simply her pride and her feelings of entitlement that she should have her way in all things. He had the distinct impression that Lady Crowden was more perturbed at not having him under her thumb than not having him in her bed. "My reasons are my own, but my answer stands. I will not embark upon an affair with a married woman. The kiss we shared was a case of mistaken identity on your part in a darkened pleasure garden. For my own, I had indulged in too much brandy to react as quickly as I should have. And it is a regret I shall simply have to bear."

"A regret? Whatever do you mean? I will have you know, my lord," Lady Crowden said, her tone quite sharp, bordering on shrewish, "my favors are highly sought after. If you will have any regret, it's that you refused me!"

The woman simply would not let it end without getting her way. She was like a spoiled child. "I am certain it is true, Lady Crowden, you are much sought after. My decision not to pursue a further acquaintance with you has nothing to do with how desirable or undesirable your favors and charms may be. You are quite lovely. You are also quite married. Kissing you in that darkened spot in Cremorne Gardens was an error on my part—one I shall not compound with further misdeeds. I need to focus my attentions on finding a wife this Season, not on finding a paramour. While it may be possible to do both, it would not be possible to do them both well."

She drew back almost as if he'd struck her. "I see. You would prefer some younger, fresh-faced child-bride straight from the school room. Some virginal miss who knows nothing of pleasing a man. Not a woman of experience. Perhaps it's your own lack of prowess as a lover that has you seeking ignorance in your bed partners."

That was not what he had said. It wasn't untrue, except for the child-bride bit, but still he hadn't said it. And while he did not require a bride fresh from the school room, he did require someone younger, certainly than Lady Crowden, who was closer to his mother's age than she was to his. With a title so recently bestowed upon him, he needed to look to getting an heir. As for his lack of prowess, let her think him a terrible lover. If it would end the nonsense sooner and cease the stream of vitriol from her, so be it. His vanity could withstand the blow. "I mean no offense to you. You are a charming and lovely woman. You are simply not available to me in the way that I need. I am quite firmly set on looking to finding my own wife. Not someone else's."

She shrieked at him. Literally. Shrieked. Like a banshee or some harpy from the wretched stories his Scottish nanny had told him as a boy. She wasn't simply an unhappy and unfaithful wife. He thought she might actually be a madwoman. And now, trapped in a library with her, a crowded ballroom full of people only a few yards away, and he hadn't the faintest clue how to extricate himself from this wretched situation that too much brandy and too little light had gotten him into. She'd thought he was someone else entirely, after all. Surely kissing a stranger by mistake did not necessitate such a degree of emotional disturbance?

Unable to make sense of her, and she was quite clearly unwilling to have sense made *to her,* Caleb simply pinched the bridge of his nose to ward off a headache and girded himself for the haranguing that was to come. He wished, almost, that he'd remained in the North, enjoying the simple society of a much smaller city. It was surely less complicated. But the memory of the dark-haired beauty in the ballroom teased his mind. He might have missed that tantalizing glimpse had he not come to London and he felt, despite the present unpleasantness, that it was surely worth it.

MARINA MOVED CAUTIOUSLY down the corridor, intent on making her way back to her Aunt Willa's side. She had determined the best course of action would be pleading ill and retreating to her home… or possibly to the Continent, for surely she would have to go so far to escape Elizabeth Whitmore's spite and any potentially awkward encounters with Stanford. In fact, she was just thinking that a month or so in some exotic location might be just the thing. Spain was lovely, she'd heard. And Portugal. And Greece. Really anywhere but London. All those options were running through her mind when her thoughts were interrupted by a pair of all too familiar voices.

Elizabeth was leading Mr. Nutter directly to her.

"Mr. Nutter, you are so charming!" Elizabeth said far too loudly, likely intending for her voice to carry. She wanted Marina to know, after all, that it was she, her nemesis, who would be the instrument of Marina's downfall.

"You are too kind, Miss Whitmore. I declare that Miss Ashton is devilishly good at avoiding me. I was beginning to think she was doing so purposely," he replied, laughing in a way that sounded not unlike a braying donkey.

No, Marina thought. No. She would not allow herself to be trapped by him, with him, or for him. And, of course, Elizabeth knew that. Elizabeth knew she would turn the man down flat if he had the poor sense to actually propose. And that would only serve to confirm everyone's opinion of her—that she was a high in the in-step, too proud, too vain young woman who thought herself far above her ignoble origins and tenuous place in society. Another refusal of a marriage offer, after having abandoned Stanford at the altar, would ruin her.

Rushing to the other end of the corridor, she started to step outside, but caution prevailed. She parted the heavy drapes and peered out, taking note of a lone man standing on the terrace beyond. Then that man lit a cheroot with a match and in that red glow she could see his face. *Stanford.* Why was he always lurking on terraces? That thought brought a wave of bitterness, but it was hardly the time to indulge it. Instead, she dismissed that as her avenue of escape.

Marina had never told him, nor anyone else, why she had been unable to go through with the wedding. It had been too humiliating to admit that she'd been so easily duped by him. Of course, he had not been quite so circumspect. He'd been quite free in expressing his opinions to anyone who would listen about what sort of person she was, how fickle she was and what a terrible flirt she was, how fast she was. Countless lies and rumors had been circulated about her by him. And in all of that, she had not spoken to him, communicated with him, nor had she laid eyes on him since. Not knowing how angry he might be, and having learned the hard way just how little she actually knew of him, she'd elected not to risk it.

Rather than be cornered and forced into a conversation she had absolutely no wish to participate in or facing off against a man who could very well pose a threat to her, Marina took the only reasonable option available to her. She hid.

Ducking into the nearest door, she closed it softly behind her and then turned the key in the lock. Leaning against it, she exhaled sharply and then turned away. Had she not been so desperate, it might have occurred to her that when she stepped into that room, it was not entirely dark. There was a small lamp burning low on the desk. That soft glow was damning enough. It meant she had interrupted a tryst in progress or had perhaps usurped a prearranged trysting location earmarked for others. Looking about, she saw a shawl draped over the back of a sofa—a fan laid casually next to it. But as her gaze wandered, the situation went from moderately embarrassing to utterly catastrophic. The room she had entered was not only occupied, it was occupied by one of the very last people whom she would wish to see her in such a state. Lady Crowden was there with some unknown gentleman who remained in the shadows.

The realization of what had happened was completely mortifying. Somehow, in her efforts to avoid Mr. Nutter and Miss Whitmore, and to keep her distance from Stanford, she'd interrupted a scandalous and romantic interlude between her hostess, and arguably her nemesis, and a mysterious gentleman who, based upon his height, was most certainly not the diminutive Lord Crowden.

"Oh, dear," she whispered.

"Whatever are you doing, Miss Ashton?" Lady Crowden demanded haughtily. *As if she hadn't just been caught having a tryst with a man who was not her husband.*

"My apologies, my lady. I was merely trying to avoid having an unpleasant conversation with an unwanted suitor," she said. After all, it was to no one's benefit to antagonize the woman. "He has been most persistent despite my every effort to dissuade him. I am so terribly sorry for the intrusion."

Lady Crowden appeared slightly mollified. Or she did until her companion uttered something under his breath that sounded shockingly as if it included the words "epidemic of unwanted attentions." Instantly, Lady Crowden whirled on him in anger, letting out a shriek that would have done any fishwife proud.

It was shocking. Even had it been any other society matron, to see a well-respected and mature woman behaving in such a fashion would have been quite unbelievable. That it was Lady Crowden, who only two years prior had pleaded and begged with Stanford to throw her over? Where had that weak, clinging woman gone and how had such a harridan replaced her? Marina could do nothing but blink in confusion. What on earth had she stumbled upon?

Horror dawned then as Marina heard the sound of rushing footsteps in the corridor. Anyone nearby would have been alerted by her shrieking and would come to offer aid—or witness disgrace. And as the people nearby were the very last ones she'd wish to face, there was simply no positive outcome to be had.

Within seconds, there was pounding on the door beyond. Mr. Nutter, with his slightly nasal voice was demanding to know if she was injured. "Miss Ashton? Are you well? I will fetch Lord Crowden and have him open this door instantly!"

Lady Crowden's eyes widened with the terror of a woman well and truly caught. And that was when she did the most unexpected thing of all. She marched to the door and opened it. "Mr. Nutter, thank goodness you have arrived. I have caught Miss Ashton and the Earl of St. Aiden in the most compromising of positions."

"What?" Marina whispered in shock. Her gaze swept to the darkened corner of the room where the gentleman remained in shadow. Was it truly him? The man she'd been so intrigued by in the ballroom? Why on earth had he been flirting with her only to then be closeted in a room with their very married hostess?

Lady Crowden ignored her entirely. "You should go immediately, Mr. Nutter, and fetch her aunt and uncle. No doubt they will have something to say about all of this. How shameful you are, Miss Ashton! Really. To behave so brazenly in my home when I have invited you here against my better judgment."

Realizing that there were far more pressing matters to deal with than the apparent faithlessness of a man she hardly knew at all, Marina protested, "No. No, that's not what this is at all!" How had it all gone so terribly wrong so very quickly?

"Save your denials," Lady Crowden said coolly. "How could we possibly believe you, Miss Ashton, with your reputation? And your late mother's. It appears that the apple did not fall very far from the tree at all!"

Marina stared at the woman in horror and then looked past her to see Mr. Nutter glowering with disapproval. The only consolation was that Elizabeth looked as though she might actually faint dead away. Then Mr. Nutter turned on his heel and made off to do Lady Crowden's bidding. And in the corridor beyond, Stanford was looking on with an expression that one could only classify as smug. That was when Marina realized something truly horrifying. None of it was accidental. She'd been managed into this predicament, just as the Earl of St. Aiden likely had. But to what end?

The reality of it all sank in. She would have to marry a stranger, assuming he would be willing to marry her. Being a confirmed spinster would not be the worst fate that would befall her. She would be a pariah. And with Stanford back amongst the *ton*, she would be forever looking over her shoulder, waiting for whatever dastardly revenge he might have in store for her.

Thinking of the gossip after she'd broken the engagement, it wasn't a stretch to imagine what would be said of her given the very damning picture Lady Crowden had just painted. There were worse things than being labeled as fickle and foolish and vain by society. She would be labeled as fast, and that sin was always unforgivable. Her mother's sad fate had proven that. And not even her uncle's vast holdings would be sufficient to bury such a scandal.

Chapter Eight

Two wrongs do occasionally make a right...

INITIALLY, CALEB HAD been confused. But then his brain had ceased to function properly somewhere after Lady Crowden thoroughly misconstrued or remained intentionally obtuse in the face of his every attempt to let her down gently. Now, having rallied, he understood it far too well. Lady Crowden was tossing both him and the lovely but clearly quite dumbfounded Miss Ashton to the wolves to save her own deceitful hide. Better to have caught someone else in the act than to be caught in it herself. It seems that Lord Crowden was perhaps not as under-standing of her extramarital pursuits as she had intimated.

He might have protested. Might. But there was good reason not to do so. His initial quandary had been solved entirely. He no longer needed to seek an introduction to the dark-haired beauty. They were now embroiled in a scandal together. Miss Marina Ashton had been presented to him almost like a gift. Additionally, and perhaps most importantly, *she was not Lady Crowden.* That was a rather significant point in her favor. Fairly rational, seemingly avoidant of conflict and overly dramatic displays—Miss Ashton might well be a Godsend.

While he remained somewhat concealed within the shadows, Miss Ashton was perfectly visible in the light spilling in from the corridor. It gave him the opportunity to study her with more leisure than had been afforded in the ballroom. Taking in every detail of her appearance, he noted that he could not find a single flaw. To call her beautiful was too pale a term for her appearance. With her black hair pulled back in an elaborate coiffure with soft tendrils left loose to curl about her face, the style accentuated the soft curve of her jawline and her chin, marked with the faintest cleft. He much preferred the softer method of dressing a woman's hair to the dowdy style favored by so many young ladies. They pinned all their hair up in symmetrical clumps atop their ears until they looked like spaniels.

Caleb couldn't quite make out the color of her gown in the room's dim light beyond it being pale in shade, as befitted a young unmarried woman. In the ballroom, he hadn't bothered to notice anything beyond the perfection of her face. The color of her gown had been trivial in comparison. Now, with an opportunity to study her, he could see the cut of it displayed a graceful neck, the gentle curve of her shoulders, and the barest hint of décolletage.

He might have liked a bit of time to make a decision about whether or not he actually wished to pursue marriage to her. But as she was the first woman he'd encountered amidst the glittering display of London society who had tempted him in the least, it wasn't that much of an obstacle to his mind. Barring some great disparity between her character and her form, he had no concerns.

Caleb did not believe in love as poets wrote of it. It wasn't some flash of lightning—some loincloth swaddled cherub flinging arrows at people. Love, to his mind, was not something one fell into. It was something one built. If she was of a practical mind, as he was, then they might truly have an opportunity to make a good and happy life for themselves. And yet it seemed fate, in the form of Lady Crowden's impulsive but convincing lies, had allowed him to find himself in his current untenable position of having compromised the very woman he'd set his sights on.

Of course, there were far better ways to get one's self betrothed than through the twisted machinations of another man's faithless wife. As for the pair at the door, he had no notion what they were about. The young woman appeared quite disappointed, but not for the same reasons the gentleman did. It was quite obvious that Mr. Nutter, as Lady Crowden had addressed him, had harbored some tender feeling or at least romantic intentions toward Miss Ashton. Why another young woman, one who clearly was no friend to Miss Ashton, had accompanied him to find her was something of a mystery. Curious as it all was, there was no denying that their current situation went far beyond farcical. In short, it was nothing less than an utter fiasco. And all of it, every last bit of it, harkened back to a moment of too much brandy and Lady Crowden having mistaken him for someone else entirely. Whether that event was his salvation or downfall remained to be seen.

"We must not leap to conclusions," the young woman beyond the door said. "There could be a perfectly reasonable explanation as to why Miss Ashton was in this room, unchaperoned, with a man who is hardly known to any of us."

If she was trying to improve the situation, she was failing greatly. But then Caleb suspected, a suspicion fueled by the wicked gleam in her eyes, that making things better for Miss Ashton was the very last thing the young woman wanted. The current predicament might not have been what she'd imagined for Miss Ashton, but she was certainly willing to exploit the situation that had been presented.

Lady Crowden stiffened. "And what else could it be, Miss Whitmore? Do you dare question my understanding of what I observed here? A married woman who is far more worldly than a mere miss such as yourself could ever presume to be. They were behaving with great impropriety. I shall not sully your innocent ears with further details on the matter. That will be for discussion with Lord and Lady Deveril. You will return to the ballroom, Miss Whitmore, and say nothing of this. I shall not have it be said that my home was the origination of such wickedness or such nasty gossip!"

To that point, Caleb hadn't uttered a word. In all honestly, there had hardly been a second's silence not eaten up with Lady Crowden's prattling. "Lady Crowden, do be so good as to provide me a moment of privacy with Miss Ashton. I assure you it will all be quite proper. You may even leave the door open if you will simply step outside. I think we should have a moment to discuss our plans since our names and our futures will now be closely linked."

Lady Crowden turned to him then and the fury that burned in her gaze was staggering. It was disproportionate to the situation in a way that simply made no sense. Could it really be that a simple misunderstanding and what he'd hoped would be a very gentle rejection could make her hate him so much? But when he looked at her once more, her gaze wasn't on him, or even on Miss Ashton. She was looking out into the corridor, to the man lurking in the shadows there. Who was he? And what had he wandered into the middle of?

Given the lengths she'd just gone to save her own reputation, it was obvious she was a master schemer. And he had no doubt her machinations would reach far beyond the room they currently occupied. But who else was involved in the mess she'd created for them? Regardless of where her animosity truly lay, he knew that he'd made an enemy of her. And now she would be the unfortunate Miss Ashton's enemy as well.

There was no opportunity for that private moment. Mr. Nutter returned and with him was a very handsome couple, the man tall and proud, the woman petite and delicately beautiful. They complemented one another in both their appearance and manner. And Miss Ashton bore some similarity to the gentleman.

"Lord Deveril, I have the most distressing news," Lady Crowden said. "I happened upon your niece, Miss Marina Ashton, in a most compromising position with the Earl of St. Aiden. I shall leave it you and Lady Deveril to handle the situation moving forward. I will go and attempt to curb Miss Whitmore's penchant for gossip. Sadly, I must assume the news is already making its way around the ballroom."

Caleb braced himself for the dressing down of his life, which if circumstances were as Lady Crowden had painted them, would have been well deserved. But nothing could have prepared him for what actually occurred. The three people gathered there ignored him entirely.

Chapter Nine

The Plot Thickens...

MARINA HAD BEEN so stunned when the Earl of St. Aiden had stepped from the shadows that she could barely think. The moment that Lady Crowden had identified him she'd been mortified. It all seemed too convenient. The man whom she'd thought was flirting with her was suddenly in a tryst with the very woman her former betrothed had been secretly—well, not wooing. Clearly Lady Crowden had been quite wooed already. It had to be some sort of elaborate plot or scheme. Otherwise, why were they all there? Elizabeth, Lady Crowden, Stanford, Mr. Nutter. How was it that every person whom she detested had all come together in this one moment? Surely it could not be a coincidence!

"What has that wretched girl done now?" Willa demanded. "And was that Stanford lurking in the corridor? What is he doing back in town?"

It took Marina a moment to answer, a moment to formulate her thoughts. She couldn't tell the truth. It sounded positively mad. So she did something quite out of character for her. She lied.

"I didn't see him," she denied. "I ducked into this room because I was trying to avoid Mr. Nutter."

"And Miss Whitmore? What was *she* doing here?" That snapped question had come from her uncle.

Marina realized she'd been silent for too long, all the strange circumstances running through her mind. Meeting Willa's worried gaze and shying away from Devil's perturbed one she shook her head. She hated to admit it, to admit what she had done, especially to her aunt. In truth, Willa was the only mother she'd ever known, and she would be so disappointed. But the woeful tale simply tumbled out. "I had words with her in the ladies' retiring room earlier, along with Charlotte. And when I was making my way back to the ballroom, I heard her speaking with Mr. Nutter. She was assisting him in his search for me, likely because she meant to put us in a situation where he would propose and—"

"And you would refuse because the man could bore a corpse," her uncle concluded. "So you hid in here not knowing the room was occupied?"

"Yes," Marina nodded. "Precisely."

"And how is it that Lady Crowden discovered you here?" Willa asked.

"She was already here," Marina stated.

At that point, the three of them turned to the gentleman who had waited silently and patiently while they examined the situation. He was a key player in the farce but, thus far, had been largely ignored by everyone to that point. Beyond her brief interaction with him in the drawing room, he wasn't known to any of them, well certainly not to her or her aunt. He'd indicated before that he was acquainted with her Uncle Valentine which meant he might very well be acquainted with Devil.

"St. Aiden? I wasn't aware the old man had any sons," Devil said.

"Nephew," the earl replied. "Well, great-nephew. To be perfectly frank, I was rather surprised by it, as well. Apparently 'the old man' and my own grandfather bad been estranged for some time."

"I see. I hear Yorkshire in your voice," Devil observed.

"True enough. I was raised in Copley. My grandfather owned a small coal company there. While I have not been in society for very long, Lord Deveril, I do understand how all of this will look. I'm fully prepared to do the only honorable thing that I can and offer for Miss Ashton's hand."

"That won't be necessary," Devil said stiffly.

Marina's stomach dropped to her toes, and she looked to Willa in a panic. All her protestations of not wanting to be married had apparently taken root in her uncle's mind. But the situation was quite different now, both for the very obvious reason of impending ruination but also because Stanford Williams had returned and would only have done so with a purpose in mind. And until she knew what that purpose was, she had to assume he posed a threat—whether to her life or merely the tattered remnants of her good name was a mystery.

Immediately, her aunt stepped forward and addressed the earl. "My lord, if you would be so kind as to wait in the corridor for just a moment while my husband and I discuss Marina's options with her?"

The earl sketched a neat bow and quickly exited the room, closing the door softly behind him. Marina turned to her uncle. "I have to marry him. I have to, at the very least, be betrothed to him or I will be utterly ruined."

"You will never marry where you do not wish to," Devil insisted doggedly. "I made that promise to myself when you were very young. And I kept it when you collapsed in that church the day you would have married Stanford. I would not see you bullied and browbeaten by a man who did not deserve you nor would I turn down a man's request based on station or fortune. My only concern, Marina, was that you marry for love. This man is a stranger to you."

"If I do not accept his proposal—assuming he was offering sincerely—I will never have the option to marry at all," she insisted. "It is my third Season, uncle. Third. I've jilted one betrothed at the altar after I had already refused some of the most eligible men of the *ton*. So many in fact that now no other offers will be forthcoming… well, not any worth considering." Taking a pause and inhaling deeply, she uttered the admission that would likely change his opinion greatly. "With Stanford once more moving freely in society, all those hideous things he said—"

Devil's frown deepened, his jaw hardening. "Did he say something to you?"

Marina shook her head. "No. Not directly. He doesn't need to speak to me directly. He only needs to be present, and every unpleasant word ever uttered by him will be resurrected and bandied about. His presence here was no coincidence."

Willa's frown deepened. "Do you really believe that he's here plotting against you?"

Marina nodded. "I do believe that. He's here for revenge… Whatever form it may take."

"If you told us why—" Willa began.

"I cannot!" Marina insisted. "I simply cannot. Suffice to say my reasons were and are very good. He is not the man I once thought him to be, and he is not to be trusted. Perhaps, being betrothed to someone else will help to shield me from whatever schemes may be afoot."

"I realize it's not ideal, but you do have another option, Marina," Willa offered gently. "If the situation were explained to Mr. Nutter, with only the tiniest deception about your reasons for ducking into this room, of course—perhaps that it was Miss Whitmore, you hoped to avoid?—I'm certain his pride would eventually recover and he might make that offer. He is at least known to you."

A shudder rippled through her. She couldn't say precisely what it was about Mr. Nutter that was so terribly off-putting for her. Yes, he was boring. But many gentlemen were and none of them incited such a sense of dread in her. "I'd rather die a lonely spinster. Or live in disgrace as a social outcast. I cannot marry him," Marina insisted.

"You cannot marry a stranger," Devil insisted, his tone uncharacteristically firm. It was clear from that how distressing he found the situation.

Marina nodded. "You are right… I cannot. But I can accept his proposal and get to know him. As our wedding date draws near, should we determine that we will not suit one another, then we shall call off the engagement—quietly, of course. Perhaps by then other gossip will have taken center stage and this foible will be forgotten entirely." It didn't bear mentioning that crying off once more would leave her utterly ruined, just as well, though perhaps not quite as disgraced.

"I don't like it," her uncle reiterated, but it was clear from his tone he was starting to come round.

Willa put her hand on his arm. "It's a reasonable solution… the only one with even the slightest hope of an acceptable outcome."

With her aunt on her side, Marina knew it was an argument they could win. "It is the only solution, uncle. Really. The only one."

"It is the best option, Douglas. It may be one we dislike, but it's the only one that allows any possibility for Marina's future happiness… and as she said, a betrothal does not necessarily mean marriage. It can still be called off."

"We know nothing of him," he said. "He was clearly in here for a tryst with Lady Crowden—"

"I don't think that's what it was," Marina interjected, hoping to alleviate his concerns. She also prayed that she was correct. Despite her earlier suspicions, upon reflection it had appeared as though he had been somewhat annoyed by Lady Crowden's dramatics. She'd certainly been annoyed with him if her shrieking had been any indication. "They seemed to be quite at odds. I do believe, based on the small bit I overheard, that Lady Crowden may have been under a mistaken impression about the earl's intentions or interest in her."

"That's a point in his favor, at least," Devil muttered. "Can't stand the woman myself."

On that point, Marina and her uncle were in complete agreement.

"Let me get the earl for you, dearest," Willa said. "We will sort all of this out. I promise."

That was likely a promise her aunt would be unable to keep, despite the very best of intentions.

MARINA WAITED IN the small library, Devil and Willa just outside. The Earl of St. Aiden, whose given name she now could not recall for the life of her, had just entered. He closed the door partially, leaving it ajar by a matter of inches. Enough that it would offer privacy but still maintain propriety. Though in truth, that was a bit like shouting "fire" when only ash remained.

"Miss Ashton," he said, entering the room, "I'd like to begin with an apology. Through no fault of your own, you now find yourself in quite an untenable situation. But it need not be a disastrous one."

Marina took a moment to study him. The room was no longer dimly lit. Her uncle had taken it upon himself to light every taper and lamp in the room. In the ballroom, she'd thought him handsome in a rugged fashion. But his face was far more than simply symmetrically pleasing with masculine proportions. *It was interesting.* His skin was bronzed, slight crinkles appearing at the corner of his eyes. A small scar marked his left eyebrow, slashing through it in a thin line. Now, having a chance to see him fully, without feeling compelled to quickly avert her gaze lest she give someone the wrong idea, she could examine the rugged bone structure that she found so terribly appealing. He might have been carved from granite. Marble would not do for a man such as he.

The Earl of St. Aiden. At least, she thought, if she had to be betrothed to a man, it would be one who intrigued her. With a shock of thick wavy hair that would likely change shades with the season, darker in winter and tending to blond in the summer months, he did not look at all like most of the gentlemen of her acquaintance. There was nothing soft about him. He didn't appear pampered and primped. There was no elaborate hairstyle, no bizarre arrangement of facial hair. He was clean shaven. But then a man with his chiseled jawline and squared chin had no need to hide behind whiskers.

Recognizing that she had been silent for too long, she cleared her throat and addressed his statement. "And is it your fault, my lord? You did not lure me to this room, nor did you arrange for Miss Whitmore and Mr. Nutter to discover us here. I can state with complete certainty that you did not instruct Lady Crowden to fabricate her Banbury tale about our actions. I fear it is my own enmity with certain individuals which has brought us to this juncture."

He inclined his head with a soft chuckle. "No. Let neither of us take responsibility for the sins of others, then. Indeed, I should think had I instructed Lady Crowden to do anything, she might have done the opposite for naught but spite."

That rather dry quip prompted a snort of laughter which promptly disintegrated into a peal of giggles. Given the gravity of their current situation, neither of those responses was appropriate. "I am sorry," Marina said. "I should not laugh. I fear it's a nervous habit."

"Better laughter than tears," he said.

Sobering, Marina said, "I had thought the situation with you and Lady Crowden to be a misunderstanding on her part. Given her rather emphatic response, I hope that I have not misread the situation… perhaps I am wrong, and your romantic interests do lie elsewhere? With Lady Crowden, even. And now you will have no chance to pursue her."

"I had no romantic interest in Lady Crowden. I had too much brandy and she made a grave error in judgment that I now find myself unable to regret," he admitted.

"That requires a certain amount of explanation, my lord."

He sighed heavily. "I was attending a fete at Cremorne Pleasure Gardens… and in the name of frivolity had consumed more brandy than was advisable. It was that which prompted my somewhat slow reaction when the lady in question cornered me on a darkened path and claimed a kiss. I did not respond as expeditiously as I could have in that moment and my delay was misinterpreted as interest.

"I will confess to you that my primary reason in dashing Lady Crowden's hopes in that particular direction, and in fact the very reason I came to London, is that I am in search of a wife. In a roundabout fashion, I suppose she may have done me a favor. Presuming, of course, that you are inclined to accept a proposal from a man you do not know from Adam."

She had once accepted a proposal from a man she thought she knew very well. In that instance, she could not have been more wrong. At least in knowing he was a stranger she would not let her guard down. But the bit of humor she heard in his voice, the dry delivery of his last observation, gave her hope. Not for the love match she thought she would have had with Stanford, but perhaps for future contentment. Of all her options—spinsterhood, ruin, Mr. Nutter, victim to Stanford's latest scheme, or bride to a total stranger—the latter was the most palatable. Which certainly said something about just how dire her situation truly was.

Reflecting on it, she realized her one true complaint with Mr. Nutter, aside from the fact that she felt absolutely nothing beyond dread when forced to bear his company, was that he droned endlessly. There was no inflection, no humor, no emotion of any kind in his speech. It was like listening to someone read aloud when they had no interest at all in the subject matter. It was all so horribly monotonous. Still, Marina did not wish to be dishonest, and he certainly deserved to know that, despite her dowry, she would not be considered an excellent match for a gentleman with such an exalted title. "I fear you may not feel as though she has done you a great service when you learn of the scandal—scandals—attached to my name. My parents were never married… oh, they had a ceremony as I understand it, but it was a sham of one. My mother died, disgraced and disowned, in a hovel in one of the worst areas of London. I have been very blessed that my Uncle Devil and my Aunt Willa have sheltered me from the more cruel aspects of that gossip, but even they could not keep all of it from my ears… And, for my own part, I have been labeled as a bit fickle. And a jilt."

"A jilt?"

She sighed. "Yes. I was betrothed at the end of my first Season but when it came time to marry… well, things had changed rather dramatically. I could not go through with the wedding."

"Why choosing not to marry someone when feeling the union would be destined for unhappiness should mark you as scandalous, I cannot fathom. There is much about society that I am still learning, and I confess to disliking a great deal of it."

Marina felt a wave of relief at his very reasonable response to that. But still, given his admission of his newness to the *ton*, she had to warn him. "Were we to embark upon an engagement, the gossips would be most unkind, especially as my former betrothed has recently returned to town."

He nodded and was quiet for a moment. "And do you wish to reconcile with your former betrothed?"

"Oh, heavens no. I don't want that at all, and even if I did, there are other factors to consider."

When he spoke again, he did so with certainty. "I can only tell you that such things as gossip and scandal matter not at all to me, but only time will prove that to be true."

She blinked in surprise at his complete dismissal of what, in many cases, would have rendered her completely ineligible. In truth, she'd never once anticipated that, given the status of her birth, she'd marry a titled gentleman. Her expectations had never taken her much beyond mere misters. "Not at all? My lord, I do not think you are grasping the ramifications of this. Not that I mean to dissuade you, but I do not wish you to feel that I have been deceptive by omission. With this scandal, in addition to my already questionable reputation, you could well be ostracized."

He nodded. "I am fully prepared for that, Miss Ashton. Quite frankly, with what I've experienced of London society so far, not to be shunned by them might be more of a punishment."

Marina gaped at him. "You cannot mean that, surely! You've traveled very far to partake of society here. I should hope not every aspect of it has been so terribly disheartening."

He shook his head. "I was not after society, Miss Ashton. I came to London to find a bride… and in the interest of being fully honest, I will tell you there are financial considerations for me. I have no interest in your fortune, but I must marry in order to receive the full inheritance of my uncle's estates and wealth. His requirements were simple—a society miss from London. A woman with connections to the aristocracy. As for whatever scandals may be attached to your name, those were never addressed in his will and are… well, they are unimportant to me."

"Why would he do such a thing?"

The earl shrugged. "I never met the man, so I cannot say with certainty."

"I cannot imagine that he would be pleased with the current circumstance we find ourselves in," she mused.

His expression shifted, transforming into something that was quite inscrutable. While she had no notion of what he was thinking, his gaze was very focused upon her as he replied, "Well, he's not here and we cannot ask him, Miss Ashton… You are not alone in having what others would view as a shameful secret. I, too, bear the scorn of those illustrious guests gathered in the ballroom."

"Whatever for?"

He shrugged, "I did not grow up in this world. Being in society such as this was never something that I imagined would happen in my life, nor is it something I ever aspired to. My grandfather was quite scandalous, you see… marrying against his family's wishes and dabbling not only in trade but dirtying his hands in an industry that is both necessary and despised. Coal fields, Miss Ashton, are harsh, often ugly, and, while they may be deserving of the disdain, I feel at home there."

"But you do not speak of them with disdain," Marina pointed out. In fact, if she'd been hard pressed to decipher his feelings on the matter, she would say he was proud.

"Indeed. I like an honest day's work, no matter how dirty it might be." He gestured in the general direction of the ballroom. "They'd rather I had lived in constant debauchery, dueling my way across the continent than to lift a spade and dig alongside those who work for me."

His reply sparked something in her beyond just attraction or curiosity. It sparked admiration, but also commiseration. "So you are a bit of an outcast, also."

A soft chuckle escaped him, but it was dry, expressing a wry sort of humor. "Indeed, Miss Ashton. I've worked most of my life. Not in some clerical capacity which would be moderately acceptable, but getting my hands dirty. I've dug for coal and hauled sacks of it shoulder to shoulder with the men my grandfather employed. And I am, much to the consternation of most people in this elevated sphere, not at all embarrassed or ashamed… Just as I am unashamed of now possessing a title. I am who I am regardless of my social standing… I would likely have refused the inheritance but even in doing so, I would not have been able to escape the obligations to the taxman. Death taxes, Miss Ashton, are the very devil. I'm beginning to have a far greater understanding of what prompted the Americans to revolt."

Marina felt her smile growing, spreading. It wasn't simply that he amused her with his rebellion against the rules of society. His answers, and his rebellious nature, were not flaws. Not in her eyes, at any rate. It set him apart from others. It marked him as a man who would see her worth as a person and not simply the dollar signs of her dowry nor the sins of her parents. In short, his reply had given her hope. "Pharisees, my lord. We are surrounded by them. Many reap the benefits of others' hard work while holding themselves superiorly above it... in both society and in government."

"Indeed, we are. I would offer you a proposal of marriage, Miss Ashton. I can get down on one knee and play the part of a devoted swain, but I think neither of us is one for putting on a front. Instead, I should like to speak with your uncle at length regarding the sort of arrangements we can make to ensure your future. We will announce our betrothal and spend the next few weeks getting to know one another to discern whether or not we truly wish to wed... If that is amenable to you?"

"It is amenable, my lord. I said much the same to my uncle, my lord."

"Caleb," he corrected her. "My name is Caleb Halliwell. I fear I have not become entirely accustomed to hearing 'my lord' and assuming it is directed at me."

"I suppose, as we are supposed to be a betrothed couple, given names would be more convincing, wouldn't they? You must call me Marina... Caleb."

"I will call on you tomorrow morning, Marina. For now, perhaps we should consider taking our leave from the Crowdens' ball before the gossip is spread far and wide."

She sighed. "The gossip is already far and wide. It does not take any time at all for such news to spread. But yes, I think leaving is for the best. I haven't the courage to face the stares and whispers in the ballroom."

CALEB WATCHED HER exit the room first. Her composure, her forthrightness—those things spoke well of her. And boded well for him. The last thing he wanted was to find himself married to a woman like Lady Crowden who screamed and harangued with little or no ability to hear reason.

He hung back for just a moment, allowing her a chance to speak privately with her relations once more and to make what he could only hope, for her benefit, would be a discreet exit. It dawned on him, as she departed in their company, that there was no one for him to speak to. His life was drearily solitary at present. Every invitation had been issued solely on the fact that he was a titled bachelor. There wasn't a soul in all of London who knew him—save for Jacob and lately that had been called into question—who cared for him. It wasn't self-pity, but simply an acknowledgment. If he intended to make a life for himself here, then it was on him to build those connections. And the first one would be with Miss Marina Ashton. Half the battle was won, after all. She'd given him a tentative yes.

When a suitable amount of time had passed, Caleb left the library and headed for the entryway of the Crowdens' home. He avoided making eye contact with anyone along the way and simply ignored the curious stares and whispers. He'd spent less than a month amongst the upper-class society of London. He didn't hold them in disdain, but he did accept that his point of view, his values, would always be somewhat divergent from theirs.

"My lord?"

"I need my coat and my carriage," he instructed the butler. For a moment, he thought about sending word to Jacob about his departure but decided against it. No doubt the gossip had reached his friend already.

With a nod, the servant stepped away to see to the task. As Caleb waited, he felt the prickling sensation of unease, of being watched. Glancing behind him, he could just see the edges of the ballroom through the wide doors. Within that frame, he could clearly see Lady Crowden glaring daggers at him. Just past her was the scheming Miss Whitmore. And yet, even making eye contact with the pair of them, and having both of them look away, that feeling persisted.

Dismissing it as nothing more than the lingering stress of the evening, Caleb accepted his coat and hat from the returning servant and then exited the home. As he headed for his carriage, he was unaware of Mr. Roger Nutter stepping from behind a potted palm, his face set like a stony mask, revealing nothing. But no man watched from the shadows without wicked intent. Not even the boring ones.

Chapter Ten

Et tu, Brute?

JACOB SIPPED BRANDY in the billiard room, content to watch others play. The evening was winding down. He was far more concerned with continued consumption of the quality libations on offer than playing a silly game or seeking the loneliness of his own quarters.

"Mr. Danvers?"

Looking up, Jacob took note of the well-dressed gentleman before him. He was not known to him, but clearly that did not matter. "Are we acquainted, sir?"

"Not as of yet, but we shall be. I am Stanford Williams… and I have acquired your markers."

Jacob squelched the panic welling inside him. "I see. And you are here to demand payment?"

"We are gentlemen. I need not demand anything," Williams said. "It is a debt of honor, after all."

Jacob didn't quite relax. How could he when the man he was speaking with had the power to utterly ruin him? But he did feel some of the tightness dissipate from his chest. "It is a debt of honor, and you are remarkably laissez-faire about such a large debt."

"I have money, Danvers. I've no need of yours."

"Most excellent… for I have none," Jacob admitted. He was being intentionally goading.

Williams smiled, but it was a cool expression, filled with disdain. "There are things more valuable than mere money. Your acquaintance with the Earl of St. Aiden for starters."

"Caleb?"

"Indeed. Were you aware of the scandal your compatriot has embroiled himself in this fine evening?"

Jacob laughed. "Did he get caught with our rapacious hostess?"

"After a fashion… it seems he was caught by her in a most compromising position with a young lady by the name of Miss Marina Ashton. Dark hair, blue eyes, quite lovely if terribly common," Williams said.

"The chit from the ballroom… I warned him about her. Trapped him, has she?"

"Something to that effect," Williams said, leaning back in his seat. "I have a rather unfortunate history with Miss Ashton. She has embarrassed me publicly in a way that I am loath to forgive. And I would spare any truly worthy gentleman from her machinations."

"Is she really that bad?" Jacob asked.

"I suppose it depends on one's perspective. It is certainly to your benefit to see things my way… A bit of retribution with your aid could result in the forgiveness of a significant amount of your debt, Mr. Danvers. And you wouldn't really be disloyal to your friend. After all, it is in his best interests not to be saddled with her for life."

"He needs to marry. Contingencies in the will," Jacob explained.

"Then he should look elsewhere for a bride, Mr. Danvers. For both your sakes," Williams rose. "Consider it, sir. You may reach me at Brown's. I'll be there for the Season. Do enjoy your evening, Mr. Danvers."

"Mr. Williams," Jacob acknowledged. "We both know I'll not

enjoy a damned thing about this dull affair save for the brandy, of course. It's most excellent… and I'll consider all that you've said. That is all I can promise."

The other man smiled tightly. "Naturally. One would expect no less than excellent brandy from the Crowdens. I should advise you, Mr. Danvers, that while your significant debt may be forgiven if you comply with my wishes, it will be pursued to the full extent of the law if you do not.

"I'm aware," Jacob acknowledged, taking a deep draw from the glass. "I didn't think you were offering only out of generosity. I will get the funds. Soon."

"From St. Aiden, I presume?" the man asked, his eyes alight with speculation.

Jacob laughed bitterly. "Unless I suddenly develop the ability to produce it from thin air, it will have to come from him."

Williams was quiet for a moment. "There is an easier way. Think about it."

Jacob's heartbeat pounded loudly, the sound echoing in his ears. Even as he hated himself for it, he heard the words coming from his mouth. "How? Precisely, please."

"You must simply dissuade him. Convince him that she is not the one, that she is flawed, fast, of loose morals—whatever is necessary for him to abandon her at the altar," Williams said, waving his hand dismissively, rather like he was declining supper than trying to destroy a young woman's life.

"He'd never do that," Jacob said. "It's not in his nature."

"Leave that to me."

Jacob wanted to protest, to deny the other man's request on principle alone. But he couldn't. Because desperation won out. And along with his desperation was something else. Something dark and ugly growing within him. Resentment. Anger. Covetousness. They all mixed together in a poisonous stew that fueled the whispers in his mind. *Why did he get to have everything? Why did Caleb deserve it all while he had nothing?*

"I'll do what you've asked. But you'll forgive the debt in its entirety, not simply a portion," Jacob insisted.

"Fine. As you wish… but make it worth it, Danvers."

LEAVING THE CARD room, Stanford moved through the ballroom as unobtrusively as possible. He was far from persona non grata, but that didn't mean his presence would go unremarked upon. And given that his former betrothed's name was on nearly everyone's lips, there was little doubt that he would become a topic of conversation, as well.

When he reached the doorway that led to the orangery, he opened the door and slipped inside, securing it behind him. It was a popular spot for trysts, hence the impressive latching mechanism that could be engaged from inside the room.

Stepping deeper into the dense foliage, he found his quarry seated on a bench, her pretty face pinched with worry. She glanced up at him. "This was not what I had envisioned, Stanford, when you suggested I challenge her to that ridiculous wager! She'll be a countess now."

"It will never happen, Elizabeth," he promised her. "Betrothed is not married. Whatever it takes, I will keep them from actually being wed. Whether that is to Nutter or to the earl, she will never be any man's wife… She need only be betrothed so that she too can feel the sting of abandonment in front of the entirety of the *ton*."

Elizabeth's frown deepened as she accusingly uttered, "You loved her."

"No. I did not. But I was forced to toady to her and her ridiculous uncle so that I could get my hands on her sizable fortune… I resent the embarrassment and wasted efforts, Elizabeth. I do not pine for her nor am I avenging a broken heart."

"Do you love me?" she asked, sounding like a petulant child.

Stanford smiled and held his hands out to her. Then he lied.

"Of course, I love you. I should never have even looked twice at Marina Ashton, but I was blinded by that obscene marriage portion her uncle had settled on her. Had I even a whit of sense, my darling, I would have pursued you—choosing happiness and love over wealth."

"I'm not a pauper, Stanford. I have a sizable fortune, too, you know. We could marry!" She smiled. "Think how utterly miserable she'd be having to apologize to me in front of everyone when I married *you!*"

It was a tempting thought. It, along with Elizabeth's very useful long-standing feud with Marina, was the primary reason he'd cultivated a secret courtship with her. "I will marry you, darling, and you may lord it over her as you please. But first, she must stand in utter disgrace. That will restore my reputation to a degree that no one would ever dare besmirch either of our names. I could not, in good conscience, marry you when it might make you an object of gossip and ridicule. That's why we must keep our romance secret a bit longer. I vow to make it all worth it," he said, sounding sincere even to his own ears. She was a dupe, but an important one. Best to keep her happy until he had no further use for her.

Chapter Eleven

Infamy...

January 15, 1842

S HE COULD FEEL the weight of their stares. In a desperate attempt to act as if everything were perfectly normal, they'd gone for a morning stroll in Hyde Park, as was their custom. Her aunt and uncle flanked her, while her cousins walked several steps ahead, cavorting as only exuberant adolescent boys can. She'd worn a day dress of red tartan, trimmed with black velvet ribbon and she wore a black velvet pelerine pinned with a tartan rose to match. The bonnet of black gathered silk was saved from austerity by the bright red plumes and ribbons that trimmed it. In short, she'd dressed as though she had every wish to be the center of attention. She couldn't very well hide, after all. At least, dressed to the nines as she was, they'd have something to talk about other than the salacious speculation about what had truly occurred in the library at the Crowdens'.

"It's dreadful," Marina murmured. "Everyone is staring."

"Let them stare," Willa insisted. "By strolling through this park, unbothered by the lot of them—and looking quite lovely—you are signifying both your innocence and your unwillingness to be bullied by anyone. You've done nothing wrong, my dear. Unwise, certainly. But not wrong."

"If this fellow doesn't arrive at the house by luncheon, I'll take matters into my own hands," Devil offered, his voice quiet but his tone chilling.

Marina shook her head. "No. No, you will not. While I appreciate your desire to protect me from… this, he didn't actually do anything wrong either. He was attempting to break off a relationship with Lady Crowden which existed primarily in her own mind. And if I had been bold enough to do the same in disabusing Mr. Nutter of any chance of our making a match, then perhaps I wouldn't have felt inclined to hide from him, thus wreaking havoc in all of our lives. Though surely Elizabeth Whitmore would have found another way to create strife and turmoil." She didn't include that the library had been her only avenue of escape due to the presence of Stanford outside. In truth, she wasn't certain what to make of his presence out there. It seemed a bit too contrived to be merely coincidence. She was still puzzling about it.

Willa linked arms with her. "You couldn't have known, Marina. Who could have? Miss Whitmore's machinations are positively Machiavellian. If ever a young woman needed a husband, it is her. Perhaps if she had a household to run and children to raise, she'd be content to meddle in their lives and leave other people alone. Idle hands and all that."

"Pity the children," Devil muttered under his breath.

Suppressing a slight giggle at her uncle's response, one that was wholly representative of his typically sardonic view, Marina shook her head. "I hardly think she'd be content with such wholesome activities. I firmly believe the only joy she takes in life is to make it a misery for others." In fact, Marina was quite certain of that.

For the short time in which she'd attempted to have a friendship with Elizabeth Whitmore she'd seen firsthand just how much glee the girl took in tormenting others. While lying and scheming were always wicked, she could perhaps at least understand it if it benefited the other woman in some fashion. But Elizabeth was cruel for the sake of it, often directing her ire at people who ought to have been beneath her notice. Young women who were perhaps not as pretty, or whose fortunes were such that even beauty could not fully atone for the lack—those were her targets of choice. Or they had been until Marina had confronted her about the behavior and thus courted her ire. Now her pettiness and spite were quite firmly targeted in her direction.

"She can't be all bad. Perhaps she is merely misguided," Willa posed. "I can't help but feel anyone who would court such unpleasantness in life must be a very unhappy person."

"You are too good, Willa," Devil said. "You assume others have a good heart when they do not. There isn't an ounce of kindness or compassion in that wretch of a girl. Only hatefulness and menace."

"Uncle Devil is right," Marina agreed. "But I have no wish to further discuss Miss Whitmore, the Earl of St. Aiden, Lady Crowden, or Mr. Nutter. We can talk it all to death and still the situation will simply be what it will be. But I do believe that we've displayed ourselves enough for one day and I'm tired of feeling like an animal trapped in a menagerie. I wish to go home, eat an entire plate of Cook's cinnamon scones, and bury my nose in a good book."

"A most excellent plan."

They walked on, ignoring stares and whispers. Despite their noble efforts to remain unaffected, certain phrases whispered by those they passed still found their mark like well-aimed arrows. *Not an ounce of shame in any of them. Just like her mother, of course. Heaven knows who her father is. And raised by a penniless governess who puts on airs. A poisoned tree bears poisoned fruit. Do you think she'll make it to the altar this time or will she discard yet another one? How many proposals must one girl receive before she settles down?*

The litany of insults and slights was familiar. Even the smallest misstep Marina had made in life had been received with those same comments. Uttered by different people at different times, they always carried the same message. She was something different, something other. *Something inherently wicked and prone to vice and disgrace.* No matter how much she tried to follow the rules, no matter how perfectly she behaved, the nature of her birth would never be forgotten. The *ton* had long memories of everyone else's public sins while committing far worse in secret. And all of their censure was meted out without the merest hint of compassion.

Exiting the park was a relief, as if she were casting off the weight of their judgment. Their house on Park Lane would offer a reprieve from prying eyes and she longed for the solace it would provide as they walked steadily onward. It was within sight when an unfamiliar carriage halted before it. A familiar figure emerged, and Marina felt a rush of relief.

Caleb Halliwell, the Earl of St. Aiden, was indeed a man of his word. He'd come to call.

HE'D THOUGHT HER beautiful the night before in the ballroom and more so still in the Crowdens' library. But now, seeing her in the bright light of day, the contrast of her vivid blue eyes and dark curls was striking. He could only assume that it was the walk in the park that had put the roses in her cheeks. And it occurred to him in that moment that he would like to be the cause of such high color, to see her blush prettily in response to something he said… or did. The instant attraction he'd felt for her was growing, solidifying into something much more insistent.

The events of the night before had been so chaotic that, while he'd appreciated her loveliness that had piqued his interest from the start, he hadn't truly recognized the depth of his attraction to her. The desire for her that thrummed in his veins was unexpected. He'd never been given to flights of romantic fancy, but perhaps he'd simply never encountered a woman who could prompt such thoughts. He needed to woo her, to convince her that, as a looming wedding date neared, making the match would be the best course. But how? The situation they found themselves in could hardly be conducive to any sort of romantic feeling. Even when they'd been alone the night before, they hadn't truly been private. Her family had been just beyond the door. That was hardly the time to tell her he thought her exquisite.

"Miss Ashton," he said in greeting. "Lord Deveril, Lady Deveril."

"I see you're a man of your word, St. Aiden," Lord Deveril observed. "A point in your favor."

"Thank you, Lord Deveril. I think." He wasn't blind to the man's doubts. Indeed, he'd have had to be a complete idiot to miss them. "If it would be permissible, I should like to take Miss Ashton on an outing. Chaperoned appropriately, of course."

Marina looked to her aunt. It was a telling gesture. While her uncle was clearly a man of significant power and authority, it was quite clear that his wife held a certain amount of sway. "You can send Stephens with me, Aunt Willa. Heaven knows she's certainly an adequate chaperone."

Lady Deveril nodded to her husband who then sighed in capitulation. "Very well. We need to have a conversation when you return, St. Aiden. There are details to be discussed."

Caleb reached into his pocket and retrieved a neatly tied sheaf of documents. "I think you'll find everything in order there, my lord. Having a moment to review it all prior to our conversation might be helpful."

The other man accepted the documents with a nod and then disappeared inside the house. Only a few moments later, a middle-aged woman with steel-gray hair and a stern expression appeared. She took one look at him, and it was apparent that she found him wanting.

"She looks at everyone that way. Well, except for my aunt. She adores her."

Those whispered words of encouragement had come from Marina and while his lips quirked, a full-on smile or laugh would likely turn Stephens against him forever. So he suppressed the urge. It felt a bit as if they were conspirators in a caper rather than strangers thrown together by chance and the machinations of two deceitful women.

"Perhaps we could ply her with sweets at Gunter's," he suggested. "Isn't that where the fashionable young men escort the ladies they are courting?"

The blush on her cheeks deepened ever so slightly. "It is, indeed. I think I should like that, though I cannot be certain of Stephens. She tends to frown upon anything that brings joy to anyone."

Caleb fought back yet another grin as he offered her his arm. When she placed her hand upon his sleeve, even through the layers of fabric, he would swear that he felt a spark of something there. But he was a rational man. She wore gloves. He wore a heavy overcoat in addition to his frock coat and shirt. It was impossible. But the awareness of her innocent touch remained as they set off for their outing, the dour-faced lady's maid trailing behind them.

Chapter Twelve

In the shadows...

THE INTERIOR OF Gunter's was lively. On such a cold day, one would think that ices were the last thing people wanted, but then it, much like Hyde Park, was simply a place to see and be seen. The frozen treats were not the primary attraction.

So much of their daily lives was simply for show, Marina reflected. And she detested all of it. She didn't know enough about country living to say whether or not she'd prefer it. Her aunt and uncle were very much city dwellers, after all. But she thought she might like to at least give it a go. It certainly couldn't be worse than being stared at as though one were a specimen to be examined in a laboratory.

"Are you fixed on remaining in town after the Season?" she asked, striving for a casual tone. She was deeply aware of Stephens hovering nearby, hanging on their every word. No doubt she would run home and report even the slightest of improprieties. Not that Willa asked her to do such things. That was simply Stephens's way.

"I have not yet decided. I rather think that decision, and many others, will be better made at a later date with proper contribution from all parties involved," he answered. His tone wasn't casual at all. It was laced with meaning.

"I see." Rather than ask further questions that would make their situation even more awkward, Marina simply took a bite of the cherry ice he'd ordered for her. "It is rather delicious. One of my favorite treats."

"I shall commit that to memory then," he said. "Are there other things you enjoy? Chocolates? Art? Particular authors?"

"Oh, you would be hard pressed to find any young woman who doesn't love chocolate," she admitted with a laugh. "As for art, I greatly appreciate the endeavors of others but have next to no skill myself. Even my aunt, who is an excellent artist herself and quite accomplished as a teacher, gave me up for a lost cause. But reading… that is my vice, I fear. I could spend entire days with my nose buried in some fantastical novel or other."

"Do you have a favorite?" he asked.

Marina looked at him, worried that he was only asking to be polite. But when she met his gaze, it seemed that he was genuinely interested. "You'll think me a ninny when I admit it, but I do love any book that frightens me. I recently read *The Horror of Oakendale Abbey* and it was simply mesmerizing."

"I don't think it silly at all. I'm a fan of Mary Shelley's, personally. I think she was infinitely more gifted than her husband, and likely Byron as well. Though that opinion was hardly popular when I was at university."

"Did you attend Oxford or Cambridge? Or did you stay in the North?"

"Oh, it was definitely the North," he confessed with a grin. "It was the University of Edinburgh. My grandfather was quite insistent that I not attend Oxford or Cambridge. He was rather firm in his dislike of the aristocracy that he'd fled as a young man, I'm afraid."

Marina smiled at his rueful tone. "Were you there for the Snowball Riots?"

"I'm surprised you know of them! But no. Alas, I had left university the year prior and was working in my grandfather's coal company by then," he explained. "In truth, I am sad to have missed it. It certainly seems as though it would have been an event worth remembering."

"So it would. Does it snow very much in Copley?" she asked.

"It does. I believe we get more snow there than anywhere in all of England. It's a small village. But quite pretty, especially with new fallen snow. Marina… if you are concerned that I mean to take you from London, well, naturally there will be times when I must return to Copley to see to business matters, but I do not expect you to give up your life here."

"What if I wanted to?" She'd voiced the question softly, but the weight of it was very real. For so long, she'd been avoiding any real prospect of marriage, terrified that she would find herself once more in the sights of some well-camouflaged fortune hunter. But their current situation wasn't one of his planning. He hadn't strategized all of this simply to trap her for his own personal gain. And he'd been incredibly forthcoming about his reasons for marrying her. It was refreshing not to be lied to by a man.

"Is your life here in London really so terrible?" he asked softly.

Shaking her head, she replied, "I love Aunt Willa and Uncle Devil. I love my rapscallion cousins. And Charlotte is my dearest friend. But the truth of the matter is that I do not have very much of a life here at all." She paused, drawing a deep breath as she admitted something to him that she had never said to anyone else. "I detest being an object of curiosity and ridicule, a person to be scoffed at by others because they think the gossip about me is true or that I'm somehow beneath them. So many people in the city are simply watching and waiting for me to do something so scandalous that they can pat themselves on the back for looking down their noses at me all my life long."

CALEB WAS QUIET. For most of the outing, he had been answering her questions but not initiating any of his own. It wasn't as if he were lacking in conversational skills, but rather that he was too distracted watching the delicate slide of the small silver spoon between her berry-pink lips. In that moment, he pulled his gaze away long enough to actually formulate a response to what she had said. It felt significant—important to their future.

He would admit, at least to himself, that the shine had worn off London for him as well. Initially, it had been exciting. And there had been some notion for him that with a title, that was where he belonged. But the title did not ultimately change who and what he was... and that was a collier from the North Country. But the city was far dirtier to his mind than any coalfield ever would be. That was at least honest work. The city, in contrast, had streets running with refuse from humans and animals alike. Dark alleyways, where the worst sorts of horrors took place by the minute, abounded. The starvation and misery he'd seen since his arrival was simply astonishing. He was not so naive as to think one man could change it all, nor was he so naive that he didn't recognize that the group of people who had the power to effect such change were disinclined to do so. At least in County Durham, he had the ability to do something about the misery he saw, even if it was simply offering employment or supporting the church's funds for widows and orphans with a substantial contribution.

"I don't care for London," he said simply. "I thought perhaps I would, and it was certainly exciting enough when I first arrived. But the longer I am here... well, it's like anything else when one looks under the shiny surface, isn't it?"

"Indeed it is," she replied. "I've never been out of London for very long at a time. We'd spend time at my uncle's country estate in the summer, but he's a city dweller. He enjoys the excitement of it all. I think he even enjoys society to some degree, but more at its expense than as a participant."

He looked thoughtful for a moment. "I don't care for this

kind of forced gaiety amidst the misery of others. It saddens me to hear that you have faced such censure when you have done nothing—when you could have done nothing—to deserve such treatment."

She looked as though she wasn't entirely so certain. "You are a kind man."

"Not especially," he said, not wanting to foster any idealized notion she might have of him. He had his share of faults, more than most according to some. "I'm a fair man, or I strive to be... If you have finished your ice, I think perhaps we should make our way back to Park Lane. No doubt your uncle will have questions for me by now."

"I'm sure you're correct."

Caleb watched as she placed her spoon in the small bowl and delicately wiped her lips. He was jealous of that piece of fabric, he thought, envying its proximity to a mouth he now desperately wanted to kiss. He understood that such desires were primarily one-sided—at least for the time being—he hoped that the attraction he had for her was not. And he hoped desperately to have an opportunity to nurture that attraction until his desires were reciprocated. But she hardly knew him. If he couldn't stop salivating over her long enough for her to get to know him, it might never change.

Rising from his chair, Caleb offered her his arm, bracing himself for the jolt her touch would create. Like before, it was electric. Perhaps it was that which had him so distracted as they began the short walk back to her home. Or perhaps it was his curiosity at why he was responding to her in such a manner when no other woman had ever had such an effect on him. Was it his own frame of mind as he knew that he wished to find a bride? Was it some sort of primal masculine possessiveness because she had now been promised to him? Regardless, he felt compelled to tell her that what was happening between them may have been brought about by the events at the Crowdens' ball, but that it was certainly not the entirety of it. He wanted her to know that he wanted her for her and that he'd been attempting to seek an introduction to her from before their encounter in the library.

"Marina...?"

She turned back to him. "Yes, Caleb?"

He was so focused on her, on her bright-blue eyes and delicately beautiful features, that his distraction was such that he didn't see the carriage. He didn't take note of it coming toward them at a truly reckless speed. It wasn't until he heard the frightened scream of an onlooker that it penetrated the haze he was under. It was instinct alone that saved them. He simply grabbed Marina about the waist and hauled her backward, both of them falling to the pavement with a heavy thud as the carriage sped past, only narrowly missing them. So narrowly that tracks from its wheels had marked her skirts.

Bruised and winded, he was still acutely aware of the weight of her pressed against him. Even through countless layers of clothing, it was a feast for his senses. But despite taking that moment to savor the pleasure of her closeness, his mind whirled with one thought. Someone had tried to kill them. But which of them was truly the target?

Chapter Thirteen

An unlikely coincidence...

MARINA WAS BREATHLESS. Shamefully, it was less from the fall than from the sensation of having Caleb's arms wrapped around her. The firmness of his chest beneath her and the hard length of his thighs which were pressed between hers was both foreign and enticing. She had never touched another person so intimately. It was as shocking to her as the moment of terror when she'd seen the carriage coming at them.

She was vaguely aware of Stephens standing nearby, wringing her hands and muttering pleas to the Lord Almighty. In any other circumstances, seeing that particular woman so overset by any event would have been a rare treat. Since the event in question had very nearly left them injured at best and potentially killed at worst, her amusement was tempered.

"Are you hurt?" he asked.

"No. No, I don't think so. Were you injured?" she asked, her voice tremulous and breathy.

"No. I'm quite well. Let's get you off this cold pavement, shall we?"

Marina blushed hotly. "Oh, yes. Of course. Forgive me. I was simply so startled that I—" She didn't finish. Thankfully she didn't have to because one of the bystanders came forward to help her up. "Thank you, sir. You are most kind."

"You're very welcome, miss. Though I must say that strapping gentleman of yours is the hero. That carriage would have run you both down for certain. Mad drivers. No business on the roads at all."

Caleb had gotten up by then and took her by the elbow. "We'll take a hansom cab the rest of the way. That was a nasty spill you took."

"You bore the brunt of it," she said. "But yes, I agree. We should take a hansom cab. This all feels very, very wrong. There was no traffic at all. Where did it come from?"

His expression firmed, his jaw clenching tightly. "I cannot answer that. But I mean to find out… First and foremost, let's get you home and handle the necessary business matters with your uncle."

Marina heard his words, and yet the meaning of them was unclear to her—because her attention was focused on a point across the street. In a shadowy doorway, Stanford Williams stood watching them. When their gazes locked, he tipped his hat to her, then he turned and was gone.

"Marina, let's get you home," he said again, his tone incredibly gentle and obviously concerned.

"What?"

"Home. I'll speak with your uncle while you recuperate from this… incident," he offered.

In the upheaval of the last moments, their reasons for returning to her home had almost escaped her. As he hailed a cab for them and then helped her inside, it all came rushing back. With Stephens occupying the position opposite her, there would be no chance to discuss it with him in any depth. Everything they said would be reported back to her aunt and uncle. While she loved them both dearly, they did have a tendency toward wrapping her in woolen cloth as if she were some sort of fragile doll.

The situation with Lady Crowden, Mr. Nutter's unreasonable anger, Elizabeth's machinations. And the appearance of Stanford just as they were nearly run down by a carriage. Those were not facts that could be easily ignored. While she was not one given to paranoia or flights of fancy, one still had to wonder if perhaps the runaway carriage that nearly hit them hadn't been an accident at all. Was someone out for revenge? Did someone intend to sabotage the potential marriage for their own petty reasons? After all, it wasn't the first time in her life that someone had plotted her death.

Even acknowledging that fact, it sounded outlandish to her own ears. Perhaps if she hadn't kept Stanford's previous scheme a secret, uttering it now would not seem so desperate. But she hadn't shared her reasons for breaking the engagement, and to do so now would be suspect at best. Others might well call her a liar outright. She had no proof of anything. Her only knowledge of his plot had come from eavesdropping on a whispered conversation between him and whoever his unknown paramour had been. It sounded completely implausible. So much so that she dared not utter it aloud.

Part of her hoped it had been an accident. An accident and a coincidence. After all, they were in a very busy shopping district. It was quite possible that he'd been there for an entirely different reason that had naught to do with her. Anyone nearby would have been drawn by the commotion. But she'd lived in London all her life and never come so close to a nearly catastrophic incident. She remained quiet, contemplating the matter on the ride home. Caleb was also silent. A new fear emerged then. What if he was having second thoughts? What if, upon reflection, he found her an unsuitable choice after all? Scandal was one thing to tolerate, but for an association with her to make him a target? That was something else altogether.

CALEB'S THOUGHTS WERE scattered, bouncing all around in a

chaotic fashion. There was one thing he was certain of, however. What they had just experienced could not, with any degree of plausibility, have been an accident. He had no wish to frighten Marina by voicing such suspicions, but with all his heart he believed that someone had just tried to kill them. But then he had to consider, perhaps the attempt hadn't been meant for both of them. He had stopped her and she had turned to him. So had the driver meant to kill him… or her? Without ascertaining which of them was the true target, there was little he could do to identify the actual source of the threat.

He would have to tell Lord Deveril, he decided. The man needed to know that someone was conspiring to harm Marina. But the question was why? Had she been targeted in any way prior to their current predicament? If not, then could it be that their impending marriage was the motivation for someone to harm her?

When the cab slowed to a stop before the palatial Park Lane home, he climbed down first, helping the dour-faced maid down, and then offered Marina his hand which she accepted. Somewhere in the chaos of the day her glove had torn and she had removed it. For the first time, he touched her bare skin, felt the jolt of that connection in its full force. It nearly rocked him back on his heels. He also recognized one very important fact. She felt it too. Her sharply indrawn breath and the way her stunned gaze lifted to his face told the truth of that.

With no small degree of reluctance, he let her go. "Let's get you inside."

Escorting her up the steps, the door was opened before they ever reached it. The butler took one look at the pair of them, raised his eyebrows, and then simply stepped aside. They were, Caleb admitted, quite noticeably disheveled from their ordeal.

"You look like you've been run over by a carriage!"

Caleb looked up to see a boy on the stairs, no more than fifteen or so. He bore some resemblance to Marina, but he had the fair hair of Lady Deveril who he assumed was the boy's mother. "We very nearly were," Caleb replied to him. "It's been an eventful day."

"It certainly has." That droll quip had come from Lord Deveril who had emerged from his study. "I take it there is some reasonable explanation for your current dishabille?"

"We'll discuss it in your study if you do not mind, my lord. I'm certain that Ma—Miss Ashton wishes to refresh herself after the tumble we took."

If Lord Deveril caught the slip of her name, he chose to ignore it. Perhaps in favor of getting to the bottom of why they both looked as though they'd rolled in the street. In some ways, he supposed they had. With a deep breath, he followed the man into his study with a backward glance at his nearly betrothed as she made her way up the stairs.

"What the deuce is going, St. Aiden? And I'll thank you to be straight with me on the matter. I've no patience for prevarication."

Caleb nodded. "I believe, my lord, that someone just tried to murder either Miss Ashton or myself. Possibly they could have wished to see us both eliminated, but I think it unlikely. From the way the incident occurred, I cannot actually say who was the intended target. I can only say that a carriage came out of nowhere. There was no traffic, the street was not busy. There had been nothing. And as we stood at the edge of the sidewalk, it came barreling out of nowhere and nearly swept us both down with it."

Lord Deveril slammed his fist down on the top of his desk. "Why? I want to know why?"

"I wish I could offer a conclusive answer. Perhaps it is jealousy—Until last night, I had no enemies. Now, there is Lady Crowden whose pride was wounded by my perceived rejection of her. There is Mr. Nutter who seems not at all pleased by this turn of events. And then of course there is Miss Whitmore who seems to hold Miss Ashton in no small amount of dislike. For the life of me, I cannot imagine any one of them choosing to commit murder over that and certainly not to have carried it out so efficiently that the first attempt would happen barely more than twelve hours from the events that have brought me here to your home today."

"No. I can't see that either. You may not have enemies, St. Aiden, but I do. And Marina's life has not been an easy one. Her father—and she does not know this—was a traitor. A man with many enemies. He may be long dead, but many of those he wronged remain and they are quite embittered. This is no simple thing. There could be any number of culprits but that is best left for another day... There is also her former betrothed."

"Her former betrothed?"

"Yes," Lord Deveril said. "She cried off the day of the wedding—well, in truth, she fainted dead away at the altar and I carried her out. When she came to, I offered to take her back to the church, to speak with the man and try to smooth things over, but she declined. She stated, very calmly and with perfect composure, that she'd learned something about her intended which indicated that he had not been honest about his feelings for her. It was something she'd wrestled with for several days and had only been willing to see it through to avoid scandal. With her collapse, scandal was a surety and thus no longer a reason to persevere."

Caleb frowned at that. "She'd told me that all of society thought her a jilt... and fickle. I assume he had something to do with that?"

"Indeed. He had no concern for her, didn't fear that she was unwell or think to ask after her welfare. Instead, he turned on her like a jackal and incited all the gossips to do the same."

He was quiet for a moment, considering all that. Finally, Caleb asked the pertinent question, "Did she tell you why she wished to cry off? Specifically, that is."

"No. She simply said she had no wish to marry a man whose affections were merely feigned and would provide no further details on the matter. I must say that she was quite firm... and he did not take it well. He ranted and raved to anyone who would listen about how she had wronged him—ruined him, even. It was the first indication he'd given that perhaps Marina's fortune was what had attracted him rather than Marina herself."

Caleb tucked that information away, knowing that it would be something he would need to tread very carefully around. "Do you think he would be out for revenge?"

"Possibly. If I'd understood the nature of his character, I'd have never given my consent to start. So it's anyone's guess," Lord Deveril said with a shrug. Then he leaned in, his expression taking on a shrewd quality. "Presently, I'm less concerned about his character than about yours."

Caleb didn't take offense. Under the circumstances, if the man wasn't concerned about what manner of gentleman he was, he would have been a fool. "I can assure you that, while marriage is a necessity for me to secure my own fortune, I've no interest in hers."

Lord Deveril tapped his fingertip on the documents spread out on his desk. "Indeed, your proposed terms for the marriage contract have illustrated that quite well. In fact, those very generous terms are the primary reason I am inclined to accept the match. I wanted her to marry for love, but barring that, I would like her to marry someone whom I can trust to provide and care for her."

"I have every intention of doing so. And for the record, I had a brief exchange with Miss Ashton in the ballroom and was set on approaching Viscount Seaburn to make a formal introduction. I had already set my mind to pay court to her. I would have pursued her as my bride regardless of the circumstances of her birth... These circumstances have simply hastened the pace at which this particular course is being run."

DEVIL LEANED BACK in the heavily upholstered leather chair at his desk and stared at the man before him with no small amount of concern. But there was also a bit of hope. Marina had not seriously entertained even one suitor since her broken engagement to Stanford Williams. In truth, he'd thought perhaps she'd sworn off the notion of marriage altogether. Whatever had prompted her sudden willingness to walk down the aisle again, he didn't know. But if it were simply the scandal, pigs would fly. It had to be something about the man in front of him.

Objectively, he was handsome enough if a bit rough around the edges. And perhaps that was his appeal, Devil thought. Perhaps Marina was attempting to marry a man as different from her former betrothed as possible. Stanford Williams was the antithesis of rough around the edges. The man had been as smooth as any charlatan peddling tonics and magic elixirs. To his mind, St. Aiden was by far the better choice. But it was all so very fast. The idea that she might marry in haste and then live a life filled with regret ate away at him. She'd suffered too much unhappiness and difficulty in her young life already. And from the moment she had come into his care, her happiness had always been his priority.

Thinking about Williams, he frowned. He didn't know the specifics of her reasons for crying off, but he knew that they'd hurt her terribly. Some of the light had gone out of her eyes since then. Her insistence on remaining unattached had caused a stir, to say the least, and gossip had been very unkind. It, along with the many scandals already shadowing her, had marked her in the eyes of society and she had suffered since. But this man before him seemed not to care at all about society. It was yet another point in his favor, and those were beginning to stack up rather nicely.

Devil retrieved the sheaf of papers St. Aiden had given him earlier. The settlement offer that had been drafted was a generous one. More generous than he could have imagined. The man was clearly very wealthy. "What are you getting out of this? Other than my niece, of course."

The earl was quiet for a moment. "My uncle's will left specific stipulations for me. The title is mine, of course, as are the estates. But to claim the bulk of his wealth, which is necessary to support those estates, I have to marry—a society miss from London with at least some tenuous connection to the aristocracy—criteria which Miss Ashton fits to the very last. While I am far from a pauper, the obligations of being a significant landowner... well, the taxes alone would beggar me."

Devil was not surprised by his answer. It had long been a way to bring young men to heel—contingencies upon their inheritance. In truth, he was relieved to know that this man would be honest with him about such things. But was he honest with Marina?

As if he'd read Devil's thoughts, the earl said, "Miss Ashton is aware of these stipulations. I felt it was for the best to be entirely forthcoming about such matters."

Devil couldn't disagree. While nothing about the earl seemed questionable, the man was still largely unknown to them. "The settlement then is contingent upon meeting the terms of the will, but this offer is made without contingency. So where does your wealth come from?"

"It isn't attached to the title," the earl responded. "It comes from the dirty coal fields that so many in the upper classes look down upon. It may be hard, filthy work, but it can be quite lucrative."

"I've invested in a few mines myself," Devil said. "Not to the same degree that you are involved with them, apparently. But I can attest to their lucrativeness. I am quite pleased with what you've offered here. It's generous. Incredibly so. But unnecessary. I've provided a generous settlement for Marina. It has always been my intent that she be well taken care of regardless of the wealth and station of whomever she married."

"Then we are of like mind. If you are amenable to the terms presented, you may have the marriage contract drawn up. You can, of course, include a clause disavowing any financial ramifications should Marina elect not to go through with the wedding. I would also ask that you include stipulations that any funds she brings into the marriage are hers alone."

Lord Deveril tapped his chin thoughtfully. "I account myself, barring that one failure with Mr. Williams, to be a very good judge of character, St. Aiden. And however this all occurred, your actions have offered me some peace of mind. It is that, and not your generosity with this settlement, which sways me. I will have the contract sent round to you tomorrow… Eaton Square?"

"Yes, Lord Deveril… You may account yourself to be a good judge of character, but it never hurts to get all the information."

Devil shrugged, quite unapologetic for having snooped. "I spoke with friends about you. That none of us have heard your name bandied about was certainly a mark in your favor. You've been in town for a month. That would have been enough time to make yourself known in disreputable company if you were inclined to indulge in drinking, gaming and… other activities. Your frequent companion, Mr. Danvers, is another matter. He's been making quite the reputation for himself."

St. Aiden sighed heavily and there was a flash of something— annoyance, perhaps disappointment—in his eyes. "Jacob is his own man. We have been friends since childhood, but I confess that he seems like a stranger to me now. As for my only misstep—to date, at least—has been the misunderstanding with Lady Crowden. But depending on how this all sorts itself out, it remains to be seen whether it was a misstep at all… If it's amenable to you, and Miss Ashton consents, I'd like to take her to the theater tonight."

"Willa and I shall escort her, but you are certainly welcome to join us in our carriage… I think, after today's events, it would be best if the pair of you did not travel alone together," Deveril explained. "There is safety in numbers, after all. Another pair of eyes to help discern where any threat is coming from might be an added benefit. After all, you cannot watch everyone, and we must determine which of the pair of you is the intended target."

Caleb saw the wisdom of his words. In truth, he even agreed with them, but he didn't like them. Not at all. The degree to which it perturbed him to have his time with her so curtailed was astonishing. But some time with her, even in the company of others, was better than nothing. He nodded, offered his thanks, and took his leave.

Chapter Fourteen

The spectacle...

AFTER HE'D FINISHED dressing, Caleb descended the stairs of the townhouse and made for the study. Upon entering, he found Jacob there. The other man was seated at his desk, feet propped up on it and sipping brandy.

"You appear to be quite comfortable," Caleb observed. Lord Deveril's assessment of his friend remained topmost in his mind. He wasn't unaware of Jacob's headlong dive into every vice the city offered, but for him to have made himself so well known to others in his pursuit of hedonistic pleasures in such a short time begged one very pertinent question. *How was he paying for it?* The bequest he'd been given was gone entirely.

Jacob shrugged, an air of insouciance emanating from him. "If I'm not perfectly comfortable in the home of my oldest friend, where could I be?"

That answer grated, the phrasing in it only too familiar. It felt as though Jacob used the long standing of their friendship as a kind of currency. "Is there some reason you are here tonight?"

"Just inquiring about this debacle you've gotten yourself into," Jacob replied. "You do not have to marry her, you know?"

"No, I do not have to. I choose to, as I should. And I will follow through," Caleb insisted. "It's the right thing to do. It's also what I want to do. I came to London, if you recall, to find a bride and now, in a somewhat unorthodox fashion, I have done so."

Jacob rose, all hints of indolence gone. "I've heard the gossip about her. A fickle flirt. And a jilt. Left a man all but weeping at the altar. A girl who would do such a thing—to run out of her very own wedding? Well, it hardly speaks well of her."

Caleb's fists clenched at his side. "That's enough, Jacob. I will not discuss the matter further!"

Jacob continued on as if he hadn't even spoken. "She's practically ruined already—there would be no shame in just walking away from her."

Caleb's temper rose. "I'm going to pretend this conversation never took place. And if you are wise, Jacob, you will never repeat the horrid things you've just said."

"What horrid things, Caleb? It's the bloody truth. Half of society thinks her foolish and the other half thinks her fast. And you know nothing of her. You've only just met her for Pete's sake!"

"And I haven't a damn to give!" Caleb's shouted reply echoed in the room. It was a rare thing for him to lose his temper and apparently it gave even Jacob pause as the man stepped back. Continuing, reining in his temper, he said, "I do not care what society thinks of her, Jacob. What matters is what I think of her. She's a lovely girl—kind, intelligent, and beautiful. Through no fault of her own, or mine for that matter, we are in a situation where marriage is the only honorable option. As she is my future wife, I will not have her name bandied about by you or anyone else. I'll thank you to remember that she will the Countess of St. Aiden."

Jacob sneered. "You've taken to being a titled gentleman quite well, haven't you? Not even two months since it came to you and already you're a different man."

Was he? Perhaps, Caleb acknowledged. He was different enough to question the motives of a man who'd been his friend for a very long time. After all, he'd outfitted Jacob for society events. He'd put the man up in an apartment at the Albany. Jacob was there on his charity. How could he help but wonder if perhaps that wasn't the source of the other man's concerns. "Tread carefully, Jacob. This will be the last time I offer that warning… good evening."

Turning on his heel, Caleb left the study and headed for the front door. Donning his great coat and top hat, he exited the house. As he climbed into his carriage, Jacob's words reverberated in his head. But it wasn't doubts of Marina Ashton that plagued him. It was doubts about his old friend and whether or not wealth and position might finally drive a permanent wedge between them.

MARINA TUGGED AT one of her elbow-length gloves. She detested them, but they had to be worn not only because theater attendance required such a degree of formality but also for the purpose of hiding the ugly scrapes and bruises from their earlier tumble. She was not looking forward to attending the theater though she understood the necessity of it. They needed for society to believe them to be a young couple, deeply infatuated with one another and on the cusp of marriage. It was the only way they would survive the scandal of having been found in such a truly compromising position. And Marina was deeply aware of the consequences that came with being judged guilty by association—or relation. After all, she could not even remember the sound of her mother's voice or recall her face, beyond the miniature portrait that her uncle had given her. The poor woman had died in a hovel, disgraced and alone save for her Uncle Devil who had arrived at the very last moment.

It was never far from her mind that, while he'd been too late for her mother, he'd certainly saved her. She could not even imagine what her life might have been had he not taken her in without a second thought. Then, of course, there was Willa who had started as her governess and who had become like a mother to her. There were so many feelings intertwined within her for them. Gratitude. Guilt. A sense that perhaps she hadn't deserved the salvation that had been afforded her. The very last thing she wanted was to cause them any pain or embarrassment.

She didn't want to further taint the family's reputation. The boys, Desmond and Gervase, would be fine. By virtue of their sex, the rules for their behavior were significantly more lax. But it was her youngest cousin, little Isabella, who was her deepest concern. At only seven years old, she was far too young to understand any of what was happening. Even then, she might be judged very harshly on it when it was her turn to enter society. Not everyone had been so accepting of her governess-turned-aunt in society. With that, and then Marina's own scandals, it could make things very difficult.

A soft knock sounded at the door and her maid opened it. After a brief exchange, Ethel returned and placed the final diamond pin in her coiffure. "The earl has arrived, miss."

"Thank you, Ethel. My velvet cloak is already downstairs. I shouldn't need another wrap. The very notion that there might be a draft in an overly crowded theater is laughable," Marina stated dryly. In truth, it would be the embarrassment and impotent fury at suffering the judgments of others that would likely heat her blood. *Or perhaps it might simply be the presence of Caleb Halliwell.*

The memory of what it had felt like to have the length of her body pressed to his had not left her. Throughout the remainder of the day, it had been perpetually on her mind. Even in the midst of that terrifying incident, it had stirred something within her that she'd never felt before. Of course, she'd been betrothed to Stanford and never experienced those sensations, but then she'd never been pressed against him intimately. Indeed, their betrothal had lasted months and he'd never so much as kissed her. Of course, she understood why now. But she didn't wish to think about Stanford and his deceptions. It was her current betrothed who was most prominently on her mind. Now, with her heightened awareness of him, she wondered how on earth she would survive the night sitting next to him in the quiet recesses of a private box at the theater.

Taking a deep and hopefully steadying breath, Marina left her room and descended the stairs to the small drawing room where everyone waited for her. As per usual, she was the last one to be ready. "Good evening," she said, as she entered. Caleb and her uncle had both risen and remained so until she took a seat next to Willa.

"Marina," Willa began, "Lillian and Val shall be joining us at the theater. It will be a bit cramped with all six of us in the box, but it will be nice to have them there I think. Afterward, we shall adjourn to their house for refreshment. If you are agreeable, of course, Lord St. Aiden?"

"I should be very glad to join you there if Miss Ashton and the hosts have no objection," he replied.

His voice was so deep and rich. It raised gooseflesh on her skin. She was so distracted by it that it took a moment, where the silence stretched to the point of discomfort, for Marina to realize that a response was required from her. "Oh, certainly. Of course. I'd be very pleased to have your company afterward."

"As we'll all be going to the same place," Willa said, "It seems rather a waste of time and good company to take two carriages. You must ride with us, Lord St. Aiden."

Marina caught the look that passed between Caleb and her uncle. After a moment's hesitation and a slight nod from Devil, Caleb inclined his head. "I'd be delighted for the opportunity to spend more time in your very pleasant company. Thank you, Lady Deveril."

They all chatted together for a moment more, no one saying anything of consequence. It was all perfectly civilized and yet completely awkward. When the butler stepped in to tell them the carriage was waiting, it was an inordinate relief.

Inside, Willa and Marina took the forward-facing seat while Devil and Caleb had taken the rear facing seat as true gentlemen should. Conversation was limited and sparse. Thankfully, the drive to the theater was a relatively short one. Waiting in line to disembark from the carriage was quite another thing. The queue was considerable. A fact only exacerbated by the way everyone was congregating in front of the theater—to see and be seen, to partake of, spread, or claim center stage in current gossip. Rumors were currency in their world, after all, Marina thought with no small degree of bitterness.

As they finally reached the entrance and were disembarking, a whispered voice murmured, "It's rather like being a caged beast in a menagerie."

Marina glanced up, heartened by Caleb's observation which mirrored her own thoughts from earlier. "I was thinking much the same myself earlier today while in the park. Perhaps if we entertain the crowd enough, they will then leave us be."

He shook his head. "They are ravenous. Insatiable when it comes to gossip… especially if it's of the salacious variety. They'd not be satisfied until we were torn to shreds."

They said nothing further until they were inside. Nothing could be heard at any rate. Once they were lost in the throng of gathered people, the noise of them all was quite deafening. Weaving their way through the mass of people was a bit like water finding its way through a narrow crack in stone. Twisting and turning, it felt like utter chaos. Once they finally reached the entrance, everyone collectively breathed a sigh of relief. However, there was no reprieve to be had inside. The lobby was as packed as the sidewalk and stairs had been outside, if not more so.

"It's an absolute crush," Willa observed.

Devil grimaced. "I hadn't intended to bring it up but there were significant stories in the gossip sheets today. No doubt many expected us to attend tonight as this particular play has been much anticipated."

Marina tried to keep her expression neutral, to wear that

affected look of coolly civil disdain. The truth of the matter was that she wanted only to run out of the theater, throw herself into the carriage, and return home. Once there, she would bury her head beneath the covers on her bed and never emerge. Since the morning where she would have married Stanford, being the center of attention had become a painful and anxiety ridden experience for her. "I hate to be the center of attention, everyone looking at me and whispering," she said under her breath.

"It will be only for a short time," Caleb replied just as softly. "Let's find our box and have at least some semblance of comfort and privacy."

She didn't try to answer. It felt as if her throat were closing—as if she couldn't catch her breath. Had Ethel laced her corset too tightly? Of course, every corset was too tight. She'd certainly never responded in that way to the familiar constrictive device. Feeling as though she were on the verge of fainting dead away, she grasped Caleb's arm more firmly. In return, he placed his hand over hers, offering welcome reassurance.

Together, they navigated the crowded lobby until they could finally reach the stairs. They climbed slowly until they reached the balcony level and located their box. Settling into their seats as they waited for the performance to start, Marina was once more overcome with a strange feeling. But it wasn't the panic induced by the crowd below. Nor was it the strange awareness she felt of her physical self when she was with Caleb. This was something wholly different. And terrifying. It was the prickling sensation that one felt when being watched, observed. *Stalked.*

Glancing around, looking for the source of that discomfort, she found herself staring into the cold, hard eyes of Mr. Roger Nutter. No longer the affable but dreadfully dull suitor—he looked at her with pure hatred burning in his gaze. With Stanford earlier and now him, she felt like prey being stalked in the wild. Danger seemed to lurk at every turn.

"Marina, you must come shopping with us tomorrow morning!" Lillian insisted. "Your Uncle Valentine has offended me deeply and so now I must go spend a king's ransom on things I absolutely do not need. You will benefit greatly from my annoyance with him."

Glancing back at her aunt, she forced a smile. "Certainly, Aunt Lillian. I will never pass up an opportunity to spite shop with you."

Marina turned back, but Mr. Nutter was gone, vanished into the crowd. It made her wonder if perhaps she hadn't imagined it all together. Only the strangely discomfited sensation remained to haunt her.

Chapter Fifteen

An introduction to the art...

THE EVENING HAD been more enjoyable than he had expected, especially when he considered the ugly confrontation he'd had with Jacob before it began. Despite the crowds and curious stares, the play had been delightful and the company exceptional. Now, in the home of Viscount and Viscountess Seaburn, Caleb finally found a moment of privacy with Marina. They were in the study, the door open, of course. In the connecting room, there was a great deal of noise as Lord and Lady Deveril played a game of hearts with the Viscount and Viscountess Seaburn.

"You have been very quiet this evening," he said. It had concerned him. He wondered if perhaps she were having second thoughts about their potential match.

She looked away, obviously uncomfortable. "Something happened at the theater and if I tell you... you will think me mad. Or hysterical. Some reactionary creature with an imagination too vivid for my own good."

He shook his head, a smile curving his lips. Though he'd known her for only twenty-four hours, he was fairly certain hysterical and reactionary were words that would never be used to describe her. "I don't believe you could say anything which would make me think that. You can tell me. I vow to listen without judgment."

She lifted her head, her eyes bright. "I was very discomfited. It felt as though I were being watched… not as I was with the gossips and scandal mongers when we were out and about today, though they were there aplenty. This was different. Menacing. I looked about and… it seems so silly and farfetched that I am reluctant to say."

He hadn't spoken to her of his suspicions about the incident with the carriage. That she felt the looming danger as well only reaffirmed for him that their situation was dire indeed. "You need not fear that I will be dismissive of your concerns. This is a situation that we are in together. What affects one impacts the other equally. We need to trust one another, Marina. You can tell me anything."

She was hesitant, but eventually gave a sharp, decisive nod. "Of course. You are quite right. As we arrived at the theater and entered our box, I saw Mr. Nutter. He was watching us… his eyes filled with a level of rage I would never have thought him capable of. I turned away for just a moment to reply to Aunt Lillian's question about tomorrow's shopping expedition, and when I turned back, he was gone. And then there was earlier today. With the accident, or very nearly accident."

"What about the accident?"

She looked down, her lashes casting dark shadows on her cheeks. "I saw my former betrothed. Stanford was standing in a doorway just across the street. He tipped his hat to me and then just walked away. Was he following me? Did he engineer the accident? Or am I just suffering some sort of delusion and I imagined the whole thing? And Mr. Nutter, as well."

Caleb shook his head, a feeling of cold dread settling in the pit of his stomach. "I do not believe it to be only your imagination. Firstly, I saw the gentleman today. I thought his behavior odd, but then it was a very odd situation. As I had no notion what your former betrothed looked like, I did not make the connection. But he was very familiar… was he present last evening?"

Marina nodded. "He was lurking in the corridor behind Mr. Nutter and Miss Whitmore. The primary reason I wound up in that study rather than escaping via the terrace was that he was already there… on the terrace."

Caleb nodded. "As for Mr. Nutter, while I did not see him tonight, I did have a very similar experience leaving the Crowdens'. I thought it was Lady Crowden or perhaps even Miss Whitmore with her unreasonable grudge against you. But now I have to wonder if perhaps it wasn't this Mr. Nutter, or it might well have been Mr. Williams. They both certainly have reason to be displeased. Mr. Nutter's admiration of you is of long standing… did he—was there an understanding between the two of you?" The idea that she might prefer to be with someone else bothered him far more than it should have.

Her eyes widened with shock, a shudder of distaste quickly following suit. "Oh, heavens no. He's been trying, regardless of any dissuading on my part, to court me for the last three years, even while I was betrothed to Stanford. Since I had my debut, he has attended all the events I have. I've never encouraged him and have avoided situations where I might be forced to say something harsh to him about any prospective match between us. Not because I wished to give him hope but because—since the incident when I was to have married Stanford, well, it's given me the reputation of being a jilt. And having refused two other thoroughly inappropriate offers of marriage, I have also been viewed as vain and overly proud. If I refused yet another… well, it would not be good."

"He's never proposed?" Caleb queried, wanting to be certain the man would have no grounds to interfere.

"Oh, no!" Marina replied. "I have done my utmost to avoid him at all costs. I have made quite certain to provide no opportunity for such an event to transpire. Aunt Willa has helped me to avoid him as much as possible, as has my dear friend, Charlotte. Whenever they saw him make any attempt to maneuver me into a situation where he might pose such a question, they intervened.

Normally, I could manage to avoid it myself, but that wasn't always an option. I didn't wish to be rude to him, you see? Despite recent events, I always thought him a nice man. Very dull, to be honest, but still nice. Perhaps my hesitance to refuse him outright has complicated the situation. Perhaps he feels as if I've somehow led him on, though that was never my intent."

Caleb frowned, a deep groove forming between his devilishly peaked eyebrows. "You say that as though you no longer view him in that light. Not the dull bit of it, but the other part. While he has given no real evidence to the contrary... yet, you no longer think him to be a 'nice man'?"

Marina shook her head with some confusion. "I wish I knew. I certainly never thought him dangerous. He looked completely furious—no, he looked at me as though he hated me," she said. "Perhaps I was entirely mistaken in the nature of his character. It would not be the first time."

"What does that mean precisely? That you've been wrong before about someone's character or being a danger to you?"

It was like the closing of a door. Instantly and decisively. Her gaze grew shuttered, her shoulders stiffened. That question had struck a nerve.

"I misspoke," she said with a slight smile, though it did not reach her eyes. "When I referenced other mistakes, I only meant in a very general manner. What if I was wrong to simply avoid the confrontation so? What if I had told him in that first Season there was no chance at all? He might have moved on and married someone else already."

That wasn't what she'd meant at all. It bothered him that she didn't feel she could be honest with him, but at the same time, the subject was one that was very concerning and would require a significant amount of trust. He'd have the truth from her eventually. "If I'd been attempting to court a woman for three years and she steadfastly avoided me, I should think, at some point or other, I would have caught on to the fact," he mused. "Any sane man would, I should think. Regardless, what you did or did not do in the past cannot be changed."

"That is true enough. I've certainly managed to put gentlemen off before with less effort," she admitted ruefully.

Caleb was quiet for a moment, considering the facts, few as they were. "I do not think it would have made a great deal of difference one way or another. What you're describing is not a man who is in love and has had his hopes dashed. You're describing a man who is obsessed... And obsession is never reasonable."

That statement rang ominously in the room. He hadn't meant to frighten her with such a foreboding assessment. He saw the shiver of fear that rippled through her and then watched as she crossed her arms protectively in front of her. He wanted to comfort her. He longed to take her in his arms and reassure her that he would look after her—he would make it all better. And those urges were something of a puzzle to him. Yes, he was attracted to her. To an extent he had never really experienced before, and certainly that attraction had intensified far more rapidly than he could have anticipated. But the possessive and protective instincts he felt for her went far beyond simple attraction or even infatuation. She stirred something inside him—something quite primitive and rather alarming in its intensity.

"What should we do, Caleb?" She posed the question softly. "Honestly, it feels as though there is danger at every turn now. Between the incident this afternoon and then seeing Mr. Nutter at the theater, it's rather like being hunted."

"We proceed as planned," he said. The sooner they married—and he intended to do everything in his power to ensure that she wished to do so—the sooner he would be able to see to her protection both night and day.

Caleb reached into his pocket and produced a small wooden box. "To that end, if we are intended to appear as a couple betrothed, then there should be a betrothal ring. It's only fitting."

"It feels quite strange to accept such valuable tokens when in truth we are little more than strangers to one another," she offered with a frown.

"It's a rock," he offered with a shrug. "A pretty one that has been cut and polished, but still… only a stone, not so different from the pebbles that find their way into one's shoes. It has value because man has decided it does. That is all."

A soft laugh bubbled from her. "What a shockingly pragmatic interpretation!"

His lips quirked slightly. "Blame it on my very middle-class upbringing."

She nodded. "I don't mind that, you know? I rather like it, in fact. You're not like anyone else I've ever known, Caleb. It's a welcome and very refreshing change."

Caleb did the thing he'd been wanting to do since he'd first seen her. He stepped closer, his hand moving to her face, cupping her cheek, savoring the silken texture of her skin. Her eyes were wide, her cheeks flushed with anticipation, and her soft, full lips parted ever so slightly on a sigh. Leaning in, he brushed his lips over hers. It was the faintest whisper of a kiss, but it set his heart pounding and had the blood racing in his veins.

When he pulled back, she was wide-eyed and quite stunned. In a hushed whisper, she murmured, "I've never been kissed before."

He smiled somewhat ruefully. "In truth, you haven't been kissed yet. Not truly. That was… a brief introduction. There is so much more to it than that and I look forward to sharing it all with you," he admitted.

"Is this real?" she asked. "Or is it simply that we are trying to lend credence to the tale being spun to save my reputation?"

"It's more than a tale, Marina. It's an intention. I haven't entered into this as merely a ruse. I've simply offered to allow you to bow out without reprisal when the time comes should you desire to do so. But make no mistake, I came to London for the purpose of finding a bride. And from the very second I saw you, there was no other woman I wished to pursue for that role."

Her lips parted on a gasp. "Surely, you can't be serious!"

"I'm not a very complicated man. I trust my instincts—most of the time, at any rate. And I instinctively knew that you were something… well, more. Perhaps our betrothal didn't occur in the manner I might have wished, but I could not be more pleased with the outcome, regardless of the methods," he insisted. Hoping that it would help her to feel more certain of his feelings toward her, he confessed, "When our gazes met in the ballroom, you saw me staring at you… quite impertinently."

"I did," she confirmed.

He continued, "I had noticed you with your friend, Charlotte. You had just finished dancing and your cheeks were flushed from the warmth of the room… I thought you the most beautiful woman I'd ever seen. I wanted to beg an introduction but the only person I knew at the party was Lady Crowden and asking her to introduce us seemed unwise, at best. Clearly a well-founded suspicion, now."

"It is suspicious, isn't it? All of it. There are things I must tell you… I haven't shared them with anyone else," she whispered.

"What is it?"

"Only two days before I was to marry Stanford, I received an anonymous note telling me that he was involved with someone else. We were attending a ball that night and when he slipped away, I followed. I overheard him professing his love to another—and that he was only marrying me for the money. The person to whom he confessed this was none other than Lady Crowden. How very strange it is that the last four people I'd ever want anything to do with were the very four people present last night!"

"Not strange. Suspect," he corrected. "Very suspect. Though I cannot imagine what their motives might have been."

"Neither can I," she concurred. "Though I daresay that Lady Crowden's upset that your disinterest in her appeared to be quite genuine."

"True enough. When I accepted her summons, I was not yet aware of the true depths of her delusional nature. In hindsight, I cannot imagine what she might have done had I asked for an introduction to you or indicated an interest or preference for you. As for our chance encounter in the ballroom… it was anything but. I intentionally put myself in your path just as your friend intentionally tossed your dance card to the floor. An act for which she will have my eternal gratitude."

Marina appeared positively stunned by his admission, but still managed to ask, "All that after only a passing glance and one simple conversation?"

"Yes. I had fully intended to find your uncle and beg, if necessary, for an introduction. Even had he refused, I would not have given up. Somehow, someway I would have found the means to get to you and to make my intentions known," he answered earnestly. "Though perhaps knowing that does not make me seem any better than Mr. Nutter."

"No. That isn't the case at all. The primary difference was that, despite my intent never to marry, I couldn't deny that I found you incredibly handsome… and intriguing. So much so that I wavered in my swearing off of all romantic inclinations."

"Then that should make accepting this token a bit easier on your conscience, shouldn't it?"

He extended the small box once more and Marina accepted it with hands that trembled. Freeing the latch, she pushed the lid back with her thumb to reveal a large, cushion-cut sapphire surrounded by rows of diamonds that formed a rectangle. "It is a terribly dear piece of jewelry. Even at the most exclusive balls, I've never seen such an item in all honesty. Well, perhaps at my debut… This is far too much, Caleb. It's so very grand."

"Do you like it?" he asked. "If not, there is a rather cumbersome and terribly ugly iron box locked away in the house. It's filled with such items. You may choose one to your liking or we can go to Garrard's and you may have one made to your specifications."

"No. This one is lovely. Truly. Why did you choose it? This one in particular, that is," she asked.

Because that brilliant sapphire had reminded him of her bright-blue eyes.

"I saw it and simply thought of you," he said, rationalizing that it was not precisely a lie. It was simply not the truth in its entirety. Given that they had concerns about Mr. Nutter's level of fascination or infatuation with her, and that his own degree of interest in her was already well beyond rational, he hardly wanted to say or do anything that might indicate he was cut from similar cloth.

Reaching toward the box now clutched in her hand, he lifted the ring out and then, as gently as possible, slipped it on her finger. It fit as though it had been made for her. That stroke of luck seemed a blessing from the fates to his mind.

"It's remarkable," she said, her voice sounding somewhat awestruck.

"It's for you… it should be."

Chapter Sixteen

Conspirators...

Astrid, Lady Crowden, huddled inside her carriage, shrouded in a heavy cloak. The missive she'd received earlier had indicated that she should be parked near the edge of St. James Park at midnight. It had not been signed by name. Not that a signature had been required. The handwriting had been quite familiar to her.

"My lady, there's a gentleman approaching," the driver called out.

"He's expected, Tyson. It's fine."

"Yes, ma'am."

Moments later, the carriage door opened and a man wearing a dark, heavy coat with his hat pulled low over his face, hoisted himself up into the vehicle. He was silent, not readily identifying himself, not that it mattered. To that end, Astrid kept her own counsel as well. Silence could have power if one was willing to tolerate the discomfort it could create. Let him be the first to speak.

"Astrid," he said.

"Stanford," she acknowledged coldly.

He removed his hat. "It's good to see you... privately."

Astrid could have crowed with delight. She'd seen him at the ball, of course, though they hadn't spoken privately that night. She'd had her sights set on another then. Of course, she'd not entertain Stanford Williams again, not after he'd made a fool of her. After Marina Ashton jilted him, he'd married the sickly daughter of some cit and hauled her off to the countryside. Now he'd returned, conveniently a widower. And he hadn't sought her out. Not since his return. He'd wounded both her pride and vanity. An unpardonable sin, to her mind, just like the Earl of St. Aiden and his clear preference for Miss Ashton.

Now he was squiring her about town, as devoted as any lap dog. Apparently, he and Miss Ashton had taken to their roles as a betrothed couple with undue enthusiasm. No doubt the presence of her former betrothed would be a thorn in their side. "Mr. Williams! How delightful to see you back in society."

"Mr. Williams, is it?" he asked with bemusement. "At one time, you spoke to me much more familiarly than that. You once cried my name very sweetly, Astrid. Of course, then you chose to bandy it about like the vicious gossip you are. What was it you said to Lady Penmore? I believe you stated that Miss Marina Ashton would surely never have waited so late to cry off without significant and sound reason to do so."

Astrid shrugged. "It is the way of society, Mr. Williams, as well you know. Partaking of and sharing in gossip is how we maintain power. And I was rather piqued with you."

"Because I married another?"

"Because you lied," she snapped. "Because your professions of love for me were as false as those you'd espoused for Marina Ashton. I was nothing but a dupe for you."

He was silent for a moment and when he did finally speak, his voice was soft but it was not gentle. "We are not unalike, Astrid. You never loved me either. I was convenient for you; I kept your secrets, and you kept mine. Now, we have other uses for one another. It irks you that the earl was so obviously ready and willing to betroth himself to Marina... you fancied him for yourself."

"What do you care?"

He leaned forward. "I care because you can get even with him for that… and with her. You simply have to aid me in my cause."

"And that is?" Astrid queried.

"I want her to know the same humiliation that she visited upon me. Despite my efforts to paint her as the villain, many people remained sympathetic to her and it was my reputation which suffered the most due to her unseemly behavior," he explained. "So I want her betrothed. I want her eager to wed, and I want, when she arrives at that church, for there to be no groom waiting for her. And you're going to help me."

She was silent, considering his offer, if it was an offer in fact. The idea of helping him with anything was unappealing on principle, except that it would entail humiliating Marina Ashton and thwarting the Earl of St. Aiden. Perhaps it was that his slight was so recent, but it stung even more than Stanford's had. She understood Stanford. They might have said they loved one another, they might have carried on as if they meant it, but the truth was that neither of them was really capable of such a fine emotion—not in any lasting way. It was the chase for them, and the usefulness of whomever they happened to be bedding at that time.

"Very well," she agreed. "But when it's all done, I want you back in my bed. At my beck and call."

"You can have me in your bed now," he replied. "So long as it doesn't interfere with my courtship of Miss Elizabeth Whitmore."

Astrid laughed in disbelief. "Miss Whitmore? Dear lord, Stanford, have you sunk so low?"

"She's useful to me," he said dismissively. "She despises Marina Ashton more than I do, if such a thing is possible. Her fortune is more than adequate… and above all, she's respectable. Beyond her own impending spinsterhood, no scandal has ever touched her family."

Astrid smirked then. "So your sickly middle-class wife has

shuffled off the mortal coil."

He nodded. "Indeed, she has."

"Naturally? Or did you aid her along in her journey to the afterworld?"

He arched one brow at her in the dim interior of the carriage. "Does that matter?"

"Not in the least," she replied. "I presume Miss Whitmore will meet a similar fate when she is no longer of use to you?"

Stanford shrugged. "I suppose that will depend on how irritating I find her."

Astrid sighed. "What is it that you want me to do, Stanford?"

"My late wife's family had a great deal of money but when she died without issue, they elected not to transfer the second allotment of her marriage portion to me. So I need to marry Miss Whitmore. I can't do that until Marina Ashton is entirely disgraced. I need all of society to shun her. In short, I need them all to think that she was the problem all along and not I."

"They already think that," Astrid replied. "This debacle with the Earl of St. Aiden aside, she'd never have received a decent offer. The few serious suitors she had were spurned and not exactly sporting about it. I imagine you are responsible for her unwillingness to shackle herself to a man... Though recent events seem to have superseded that inclination."

"They cannot marry," he insisted. "I cannot afford for her to go from being a mere miss to being a countess... not if I am to move freely in society again. She has the power to ruin me. And I will not go quietly or alone. If I must be dragged down, I will take you with me. Once she is married, there will be no reason for her not to tell the tale of how it came to be... the truth, Lady Crowden, will be spread far and wide. Your husband may be understanding about your infidelity, but only if it's discreet. He'll not take kindly to being publicly cuckolded in his own home."

Astrid felt a frisson of fear at his words. It was quite true that Nigel didn't care one whit whom she took to her bed, so long as she was discreet. If it were put around that Miss Ashton had interrupted her ill-fated rendezvous with the earl rather than being caught in her own—well, he might make good on his promise to banish her to the countryside. Frankly, she couldn't think of a worse punishment. It was tantamount to Hell on earth for her.

"Fine. What would you have me do?"

"I will deal with Miss Ashton," he said. "Your primary objective is to be certain he never arrives at the church on the appointed date."

"And how am I supposed to know when that is? I would hardly be invited after everything that has occurred!" Astrid snapped.

"I will keep you apprised of any developments. I have people watching them even as we speak. I will know their every move."

STANFORD CLIMBED DOWN from the coach and watched it vanish into the night. Only when it had gone did he return to his own carriage. He had more business to attend to that night. Jacob Danvers needed to be given his orders and then he would have his second clandestine meeting with a lady for the evening.

Elizabeth Whitmore was more gullible than even Marina had been. She was willfully blinded by her own pettiness and spite. A fact he was not above exploiting for his own needs. And since his return to town, he'd been spending a not insignificant amount of time with her. He'd balanced account books more exciting than she was, but her hatred for Marina was proving very useful. The wager she'd made had been his idea, after all. He'd told her that before the Season was out, they would wed, that he would be in a position then to proudly ask for her hand. And he might. Assuming he didn't find anyone else better before then. Her position was adequate though hardly exalted, but her fortune was substantial. She was terribly average, he thought. Respectable and still considered a beauty despite her rather nasty turn of character. It was her third Season, as well. She was still "eligible" but only just. In short, she would do.

Danvers was waiting for him at one of the more questionable gaming hells. The moment he entered, he found the man deep in play and losing funds he certainly did not have. "You'll not get another loan from me," he warned him.

"I won't need one," Danvers replied. "Not when all is said and done… I assume you've come for an update?"

"I have."

"He's presented an offer to Deveril and it has been accepted. This evening, the whole lot of them went to the theater," the other man said with a sneer. "I was not invited. Caleb is set on his course of marrying this girl. The betrothal is not simply a sham to salvage her reputation. Not that I thought it would be when he needs to wed. And as of this evening, she'll have a sapphire on her hand the size of a bloody robin's egg."

"Do you know when they mean to marry?"

"No… he means to have the banns read this Sunday. So a matter of weeks? Although there was an incident earlier today… a near mishap with a carriage that very nearly did them in. He's convinced it wasn't an accident and that someone intentionally set out to harm Miss Ashton. That could hasten their rush to the altar."

Stanford considered that. He'd seen it. After all, he'd been following her discreetly all day. Allowing her to see him after that incident had been nothing but a mind game. Let her think he was responsible. Let her live with a bit of fear. She deserved it after all he'd been put through. But if it rushed them to the altar before everything was in place, that could be disastrous.

It hadn't taken a great deal of thought to discern why she'd broken their engagement. He'd been careless, speaking to his lover—to Astrid—at the time. Of course, he'd been lying to her, as well. Women, for Stanford, were simply a means to an end. A vehicle for transferring funds from one family's coffers to another.

Oh, they had other uses and fulfilled other needs, but those required less discretion and strategy than acquiring wealth through marriage.

As for the attempt on her life—and it had been that—he didn't know who was behind it. For himself, he didn't want Marina dead. Or at least he didn't if it would not benefit him. He didn't necessarily mind if she died, but she was more useful to him alive and in disgrace than moldering in her grave—an object of pity with her many tragic tales. "Watch them. Closely. They cannot wed, but that needs to appear as if by his choice rather than because the cold hand of death intervened. She'll not get off that easily."

"Why did she abandon you at that altar?" Danvers asked.

Stanford shrugged. He knew the answer but did not feel compelled to share. "Who knows the vagaries of a woman's mind? Regardless of her reasons, there have been steep consequences, and I have paid the brunt of them. It's time for that to change… do your job, and your debt to me will be discharged." With that, he turned on his heel and vacated the club. Miss Whitmore with her dull company and insipid kisses awaited him.

Chapter Seventeen

An unfortunate run-in

January 20, 1842

"IT HASN'T SPROUTED wings and flown away."

Marina glanced up at her aunt's curious turn of phrase. Lillian was looking at her speculatively. "Pardon?"

Reaching over, her aunt picked up her hand and once more admired the ring that had been placed upon it. "Your ring, dear. I must confess to no small amount of envy. It's truly stunning. Perhaps he owns a gem mine instead of just coal?" she suggested in a teasing tone.

Leave it to Lillian to look not for a simple bright spot but for one that sparkled, Marina thought as she tucked her hands into her lap beneath the edge of the table. It would likely not help her to resist the temptation to stare at the ring, but it might make her do so with less frequency.

"I am sorry to disappoint. But he's very solidly invested in the coal mining industry, Aunt Lily. Nary a gem mine in sight."

"Pity," Lillian replied with a weary sigh. "Maybe when it's Isabella's turn to find herself a husband she can land one who will drape us all in emeralds the size of apples! Barring that, I should at least hope she loves him. What do you think, Marina? Emeralds or a love match? Or both?"

"I couldn't say."

Lily smiled. "You will know soon enough, I think. The earl

has been most attentive from what I hear."

Beneath the table, Marina rubbed her finger over the ring, twisting it on her finger. He had been attentive. For five days since he'd presented that ring, he'd been the picture-perfect bridegroom. And yet still she hadn't fully acclimated to it. It wasn't simply the weight of the bejeweled item, though that was not insignificant and felt somewhat foreign on her hand. The symbolism of the ring surely played a part in her continued fascination with it. After all, it was a means of outwardly manifesting her status as a soon-to-be-married woman. *If she were a soon-to-be-married woman.* Of course, that wasn't the reason behind her conspicuous study of it either. It was the connection she felt to Caleb and all that it signified.

He'd kissed her. Oh, not a real kiss, as he'd said that night in her aunt's library. It hadn't been passionate and all-consuming. It had been a mere brush of his lips over hers, and yet still hers tingled with the memory. If what he'd said was true—that there was so much more—then she couldn't imagine how she might respond when kissed properly. And yet, despite the many times he'd come to call on her in the ensuing days, the numerous parties and balls they'd both been in attendance at, they'd been unable to find a single moment alone in which they could recreate that act. When they were in society, all eyes were on them, watching them for the faintest hint of impropriety. It was decidedly inconvenient. How was she to know if he was the right choice for a husband if she could never kiss him, never touch him? What if that startling rush of sensation had been simply because it was her *first* kiss and not because she was kissing *him*? She didn't truly think that was the case, but there was no way to disprove it unless they were granted at least a moment of privacy.

"I do believe that, with what you have at home, and what we've purchased in the last few days," Willa said, "that your trousseau is finally complete."

It was an olive branch, a way to change the subject and spare her more of Lillian's well-intentioned but still very nosy and very pushy questions. "I'm very relieved. While I do not object to shopping, the marathon we've conducted over the past few days seems a bit excessive."

The door to the tea shop opened, the bell jingling cheerily, drawing their eye. That cheerful sounding bell with its happy tune, Marina thought, was a liar. Standing in the doorway, surveying the interior as if she were a queen inspecting her subjects and finding them wanting, was none other than Elizabeth Whitmore.

"I do believe the milk has curdled," Lillian said, entirely deadpan.

"You're sounding more and more like the dowager every day," Willa pointed out.

Lillian smiled, her shoulders squaring with unmistakable pride. "That is quite wonderful as she was both inspirational and aspirational. I miss the old wretch, let me tell you."

"She'll haunt you for that," Marina stated boldly causing Lillian to laugh. Instantly, she knew it had been a mistake. It drew Elizabeth to them like a moth to a flame. After all, her calling in life seemed to be stamping out joy whenever it crossed her path. "Oh, dear. I've done it now."

Elizabeth strolled toward them, a patently false smile curving her lips. "Viscountess Seaburn, Lady Deveril… Miss Ashton. It's quite surprising to see you out and about given the rather salacious rumors I saw in the scandal sheets just this morning."

Marina didn't need to ask. She'd seen them herself. "One should know better than to pay too much attention to idle gossip and unfounded rumors."

Elizabeth reached out and took Marina's hand, lifting it slightly to examine the large ring that now rested there. "Rather gauche, isn't it? Or perhaps it's paste?"

Refusing to rise to the bait, Marina pulled her hand away. "No, it isn't paste. It isn't gauche either. But it is a betrothal ring which, I suppose, means I will be the winner of our wager. Perhaps you should start penning your apology speech now.

There is so much, after all, for which to beg my forgiveness."

Elizabeth laughed, but it was a humorless sound, not unlike her personality. "Oh, you haven't won yet. It isn't about which of us could get betrothed first. It's about which of us will actually be married! There's quite a long road ahead for you and the earl. A road that you have traversed before without ever reaching its end! But I'm certain you'll navigate it well enough. The middle class are notoriously handy when it comes to ascending another rung or so on the social ladder... Leave it to you, Miss Ashton, to ensnare a bourgeois nobleman."

As Elizabeth walked away, Willa leaned across the table and demanded in a low hiss, "Now would be a very good time for you tell me precisely what she was speaking of."

Marina's lips pursed as she recounted the woeful tale. "At the Crowdens' ball, during our confrontation in the ladies' retiring room, she goaded me into wagering which one of us could get a husband first... And I was so angry and so exasperated with her smugness that I accepted."

Willa frowned. "If that were the case, why was she bringing Mr. Nutter directly to you?"

Marina had given that much thought. "Because she knew I would refuse him and another such refusal would only offer more proof that those who called me difficult, vain and ungrateful, fickle, high in the instep—and everything else—were correct. All the things society had already begun to whisper about me would have been proven true. In short, any of my limited prospects would have washed their hands of me or been too fearful of public rejection to pursue me further," Marina replied. "To be not only a spinster but one who has already jilted a prospective husband, refused multiple offers, and then publicly turns down what is considered her last chance for a decent match? It would be seen as the most dastardly insult to a man."

"Why on earth would you accept such a foolish wager?" Lillian demanded.

Marina sighed, rolling her eyes heavenward. "I do not know,

but I did and then all of this happened… Now, I'm on the verge of winning this wager, though that seems terribly unimportant in the overall scheme of things."

Willa must have sensed how upset she was. She reached out and patted the back of Marina's hand. "I cannot imagine what she was thinking to suggest such a wager. Where did the notion for such a wager even come from?"

Marina sighed. She didn't know with certainty, but she strongly suspected it had come from someone else. While Elizabeth was particularly nasty, she was hardly an original thinker. Someone must have suggested it to her. But who and for what purpose?

"She's a nasty young woman," Willa continued. "Foul tempered, unkind, rude, and she has an unfortunate tendency to bray like a mule when she laughs. Likely because the sound is entirely forced since she has no humor to speak of. Her jealousy of you is boundless and you should be cautious around her. Such people are not above sabotage to get what they want!"

"Indeed," Lillian concurred. "Quite right. Heaven knows Willa and I faced our share of challenges. But I have to ask the question, Marina, do you like this man even a little? Or have you agreed to marry him only because of the scandal? Perhaps because you are feeling desperate about alternatives?"

The pointed question had put her quite on the spot. It forced Marina to admit a truth that she hadn't fully come to terms with herself. "I like him more than a little, Aunt Lillian. Much more, I think." It was the first time she'd uttered such a thing aloud and it made her heart race in her chest. "He's handsome, articulate, but so… well, he's not at all like the normal gentlemen of the *ton*."

"How so?" Lillian probed. For all her affectations of being shallow and obsessed with all things that glittered, Lillian had a depth of character few would recognize.

"He doesn't care about the fact that my mother and father were not wed. He has a shockingly egalitarian point of view that is a refreshing change of pace," Marina explained. And that was only a half truth. While, yes, he did possess such a viewpoint, that wasn't truly the source of her fascination with him. She couldn't have named it even if she wanted to. Her experience in such matters was so terribly limited that she hadn't the faintest idea what attraction or desire, or even romantic love for that matter, looked like, even if she did suspect it as the root cause of her current feelings.

"I shall go see the proprietor for a moment," Willa interjected, giving Lillian a pointed look. It was a signal to dig into matters more deeply without her present. It was hardly subtle, but it was effective.

"There has to be more to base a marriage on than the fact that he simply doesn't find you objectionable," Lillian insisted. "This is your life, Marina. The whole of it. There are worse things than being scandalous. Being married to a man you detest certainly tops that list."

"That—the scandal—might have been what prompted our arrangement," Marina replied, "but I think there is much more to it than that."

"And did you reach that conclusion while closeted in the library with him the other night? Perhaps after you shared a kiss?"

A heated blush pinkened her cheeks as she glanced around to see if Willa was in earshot. "Aunt Lillian, you are scandalous!"

"Practical," she countered. "Marriage to a man whose touch you cannot abide is a prison sentence. I would not have that for you. Marriage... Willa would never dare speak of such things to you, but passion is a key component to love. And love is a necessity for a marriage that is truly happy."

Realizing that her aunt's somewhat intrusive questions were being asked entirely out of concern, Marina softened. "I can most assuredly abide his touch. More than abide, I think, although he was far more of a gentleman than I might have wished him to be." It was a mortifying admission to make, but far better to have that conversation with Lillian who, at times, was more like a friend than an aunt. She certainly couldn't have that conversation with her Aunt Willa who was, in fact, more like a mother to her.

Lillian sighed. "So that's the way of it... he is remarkably handsome. And contrary to what Willa might have you believe, neither she nor I had conventional courtships. Some might argue that Valentine and I didn't have a courtship at all. But I was still drawn to him like a moth to a flame. I could no more have stayed away than stopped the world from turning."

"You do understand," Marina conceded, bemused by it.

"Oh yes, dear heart, I understand only too well. Do you know when you shall see him again?"

"He's asked to take me driving in the park tomorrow."

Lillian grinned. "Willa would kill me for telling you this, but if you'd like to have a moment's privacy with your earl, then I shall tell you of the perfect place... it's where I met your Uncle Valentine!"

THE PRETTY BUT viperous Elizabeth Whitmore left the tea shop. Whatever her exchange with the women inside had been, it was clear that it had not gone as she planned. She was there to interfere in the planned nuptials, of course, though he didn't know why. Not that it mattered. The wedding would never take place. He'd do whatever he had to in order to prevent it. For the moment, he needed to stay alert, to maintain vigilance lest he lose them in the crowd.

It was another quarter hour before he observed the three women departing the tea shop. They walked along Bond Street, a pair of footmen trailing in their wake. There were too many of them to take any sort of action, too many to manage and control. So he settled for observing them, taking note of which shops they favored, where they paused to stare in windows. And he noted how full of packages the footmen's arms were before they trotted off to take packages to the carriage waiting nearby.

The key to effective strategy was understanding one's quarry, after all. The more information he had the more likely he would be to accurately predict Miss Marina Ashton's actions and whereabouts at a later date—a date where he could catch her alone and unaware. Or as alone as a young lady could be. One servant perhaps. A maid or even a footman could be easily subdued, he thought. Because whatever happened, whatever methods he had to resort to, she would not become the Countess of St. Aiden. He would not allow it.

"She'll pay for everything she's done," he whispered. "Every last thing."

Farther up the street, the three women disappeared into yet another shop. He settled himself in a nearby alcove to wait. Patience, he cautioned himself. He could not afford to act impetuously and jeopardize his advantage. At this point, no one knew his true motives. No one knew the lengths he would go to. He would need to keep it that way as long as possible or failure would be inevitable. And failure was simply not an option.

Chapter Eighteen

Sabotage...

January 17, 1842

CALEB WALKED ALONG the path with Marina beside him. They'd come to Hyde Park in his phaeton, ostensibly for a drive. But she'd suggested they disembark and take a short walk. Now, as they made their way deeper into the wooded area, she was quiet, somewhat lost in thought it seemed. "Was it a pleasant outing with your aunt yesterday?"

She laughed. "Pleasant is not necessarily how one should characterize shopping with Aunt Lillian. Herculean feat might be more apt. She shops with enthusiasm and endurance in equal measure. As if it were a sport, even. Thankfully, Aunt Willa accompanied us. She's a staying hand for Lillian which is helpful."

His own lips quirked with amusement. While he'd had limited interactions with the viscountess, he could certainly see that description fit her very well. "I confess that I have never been shopping with a lady before but now you have piqued my curiosity."

"I shall ask her if she can muster another such outing for you. I daresay she will say yes and my uncle will simply pour himself a rather healthy portion of brandy."

Caleb did laugh then. He enjoyed conversation with her—her wit, the way her eyes sparkled with humor, the way her lovely mouth shaped the words. It was dangerous. *She was dangerous.*

For the past six days, he'd been doing his best impersonation of a devoted swain. He was beginning to realize that it was more than simply an act. Every moment spent with her was one he anticipated with glee.

As they continued along the path, his curiosity about something else, other than the feelings she stirred within him, was growing. The trees along the path were growing thicker and they had passed very few people for the past few minutes. "Is there a particular destination you have in mind for this walk, Marina?"

"It's just up ahead," she said with a slightly mysterious smile. "But we'll need to step off the path."

With a slightly raised brow, he followed her from the path and into a stand of trees. They formed almost a perfect circle creating a secluded spot in the middle of London's busiest park.

"How on earth did you know about this place?" he asked. It was rather magical.

She walked toward a tree and pointed to a carving on it. It was a heart with the initials *V* and *L* inside it. "This is where my Aunt Lillian and Uncle Valentine met. Apparently brought together by a meddling old woman and a very ugly hat... I suppose the prospect of our getting married has prompted some sentimental reminiscing for her and she told me about it yesterday."

He walked closer to the tree, coming to stand beside her. Reaching out, he traced the initials with his fingertips. "As it should. If one cannot be sentimental about getting married, or meeting the love of one's life, then what is the point of it all?"

"The love of one's life?" she asked.

Caleb smiled. "For all his comments about your aunt paupering him with her shopping, it's clear to anyone that your uncle is hopelessly besotted with her even after nearly two decades. As can be said for Lord and Lady Deveril. Their devotion to one another is impossible to hide," he observed.

"But we are not," she said. "Besotted, that is."

That state of being entirely besotted with her was not as far off as she might think. "Neither were they when first they met," he countered. "I like you. I find you incredibly beautiful. And with time, I would hope that we will build a relationship much the same."

She nodded thoughtfully. Then she looked up at him, her bright-blue eyes filled with uncertainty. "Would you think me terribly forward if I were to ask for more than a brief introduction to kissing?"

Caleb stepped closer to her, close enough that he could breathe in the light citrus scent that clung to her. "I would not think you forward. But I would think myself incredibly fortunate."

He didn't give her the chance to say more. They were at a point where words were not necessary. It was a time to show her with actions what he truly felt for her.

He cupped her face in his hand, using his thumb to tilt her face up to his. Initially, it was simply a repeat of their brief kiss the other night—to start. He brushed his lips over hers, once, then twice, and on the third pass settled his mouth more firmly over the enticing pillowy softness of hers. As he mapped the sweet curves of her lips, he eased his other arm around her waist, pulling her closer still. He detested the corsets and hoops and petticoats that kept him from feeling the natural curves of her figure. He wanted the softness of her body beneath his hands, not the confining and confounding architecture required for the fashions of the day.

She sighed, a soft pleasured sound that resulted in her lips parting ever so slightly beneath his. It was an opportunity he would not allow to pass. Sliding his tongue over the seam of her lips, he felt her gasp, felt her stiffen with surprise. But only for a moment. Her uncertainty simply evaporated and she leaned into him, allowing the kiss to take on a life of its own.

IN ALL HER wildest imaginings, in every lurid and forbidden novel she'd read, every whispered conversation between serving girls, kissing had always been a vague notion for her. It had seemed incomprehensible that someone pressing their lips to hers might have such a profound effect. How was it possible that such a simple act could have such consequences? But now, she understood just how foolishly naive that had been. Perhaps the actions involved might be as simple as that very mechanical description of what a kiss was, though clearly some of the details in those hushed conversations and ridiculously verbose tomes had been decidedly lacking in pertinent detail, the sensations such touches evoked were far beyond anything she could have possibly anticipated.

She was breathless with it, giddy as if she'd had too much champagne. Her blood raced in her veins and her heart pounded almost violently in her chest. Without conscious thought, she placed her hands on his chest, allowing them to slide upward until she locked her fingers behind his neck. In return, his arms tightened about her, hauling her against the hard planes of his chest. Even standing on her toes with her head tipped back, his rather impressive height was a hindrance. But clearly he was a man not about to let anything, including the fact that he was more than a head taller than she was, stand in his way.

He spun them about so that her back was to the tree, her feet perched upon the heavy roots at the base of it. It put them on a much more even level. Then he was leaning in, pressing the firmness of his chest against hers. And Marina realized something about herself—that whatever she might have believed about herself before, it was clear that there was passion within her. For he'd unlocked it, freed it. And she reveled in it.

Even through layers and layers of clothing—a not insignificant number—she could feel the heat of him. And for the first time, she felt that perhaps he truly did want her, that just as he'd said, the circumstances of her birth and the scandal attached to her name truly did not matter to him.

She couldn't say how long the kiss lasted. It could have been minutes or hours because she was simply lost in it—the pleasure and intensity, the novelty, and the fact that while it was only her lips he kissed, her body responded quite fiercely in other areas that she dared not even consider.

After the longest time, he eased back from her slowly, smiling down at her. But there was hunger in his gaze. Even she could recognize it. "That is what I wanted to do the other night in the library."

"I wish you had," she murmured in response. "It was magical."

His smile shifted slightly, taking on a hint of wickedness that made it too appealing by far. "I mean to do this again. Whenever the opportunity presents itself. That's the trouble with kissing, you see? Once you know how marvelous it can be, you never want to stop. It's a Pandora's Box with no turning back."

She didn't want to go back. Not at all. Marina was solely focused on moving forward… with him.

Chapter Nineteen

With the highs come the lows...

THEY RETURNED, ALBEIT reluctantly, to the phaeton he'd left parked just off the path when it had become too dense for the vehicle. Caleb helped Marina into it and then climbed up behind her. They'd been away from the vehicle no more than ten minutes but those ten minutes had been quite revealing. Her passionate response to his kiss had left him reeling with desire for her. It also left him hopeful—hopeful that infatuation and desire might grow into something so much more.

It was mere chance that as he walked to the other side of the phaeton, he'd gone behind it rather than in front. The toe of his boot struck something. Thinking it a stone that might damage a wheel, he bent to retrieve it and remove it from the path. But it was no mere rock. It was a pin—a vital one. A quick examination of the vehicle's wheels showed him that the one on the right, the side where Marina was seated, had been sabotaged. With only one pin, it might have well gotten them as far as Park Lane. But the moment they left the park, bouncing along the cobbled street beyond, would have brought immediate disaster. She would likely have tumbled from the vehicle to the hard stones and, depending upon the traffic, been trampled by a horse or crushed under the wheels of an oncoming vehicle.

Turning back, he walked toward her. "Someone has tampered with the wheel. We'll not be driving anywhere in this. But we're close enough to your home that I think we can walk relatively safely so long as we stick to the more crowded areas."

"Tampered with?" Her eyes widened in shock, then her expression grew shuttered. And again, he knew that she was hiding something. "Do you mean in the short time we were gone, someone attempted—they're watching us, Caleb. Even now!"

He nodded, fully aware that she was correct. It was that thought which fueled his urgency. "The crowd in the park is thinning as the promenade hour comes to an end. We need to make haste, Marina. Let me get you to safety and then I will try to discern who it is that poses a threat to you."

"Don't you mean to us?"

He shook his head. "I very much fear that you are the target and I'm not certain what that signifies beyond an increased need to protect you at all costs… that means I must see you to your uncle's house before I begin a very thorough search of the park. If this person has left any clue of their identity behind, rest assured that I will find it."

"I can help you find him… her," she corrected far too quickly. "Whomever it is! Surely two sets of eyes are better than one."

He realized then that she had suspicions of who might be behind the attacks, but for whatever reason she was not sharing them.

"No. This person, *whomever* it may be, clearly has marked you as their target. The carriage outside Gunter's and now this? Marina, let me see you home safely. Trust that I will get to the bottom of this."

Caleb offered his hand, and she accepted it. He could tell from the firm set of her chin that she was not pleased. Whether by his assertion that she was the target or by his unwillingness to allow her to place herself in harm's way, he couldn't say. Regardless, his first priority was to see her to safety.

"I dislike being relegated to the background while you deal

with this. I'm not helpless," she insisted. "And by virtue of being the intended target, surely you must realize what a vested interest I have here!"

"No, you are not helpless. You are strong, capable, intelligent… but just because you can face danger does not mean you should." He held out his hand once more.

With a heavy sigh, she capitulated, allowing him to help her down. From there, they walked swiftly, making their way toward the crowd gathered near the gate. From there, they exited the park and quickly made their way up Park Lane to Marina's home. He scarcely breathed until they reached her door. But once she crossed the threshold, he did not hesitate. He turned to make his way back to the park.

"You can trust me, Marina… With both your life and your secrets," he vowed.

She glanced up at him, their gazes locking for a moment. Then she looked away.

"When you are ready," he said, "you will tell me. Whatever it is, we can deal with it together."

"When you say such things," Marina whispered, "you give me the thing I fear most."

"And what is that?"

Her voice was whisper soft as she murmured, "Hope, Caleb."

As THEY ARRIVED home, the butler ushered her inside, quickly taking her coat and bonnet even as Caleb rushed away. It was clear the aging retainer thought their behavior quite odd. And then Marina looked up to see Willa standing on the stairs looking at her quite curiously. "Is something amiss with the earl, Marina?"

She had to tell them. But how much? She'd kept the secret of Stanford's plot for many reasons. Firstly, it was humiliating to own that she'd been so blinded by his charm that every single misgiving she'd had about him during their engagement had been brushed aside with foolish optimism. And then there was the very real fact that her uncle might possibly kill him. If it were scandal she hoped to avoid, that would certainly not be the way to go about it. "I don't wish to revisit it repeatedly. Let's find Uncle Devil and I shall explain it to you both at once," she said.

"He's in the study," Willa said. "I will be right behind you."

Marina made her way down the short corridor and knocked upon her uncle's door. Inside, she could hear one of her cousins getting a dressing down. They were always into some mischief. That bit of normality made her smile.

As she entered, her cousin looked imminently relieved. But her uncle took one look at her and instantly knew something was wrong. He dismissed Gervase with a stern warning and then asked, "What's happened?"

As Willa had entered just behind her, Marina went on with her explanation. "We left the phaeton to walk for a bit in the park and while we were away from it, someone tampered with the wheel. Apparently on the side where I would have been seated. Caleb escorted me back here and returned to the park to investigate."

"Marina, this is the second such incident! Something must be done," Willa said, her concern evident in the tightness of her voice.

"Something will be done," Devil said. "None of this business started until the rumors of your betrothal to St. Aiden began making the rounds. I cannot help but think the two related. The question, Marina, is whether you have been targeted because of your involvement with him. Perhaps calling off this engagement would be for the best."

Marina shook her head. "I don't wish to call off the engagement!"

"You are not in love with him. You hardly know him," Devil protested.

"I mean to marry him, uncle," she stated firmly. "Not to

avoid scandal but because I want to marry him." It was the first time she'd voiced that thought aloud though it had been hovering along the periphery of her mind from that fateful encounter at the Crowdens'. It was shocking to her just how much she meant it. It was clearly shocking to everyone else as well for the entire room fell silent for a full minute.

When her uncle did speak, he was insistent. "Infatuation is no basis for marriage."

"Perhaps not," Marina conceded. "But he's a good and honorable man. He's a man who, even against my protests, puts himself at risk to ensure my safety. You yourself have said you can find nothing about him that would mark him as an unsuitable match… and I have met no other gentleman with whom the prospect of marriage is tolerable, much less something to be anticipated."

Willa stepped in then when it appeared her uncle intended to argue further against it. "If the betrothal is the cause of danger, there are two ways to end it. Cry off and be done. Or marry quickly… and there are reasons to do so." With that, Willa produced a bit of paper cut from news sheet which had been tucked inside the pocket of her gown. "I found this in the scandal sheets this morning. I fear there will be more to come."

Marina accepted the slip of paper and began to read, her heart sinking with each word.

A certain young lady of the ton *has made quite the spectacle of herself of late. For the past week, Miss M.A. has been squired about town by the Earl of St. A., to whom she is newly betrothed. While the banns have not yet been posted, it is being put about that their understanding is quite firm. Contracts have been signed, as well, and this author has been informed that there are clauses included in the contract to disavow any financial ramifications should Miss M.A. decide to cry off. Such doubt from the outset hardly bodes well for this tremulous union. It remains to be seen if this marriage actually takes place or whether this is simply an elaborate scheme to camouflage her loose behavior at a recent ball which was touted as the event of the Season. Of course, even if the betrothal is legitimate, that is no guarantee of a wedding actually taking place. After all, Miss M.A. does have quite the history there.*

—From the London Ladies' Gazette

Marina stared at the paper with a sick feeling in her stomach. While she certainly had no intention of crying off, and everything she had learned about Caleb in the interim had only made her more certain of the match, the gossip rag eliminated any possibility of backing out. Even her uncle would have to see that, if she failed to marry now, when it had been intimated that they were cultivating such a lie in the eyes of society, it would be ruin for both of them.

"I can't cry off now, not even if I wanted to! Everyone would assume it had been a sham all along," she said.

Devil's jaw clenched. "Damn them. Damn the lot of them. I will not see you forced to the altar by anyone."

Marina walked toward her uncle and placed her hand on his arm. "No one is forcing me. Perhaps, initially, it was more about the situation. But now, it's about him. About the two of us. Please do not worry for me."

"I do not know how to do anything else," he admitted gruffly.

"Then find yourself another purpose," she suggested and waved the offending paper before him. "This is the mystery to solve. How were these details known to the author? Is it Lady Crowden, perhaps, getting her revenge? Or Elizabeth Whitmore in a final act of pettiness and spite?"

"Or Stanford Williams?" he queried.

Marina nodded. "Yes. Or him." The mere mention of his name jangled her already fraught nerves. It brought back that feeling of panic that had simply overwhelmed her when they'd walked into the church that morning. "But I've no wish to talk about him. I want to talk about this!" She waved the piece of newsprint once more. "How could they possibly know the details of the contract? Where would they have gotten such information?"

"I do not know, Marina. But regarding the wedding, you do understand what this means, don't you, Marina?" Willa asked.

"I do," Marina said and handed the slip of paper to her uncle. "There is now only one course of action we can take to avoid ruin for myself and for Isabella in the future. Another scandal attached to this family's name will be detrimental to her future. The things whispered about me are proof that not even a decade or more is long enough to wipe the memories of society matrons... We need to marry more quickly than anticipated."

Devil scanned the article and bit out a curse.

"If scandal is the only consideration, then, yes, it would be best to marry," Devil agreed. "But scandal is not my only concern, Marina. Your happiness is paramount. If you have qualms, if you have concerns about him, scandal be damned."

Marina was quiet for a moment, thinking of how to respond to the obvious worry that both her aunt and uncle had for her. In the end, she could only speak to her intentions and her hopes. "I do not have questions, qualms, or concerns. The more time I spend with the earl, the more convinced I am that this is for the best. I know it isn't the love match you both had hoped I would make, but there are many instances where the vows precede the sentiment. While I do not love him yet, I *could* love him... without any difficulty at all, I daresay."

"There are also many instances where vows are spoken and no sentiment ever develops," Willa said softly. "What happens, my darling girl, if you find yourself unable to love this man?"

Marina was far less worried about her ability to love him than his ability to love her. "If I do not marry him, I will never marry at all. After this... I would be an untouchable in society. Shunned. There would be no hope of redemption. The idea of a love match would be lost to me regardless. And I can't think only of myself. This impacts you and all of my cousins as well. I intend to speak with the earl when he calls later. I think, under the circumstances, a special license should be procured and we should marry posthaste—assuming, of course, that one will be granted."

Willa turned to Devil. "You can arrange that can't you?"

"If not, I know someone who can," he answered. "Are you certain, Marina? We could travel. Take to the Continent. It would all be long forgotten perhaps by the time we returned."

She smiled sadly. "The *ton*, as you well know, forgets nothing. They simply ignore it when it no longer interests them. But it is always there, ready to be invoked on a petty whim. Surely the continued mention of my mother's disgrace is proof of that?"

There was silence in the room then, all of them only too well aware that she spoke the truth. Then Marina spoke, her voice solemn and low. "There are things that you do not know. Things about my betrothal to Stanford and why I elected to call off the wedding."

Devil looked past her, his gaze locking with Willa's. Then he said simply, "Go on. Tell us everything."

Marina took a deep breath and then let it out on a sigh that spoke volumes, even to her own ears. "After the way he carried on in the aftermath of my crying off, I don't think it's any secret now that he was only after the marriage settlement you had offered. But something happened the night of the Fairringtons' ball... That morning, a letter was delivered to me here warning me of Stanford's perfidious nature. And that night, after he'd excused himself to speak to a business acquaintance, he didn't rush off the card room as he'd said but slipped down the corridor toward the doors that led out to their small terrace."

"You excused yourself and followed him," Willa surmised. "You were acting very strangely that night. I'd since put it down simply to your nerves about the upcoming wedding and your doubts, but now... what did you learn?"

"I overheard him speaking with a woman on the terrace—professing his love for her and his disdain for me. Just as the letter had stated. I didn't recognize her voice at first, though I knew it was familiar. It was only after they walked inside that I knew... It was Lady Crowden," she explained.

Willa gasped in shock. "Oh, that wretched woman! And she was one of the few that openly questioned his accounting of things!"

"Because it served her purpose," Marina summed up. "She might have professed her love for him, but neither of them is capable of such a fine feeling. They are both selfish and self-serving to such a degree that they could never truly love another... but there was more in the letter. And I've never spoken of it to anyone. This letter, signed only 'A Concerned Acquaintance' hinted that if I were to go through with the wedding, Stanford would find himself a widower before long. That my death would be tragic and garner him endless amounts of sympathy and all the while, he'd have been the very one to end my life."

"Do you believe that?" Devil asked.

"Everything else in the letter proved true," Marina said. "I had no reason to doubt it."

Both Willa and Devil grew silent, her aunt in shock and her uncle in fury. So Marina continued. "And the reaction you are having right now, Uncle Devil, is the very reason I elected to keep this secret. We cannot afford the scandal that would result from you challenging him to a duel or simply killing him in cold blood."

"There is nothing cold about my blood right now, Marina," he said, his voice thick with anger and other emotions. "But I will make an effort not to call the blackguard out, if only for your sake. If he comes near you, I will act as I see fit to keep you and everyone else I love safe."

With that, Marina rose and walked around the desk. Leaning down, she kissed his cheek. "I love you. And I will be forever grateful that you've shown me what a man and a gentleman ought to be."

Chapter Twenty

Making haste...

CALEB RETURNED TO the park in search of any clue as to who might have tampered with the phaeton. It had taken mere minutes to get back but already the park was nearly deserted, the promenade hour having given way to the time for afternoon calls. Still, he walked the paths they'd traversed earlier, looking for even the slightest thing to give him some indication of who might have been watching them. *Lying in wait.*

He had all but given up hope when something caught his eye. Near the clearing where they had shared that scorching kiss, he saw a pair of footprints in the soft, peaty earth at the base of a tree. There was also a handkerchief—marked with dusty fingerprints, likely soiled when they removed the pin from the wheel.

When he retrieved the fabric, a sinking feeling settled in the pit of his stomach. It was embroidered with initials. *JLD.* There was only one person he knew to whom it could belong. Jacob Linwood Danvers.

Normally it would never have crossed his mind to think Jacob capable of such things. But nothing had been normal between them since he'd inherited the title and the wealth that would come with it, presuming, of course, that he could make it to the altar. Jacob's resentment of what he considered to be an embarrassment of riches had been instantly obvious and had seemingly grown stronger still when they reached London. Then, of course, there was Jacob's insistence that he should not wed Marina—and upon reflection, he had developed a theory.

Jacob had presumed that he would simply turn over the running of the mines to him, that he would be given the company to run and a living to be had from it. Of course, Jacob didn't realize that in many regards, Caleb's hands were tied. On his deathbed, his grandfather had pleaded with him to never let Jacob be involved in the running of the mines. The old man had feared that Jacob would run them into the ground or lose them on the turn of a card. Either outcome was both possible and plausible. But Jacob did not know that. He'd never told him so out of concern for his feelings. Perhaps that had been a mistake. Could he afford to provide a small settlement for Jacob? Assuming that he managed to meet the terms of his uncle's will, he certainly could. But if he did not and failed to secure the fortune to support those estates—and pay the death taxes, it would all be a moot point. All would be lost—the mines his grandfather worked so hard to build and the land that generations of his ancestors had maintained.

It wasn't simply greed that had prompted him to seek a bride but practicality. But Jacob wouldn't see that because he was choosing not to. Jacob was only choosing to see that he had been given something that he would not share. Now he was forced to wonder if Jacob's resentment over these windfalls and leaps in status blinded him to that fact. And, if it had, was that truly enough to drive him to murder?

Tucking the handkerchief into his pocket, Caleb walked back to his phaeton and made arrangements to have the vehicle repaired and the horses returned home safely. For himself, he walked back to the townhouse, hoping it might clear his head and offer some clarity of mind about his next steps. As he did so, he became acutely aware of that strange sensation once more. He was being watched. A glance around him showed only one possible source for the observation. Lady Crowden was seated in a cabriolet only a short distance away, her hard eyes throwing daggers in his direction. It was all growing more complicated by the second.

There was one thing he was growing incredibly certain of. If he meant to marry Marina, they did not have time to wait. There could be no long engagement for them to get to know one another. If they were to wed, they needed to do so quickly before any of those plotting against them could strike again. And the moment they were safely wed, they needed to leave London immediately along with the many dangers it held for them.

Returning home to a house devoid of anyone but servants, Caleb retreated to his study and began penning a letter that would change everything. He'd never planned an elopement before, but clearly there was a first time for everything.

MARINA RETREATED UPSTAIRS. She could feel Devil and Willa worrying for her, their concerned gazes on her all the time. While she knew it came solely from their love for her, it was over-whelming. She hated feeling that she was a burden to them. They would never say such, and likely never think it either, but that feeling persisted. If she was entirely honest, it always had.

Seated in a well-upholstered chair near her window, Marina let that realization settle in her mind. Despite all the love, lavish gifts, and unwavering support, she still felt as though she were an interloper at times—as if she did not truly belong there. Was it because of her very humble beginnings? Or was there more at play? Many things had been whispered about her over the years— old gossip about her mother, rumors about her father. She knew that every effort had been made to protect her from that truth, but she had pieced enough things together over the years to understand that her father had been a villain. His sins had gone far beyond simply abandoning his child or even arranging the sham of a marriage he'd entered into with her mother.

Would those feelings ever fade? If she and Caleb married, would she feel that she was a burden to him? Or worse yet, would he see her that way? Could the attraction they felt for one another grow into something more, or would it fade and leave them in a hollow sham of a marriage?

They were questions without answer. Predicting the future was not something she was gifted with. There would be no way to know how she would feel until it all happened. And that was the crux of it. In the end, how she would feel mattered less in the moment than the ramifications that would occur if she did not go ahead with it.

A knock at the door interrupted her morose thoughts and she called out for them to enter. It was her maid bearing a tray with a sealed letter atop it.

"This just came for you, miss. From his lordship, the earl."

"Thank you, Ethel," Marina said. "While I see what this is all about, could you have a bath readied for me? As steaming hot as possible." Perhaps the hot water would ease some of the tension that thus far had refused to abate.

The maid nodded and scurried away as Marina broke the familiar wax seal on the letter. It bore the same crest as the signet ring Caleb wore.

Marina,

I've come to the unfortunate conclusion that we no longer have the luxury of waiting to wed. I fear that until we are legally married you will continue to be the target of these vicious attacks and underhanded plots. If you are in agreement, I will speak with your uncle at your (and his) earliest convenience about a quick elopement and then decamping from London to a nearby country estate. It would allow you to remain close enough to your family for visiting but far enough that any travelers from London would be noted and remarked upon in the village. I can think of no other way to ensure your safety than to be ever present at your side. In order for that to happen, we must marry now, without hesitation.

Caleb

No flowery prose or—if not quite false but hopeful—words of love and devotion. It was all laid out practically and logically. The only time practicality and logic went by the wayside was when they kissed. And if they married, there would be much more than simple kisses passing between them.

Simple. There was nothing simple about the way he made her feel with just a touch.

Getting up from her chair, Marina moved to the small writing table and penned a note to Caleb. She had only just finished when Ethel returned to inform her that her bath was ready. Passing the note to the maid, she asked that it be delivered immediately. "Oh, and please inform my aunt we will be having a guest for dinner." Her decision was made. It was long past the point to dither or be indecisive. If she wished to salvage what she could of her reputation and, hopefully, put an end to whatever madness was surrounding them, she would need to act quickly. Perhaps, once they were officially wed, it would eliminate the mysterious motivation for the attacks on her.

Chapter Twenty-One

The decoy...

THEY WERE CLOSETED in the study before the dinner hour, Devil brooding at his desk as she paced the floor. Willa turned to him. "What have you discovered about him? Anything that would give you pause about permitting the match?"

Devil raised his head to meet her gaze. "Nothing. It seems as though he is precisely whom he appears to be... There's no indication that he has any vices of note, no scandals in his background. The business enterprises that he is part of are reportedly sound and legitimate. On the face of it, my love, we could not have chosen a better match for her. In truth, I have no objection beyond the fact that she does not love him. Do you have objections? You have a remarkable instinct about people, Willa. If you have concerns—"

It was that which bothered her as well, the remarkable speed at which everything was transpiring. Of course, she'd had misgivings about Stanford Williams that had gone well beyond simply the expedited courtship. There had been something about him that had seemed cold to her, calculating. But he'd been handsome, attentive, seemingly without fault. Still, it was obvious that something had occurred. Contrary to what people might say, Marina was not fickle or flighty. Her niece would never have agreed to Stanford's proposal if she hadn't been fully committed to the notion of becoming his wife. Now, with Marina's admission about what she'd overheard, all the pieces had finally fallen into place for her. She understood why Marina had called off the wedding. She even understood why Marina had kept the secret. Devil would have done something terribly reckless.

Thinking of the Earl of St. Aiden, Willa realized she did not have any of those same misgivings about the earl. Despite the strangeness of how it all came to pass, he seemed to be trustworthy. Honorable. But was that enough?

Marina was the child of her heart, after all. She could not have loved her more even had she given birth to her. And her future was now hanging in the balance. She shook her head. "As she said, she does not him love him *yet*. What a gamble it is to marry first and hope love will simply occur! There is so much more to it than that… I do not wish to see her hurt."

Devil rose and closed the distance between them, taking her hand. "She will be hurt if the marriage fails. She will be equally hurt if it does not take place at all. There is, much as I am loath to admit it, only one way where there is the possibility of a desirable outcome. She's willing to take the risk and is of an age where we have no sound reason to prevent her from doing so—not when the stakes are so high otherwise. And now that I know what Stanford Williams was truly about, his presence in town is of great concern to me. If she marries the earl… perhaps he can take her someplace that we will not have to worry so much about what Williams's intentions are."

"She's invited him to dinner. He sent round a note earlier but I've no notion what it contained. Respecting her privacy is torture," Willa admitted ruefully. "He should be arriving momentarily, I imagine. I looked for him to arrive earlier, in all honesty," Willa mused. "If we've seen the gossip rags, no doubt he has as well and feels compelled to act."

"As he should," Devil conceded. "He's acquitted himself quite well throughout this nonsense. And it is nonsense, Willa. There seems to be no basis in reason for any of it! And there are far too many unknowns. Lady Crowden, Nutter, Elizabeth Whitmore, and now Williams?"

On that point they were in agreement. Willa brought his hand up to her lips, kissing his knuckles, savoring the strength in him as always. "I cannot fathom why it is happening either, Devil. Marina, barring her animosity with Miss Whitmore, has never done anything to incur such wrath! Even her collapse on the morning she was to wed Williams was not something she could control. She fully intended to marry the man despite what she knew about him just to spare the family any scandal. This seems to be coming from every direction—the physical attacks, the gossip and rumors—Perhaps our mistake is in thinking we are dealing with only one foe? The gossip and the attacks may have been initiated by different perpetrators."

Devil raised his eyebrow, considering the possibility. "It's possible. Hell hath no fury, Willa. I do not think Miss Whitmore has anything to do with the attacks. The gossip? Perhaps, though that seems far more likely to be Lady Crowden's work. And I mean to take care of that particular threat myself. With a bit of help, of course."

"Highcliff?" she asked.

Devil grinned. "Of course. The man may be retired, but the lion still has his teeth so to speak."

"And the other? These physical attacks can't be laid at Miss Whitmore's door, I should think. And it hardly seems that it would be worth the risk for Lady Crowden."

"That remains a mystery," he said. "But I mean to get to the bottom of it as well."

⇢⇢⇢⇠⇠⇠

Arriving at the Ashtons' home, Caleb was shown not to the drawing room but to the study. That choice indicated from the outset that there were sensitive matters to be addressed. Upon entering the room and noting the dour face of Lord Deveril and the worried expression marring the lovely face of his wife, that was even more apparent.

"I presume that Miss Ashton informed you of the sabotage of my phaeton in the park," he said, forgoing any formal greeting.

"Indeed she did. And you've seen the gossip rags and the drivel they have printed?" Lord Deveril demanded.

Caleb nodded. "I have. And I think the only solution is for Miss Ashton and myself to marry with haste… immediately, even. I came here tonight to suggest just that. I understand you have misgivings, and rightfully so. To that end, I would not take her to Yorkshire just yet. There is an estate in Northampton where we may stay for the remainder of the Season—near enough that you can visit easily—and frequently—to be reassured of her welfare."

Lady Deveril breathed a sigh of relief. "How thoughtful! We should be very glad to keep Marina at least reasonably close by when you are wed. And frankly, given recent revelations, having her out of London and away from those who would harm her is something of a relief."

Lord Deveril remained quiet for a moment. "Do you possess the necessary connections to obtain a special license?"

Caleb nodded. "I should be able to obtain it with little difficulty. If problems arise, I will certainly ask for assistance."

The dinner gong sounded just then, preventing further conversation. They moved en masse toward the dining room just as Marina descended the stairs. Rather than the pale gowns he'd seen her in previously, that evening she wore a deep-blue velvet, her eyes gleaming like the most brilliant of sapphires. Every time he saw her, he was struck anew by her beauty. But he'd seen something else in her, something that he would never have suspected with only that fleeting glance in Lady Crowden's ballroom.

Marina did not know her own worth. Oh, without question,

she knew she was beautiful. She had eyes to see after all and no shortage of mirrors in the home. But seeing it and feeling it were very different. Understanding that there was more to be valued in her than simply her face and form, that was a different matter still. That was the root of her vulnerability, of her doubts. Whatever nasty things had been whispered about her due to the circumstances of her birth—those things had grown inside her, twisting like vines, choking out the rose that should have long since bloomed.

The nature of his thoughts startled him. He was not a man given to poetic phrasing or such flowery thoughts. Practical and pragmatic. Those were the traits most people would ascribe to him. Certainly they were things he had always strived for. His attraction to her was unprecedented for him, but he was not some lovesick swain writing odes to her beauty. Theirs was an arrangement that benefited them both. He would obtain his inheritance; she would retain her reputation. The attraction, the fact that he had some degree of admiration for her, that was all simply a stroke of good fortune. A foundation from which they could build something that might offer them both some degree of at least contentment, if not happiness.

Even as he said those things to himself, they rang false. Hollow. Because there was a sense of inevitability about all that had transpired—like a clockwork mechanism, all of them tiny cogs in the wheels. It felt as if they had been set on this path and were fated to follow it to its end.

"My lord," she said, acknowledging him with a slight smile, though it was tinged with some bitterness. "Thank you for coming."

"Miss Ashton," he replied, inclining his head. "I've spoken with your uncle—and your aunt—now you and I have some decisions to make."

"After dinner, we can walk in the garden. It will afford us a bit of privacy to speak freely… without servants listening and reporting on our every word."

THEY MADE IT through dinner. Each course seemed interminably long, especially as her nerves were so great that the thought of food was positively nauseating. That was quite an unusual event in and of itself as she normally had a very hearty appetite. Of course, her nerves were fraught. After all, she was about to suggest running off to elope with a man she barely knew.

She knew that her aunt would hate to see her married off in such a fashion. There would be no orange blossom bouquets, no perfectly fitted, embroidered gown, or elaborate veil. There would be no church pews filled with guests to watch her be married off.

As dinner came to an end, the boys left the dining room with their parents. Willa and Devil did not separate everyone by sex after dinner. The women were not relegated to the drawing room while the males were sequestered in the billiard room or library. For herself, she walked to the double doors that opened onto the terrace, throwing them open to the cool night air. "We can access the garden from here," she explained.

Marina stepped through the doors and out onto the stone terrace that ran the length of the rear of the house. Caleb followed wordlessly behind her, shutting the doors after them.

Shivering in the chilly air, she turned to face him. "Let's elope. Now. Tonight. Immediately."

"Because you wish to marry me or because you're afraid of what might happen to you if we do not?"

"Both are equally true," she replied. "I am not without enemies, Caleb. Elizabeth Whitmore detests me. But she isn't trying to kill me. Mr. Nutter? Perhaps. His perception of the events that transpired at the Crowdens' ball could have driven him into some sort of jealous rage, I suppose. But the way this villain has gone about it… it's cold and calculating. And cautious. Someone who wishes to remain hidden in the shadows. That leads me to believe they have something to gain... and that could be Stanford Williams."

"And what does he have to gain?"

"Revenge," she relied. "I humiliated him publicly. It was not my intent. When I walked into the church, I simply couldn't go through with it... not after what I learned."

"And what is that precisely? I know that you've been withholding information. I simply don't know why."

"Embarrassment, I suppose," she said. "I felt like a fool for having been gullible enough to believe his lies."

He laughed softly, without any real humor. It was almost bitter, she thought. "We've all been gullible," he said, "believing in someone we should not. Be it a friend, a lover, a family member... That doesn't make you a fool, Marina. You'd only have been a fool if you'd ignored the truth and married him regardless."

"He and Lady Crowden were lovers. He courted me, then proposed to me because he wanted the fortune that my Uncle Devil has set aside for me. And once he had it, he intended to do away with me. Well, the last part is presumed. The first part is fact. I received an anonymous letter two days prior to the wedding informing me of all this—not the identity of his lover, but that he would meet them at the Fairingtons' ball... The truth was that I was simply a means to an end to him."

"And now you feel I am marrying you because you are a means to an end," he mused.

"We are that for one another... but we aren't only that," she insisted. "Are we?"

"No. No we are not," he replied softly. "I can't say what we are to one another precisely, not yet, at any rate. But it is more than I anticipated. Certainly more than I was prepared for."

"I feel the same. All the more reason to act now," she said. "We need to marry quickly before anything else can go wrong."

He was quiet for a moment. "I've reached much the same conclusion. We do need to marry quickly. And given what I now know, I do believe that you are the target entirely. Initially, I thought perhaps you had been targeted because of me. Yet, even if I fail to meet the terms of the will, the money will simply go to various charities and causes my great uncle supported during his lifetime. I find it difficult to believe that hospitals for veterans and benevolent societies for widows and orphans have resorted to murder for their funding."

In spite of their dire situation, she laughed at that. "It does challenge one's ability to stretch the imagination, does it not?"

He reached out, taking both of her hands in his. "Some of it seems intended to drive us to the altar while other things that have occurred appear to be much more sinister in nature. Revenge. Wounded vanity. Jealousy—there is no one more dangerous than a covetous man."

"Or woman," she said. "Perhaps it is jealousy. But that doesn't eliminate Lady Crowden, Elizabeth Whitmore, or even your companion, Mr. Danvers. We have no proof that they aren't somehow involved."

"I spoke with your aunt and uncle upon arrival and told them much the same as you just told me. That we needed to marry quickly. I had suggested by special license, but I am not opposed to elopement. Assuming, of course, that they would not disapprove too terribly... They are very worried for you. For both your safety and your future happiness."

"I know they are. I can feel the weight of their concerns quite keenly... but I have concerns of my own. I fear that my presence here in this home may be placing them and my young cousins in danger."

He nodded. "That isn't an unreasonable assumption. They are clearly not above sabotaging a vehicle which would have endangered us but also anyone else on the road."

Another shiver raced through her, this one having nothing to do with the falling temperature. When he stepped closer to her, his broad frame blocking the wind, she had to fight the urge to simply lean into him. Her aunt and uncle were just inside the house after all and were very aware that the two of them were on the terrace alone. But even that knowledge could not prevent her from giving in to all of her many temptations. Tipping her head up, she rose on her toes and pressed a kiss to his cheek, feeling the rough whiskers beneath her lips. But only for a moment. Because he turned his head and captured her lips. Marina leaned into him savoring the strength of his arms around her, the heat of his body against hers. His arms closed around her, pulling her closer still as his lips moved over hers, his tongue teasing her lower lip until she parted them, granting him entrance. It was as divine as it was terrifying. Because it consumed her entirely. And in that kiss, the entire world simply fell away. All the worries and fears, for at least that moment, simply faded into nothingness.

HE WANTED HER. Desperately. In a way, he thought, that he had never desired another woman. The intensity of it was shocking. The relentlessness of it was, in a word, unsettling. It challenged everything he'd ever believed about himself.

Despite breaking the kiss, he did not let go of her. Instead, he continued to hold her close. "I will take the necessary steps to obtain a special license for us to marry by week's end," he said.

"Do you think we can afford to wait that long?"

"No," he replied. "But I also do not wish to see you cheated of having a wedding with your family present. God willing, Marina, this will be the only wedding either of us have. I wish we had the luxury of time to give you the wedding you deserve."

"I don't care about that. I wish we could marry tonight," she admitted. "I'm so terribly afraid that something will happen to stop us."

"What could go wrong?" In truth, many things could, but she sounded so terribly anxious that he didn't wish to worry her further. "We will be discreet in our movements. No one need

Caleb shook his head, dismayed at how his oldest friend had become a veritable stranger. "If you are unhappy with your current financial state then you have no one but yourself to blame."

"It isn't as simple as that!" Jacob protested. "We were the best of friends, Caleb, and now you will not even welcome me into your home!"

"I can't welcome you, Jacob. Not when you are already making free with it… and it isn't your presence to which I object. I simply dislike coming home to find you making so free with not only my home but my personal chambers. You are not the man I once knew, Jacob. Not the true friend whom I could count on. You've changed."

"I've changed?" Jacob said, his voice rising with ire. "Your newly elevated station has gone to your head. You're so puffed up with your own importance you can't even see what a prig you've become! All this talk of marriage and settling down. It's all obligations and responsibilities when you should be sowing the most glorious wild oats a man could enjoy!"

Caleb shook his head. "There is more to life, Jacob, than going from one party to the next, one card game to the next, one bawdy house to the next! We are nearing thirty. Isn't it time to do more with your life than simply sow wild oats?"

He shrugged. "Some of us haven't the luxury of settling down with a wife… After all, you've never allowed me any say in the running of the mines. Now I'll never have the sort of income required to maintain a household and support a woman in anything other than genteel poverty!"

"Perhaps finding a woman who would think genteel poverty worth it to be with you might be the answer to your unhappiness," Caleb suggested.

Jacob began to pace. "I didn't come here to fight with you or to be given advice like I'm some halfwit. I came because… I'm in a bit of trouble."

"Of course, you are. How much do you owe?" Caleb asked,

completely exasperated with the whole of it.

"It's not that sort of trouble. There was a bit of a row the other night and the gentleman who kept me from being beaten to a pulp has asked to meet with you. He has an investment opportunity he wishes to present to you, and I told him I would arrange it… It's a debt of honor, Caleb. Surely even you cannot deny me that courtesy?"

"Tell me who he is and I shall make an effort to seek him out."

"It would be easier for me just to take you there."

Caleb stared at him for a moment. *Lying.* It was obvious he was being deceitful. Feeling that he had no choice but to call his bluff, he reached into his pocket and retrieved the handkerchief he'd found in the park. "I believe you dropped this?"

"In the corridor?" Jacob asked, his expression inscrutable.

"No. In the park. Where you had just sabotaged the wheel on my phaeton. Miss Ashton could have been gravely injured or even killed. But that was rather your point, wasn't it?"

"You're mad." The accusation fell flatly from Jacob's lips, lacking any real sincerity.

A muscle ticced in Caleb's jaw. "No. I thought I was, at first. I questioned myself… what could my oldest friend possibly have to gain by attempting to murder my betrothed, after all? But then I remembered those old and terrible rumors. The ones about your parentage. That the man who worked for my grandfather was not your sire at all."

"It's rubbish." Again the denial lacked any power.

"Is it?" Caleb demanded. "We look alike, Jacob. So much so that everywhere we have gone for years people have thought us siblings. Are we?"

Jacob's expression hardened. "Does it matter? Whatever my blood may be, the pittance left to me by the old man says all that need be said."

Caleb shook his head. "You're wrong. He loved you. I know he did. But he was fearful for you… he didn't leave you more because he knew you'd squander it. He made me promise to keep you out of the running of the mines because he no longer trusted you to do what was in the best interest of everyone there. You'd cut corners and endanger lives. That is quite obvious to me now, even though I wondered then if it was the right choice."

"And now you're turning on me, as well," Jacob accused.

"No. You turned on me. You tried to kill an innocent young woman to prevent me from marrying her."

"I bloody well did not!" Jacob shouted, and it rang with truth. "I made no attempt on your betrothed's life. If you can believe nothing else, believe that I would not dirty my own hands to do such a thing... and we are both well aware I lack the funds to hire someone for the deed."

Caleb took note of that primarily because it was the first thing Jacob had uttered that contained even the faintest ring of sincerity. But he wasn't done. Not by far. "You've done nothing but try to prevent me from making a match and assuming my inheritance... from day one you've been working against me. Even more so since I informed you of my intent to marry her. Why?"

Jacob sneered at him. "Because you don't deserve it! You don't deserve to have the mines, the title, and the fortune! You don't bloody well deserve it. What about me? If I am your half-brother, and we both know the truth regardless of whether or not it is ever said, I am older by two whole months. By all rights, everything that is in your possession should have been mine!" The words rang with bitterness, with resentment and envy.

Caleb simply walked to the door, opened it, and waited. "Leave," he finally ordered. "Leave and do not return."

"You'll regret this," Jacob insisted. "You will rue this day just as you will rue your decision to marry a woman whose own mother was little better than a trollop."

Caleb held his temper, but only just. "My only regret, at this time, is being foolish enough to call you friend. And it takes more than blood to render one family."

Jacob left the house fuming. For nearly thirty years, he'd been second place, standing in the background as everything that should have been his went to Caleb. Initially, he'd been able to accept it. Bastards didn't have rights to anything. It was simply the way of the world. But watching windfall after windfall drop into Caleb's lap, it had become harder and harder to ignore the resentment. It bubbled within him constantly, like a pot ready to boil over. He was lashing out at the man who was his brother in truth, but had been his friend throughout life.

He was the eldest child of their father, though he had never been and never would be acknowledged as such. But he didn't hate his brother. He didn't despise Caleb, but that resentment was an ugly and insidious thing writhing about inside him, making him say and do things that he would only regret later. But his concerns about Miss Ashton were legitimate. Surely her reputation had been at least partially earned! And if so, she was not the sort of wife Caleb would need.

Was it truly such an unpardonable sin to stop him from marrying a woman who would likely cuckold him if rumors were true? Another voice whispered the answer in his mind. *Yes. If that is his choice.*

Jacob pushed such thoughts aside. He couldn't afford them at the moment.

Stepping outside, he had not gone far when he noted a familiar carriage waiting at the end of the street. It was Williams. The man was there for a reason and Jacob knew it was best to get on with it and find out what that was.

Making his way to the conveyance, a footman hopped down and opened the door for him just as he reached it. Climbing inside, he took note that Williams was not alone. Lady Crowden was with him. None of it sat well with him. He didn't like the lying and scheming. He didn't like that a wedge was being driven between himself and Caleb, who was his only friend and also, even if never acknowledged, his only family.

"Did you learn anything new?"

"He has obtained a special license. I heard it from his own lips," Jacob said. "He means to marry the chit by week's end… He also stated that someone had made an attempt on Miss Ashton's life. While I did follow them in the park, I did not tamper with his phaeton. Did you?"

Williams shook his head. "Of course we did not. Our goal, Mr. Danvers, is to see the woman humiliated and ruined socially. Not to see her dead. In truth, her death would be most inconvenient for us as it would make her an object of pity. He's likely overreacting."

Jacob knew Caleb was not the sort to leap to conclusions. If he'd said someone intended to see her harmed, then he believed it to be true. And yet what Williams said rang true. At least part of it did. He might not have orchestrated the attempt on her life, but he didn't view Caleb's response as an overreaction. And that could only mean that he knew more than he was willing to reveal. Given what he'd learned of the man during their short acquaintance, that made sense. It meshed with everything the man had said thus far. His former betrothed had abandoned him at the altar and humiliated him publicly. He wanted to turn the tables on her and see her as the object of ridicule. Lady Crowden's involvement was something of a mystery though. Whether Williams was being entirely truthful or not, either about his motivations or the attempts on Miss Ashton's life, Jacob understood that they were not to be trusted. Neither of them.

"You were supposed to lure him out… to get him to the carriage so he could be spirited away," Lady Crowden stated. "But you failed."

"He's not inclined to trust me right now. Or anyone for that matter since someone tried to murder the woman he intends to marry," Jacob snapped. "I'll get him to accompany me somewhere and you can do whatever it is you're planning to do. But I'll be well out of it. Out of it and out of debt." Even as he uttered the words, a pit formed in his stomach. Guilt, shame, regret—all of it coiled together inside him. He was betraying his friend. His brother, even if that would never be acknowledged publicly.

"That is our understanding," Williams agreed.

It wasn't a yes, but an evasion. Jacob realized then that he'd made a truly terrible error in judgment in throwing in his lot with the pair of them. Everything Caleb had said about his choices had been true. His present situation was entirely of his own making and that was a bitter pill indeed.

Chapter Twenty-Three

Springing the trap...

NEARLY AN HOUR after Jacob had left, Caleb's temper had cooled enough to think more clearly about what had transpired in his absence. It was easy enough to see that the desk in the corner of the room had been rifled through. Then he understood perfectly why Jacob had wished to be alone in his chambers. No doubt there would be a significant number of banknotes missing. Likely, Jacob did not even consider it stealing as he felt the funds were simply his due. Still, it was difficult for Caleb to fully accept that he could be the culprit behind the attacks on Marina. Not because he had any particular faith in his friend's morality but for the very reason Jacob had offered up himself. The man would never dirty his own hands. So how and why had the handkerchief come to be there?

Also, if Jacob's covetous nature was at the heart of it all, then why was Marina the target instead of him? None of it made any sense. But perhaps he was going at it from entirely the wrong angle. Thinking of other incidents that had occurred with having seen both Lady Crowden and Mr. Nutter watching them, neither of them was above suspicion. The only player in the mix thus far whose motivation he did not understand was Miss Elizabeth Whitmore. Perhaps it was time to have a conversation with her and find out precisely what she knew and what she didn't.

Turning, Caleb made his way downstairs once more. Grabbing his coat, he didn't bother ringing for his carriage or a mount. It would take too long. Instead, he stepped outside, planning to get a hansom cab.

As his feet touched the pavement, he felt a frisson of unease. Ahead of him, parked in the street, was a dark carriage, the curtains inside it shut tight.

"Lord St. Aiden?"

Hearing the query from behind him, Caleb turned. There was only a split second to register what was happening. Then the blunt object glanced off his brow, sending him staggering to the paving stones. Another blow and the world went dark.

THE TWO MEN stared at the prone form of the Earl of St. Aiden for a moment. Then they did as they'd been bade and hefted him up between them to deposit him in the carriage. A shadowy figure within produced a pair of coins in their gloved palm, extending it toward them.

Taking their bounty, the men turned and walked away.

"It don't feel right, does it?"

The second man looked at his companion. "Harry, we can't afford to worry 'bout how it feels. This right here is more than we'd make in six months for naught but givin' him a knock on the head."

"I reckon, Ollie, if we was to provide some information to folks who might come lookin' for him, we might get paid again."

Ollie smiled, revealing a large gap between his teeth. "Harry, you're a right genius sometimes. Fine. We lay low a bit and see who comes lookin' for him. It's bad business this... don't like working for someone when I don't even know their face. Could pass 'em on the street right now and never know. Makes me nervous."

ASTRID HAD WATCHED from her perch in the shadowed recesses of the carriage as the men loaded the Earl of St. Aiden into the nondescript carriage Mr. Williams had procured for this portion of their scheme. Now, with the lackeys paid, it was time to depart. She felt strangely vulnerable and exposed—fearful, even.

It had dawned on her while Stanford was making the arrangements for the carriage, that she was taking all the risks while he was reaping the rewards. She and Mr. Danvers were the ones who might face consequences from all their plots and schemes.

It was that realization which had her crafting her own plot. She'd be certain that someone knew it wasn't just her—she wouldn't allow him to ruin her or take the fall for his misdeeds. But he'd said it was imperative to keep the pair from being wed and she was just petty enough to want that herself. After all, she'd taken note of how he and Miss Ashton looked at one another, the closeness that seemed to be growing between them.

As a woman well past forty, she understood that others saw her as a fading, or perhaps already faded, beauty. All the creams and remedies in the world could not stop time. But his obvious preference for the youth and vitality of Miss Marina Ashton had wounded her vanity. And the price for that insult was one she would be only too happy to extract from him. That it would see Miss Ashton suffer as well was simply the decadent icing on the cake. She had never quite forgiven Stanford or that wretched girl for having the audacity to parade about society together, outwardly giving every indication of being a couple madly in love with one another. She'd fumed every time she'd seen them together.

Tapping on the roof of the carriage, she called out to the driver, "Number eight, Greenwood Street in Bloomsbury... and hurry." The last thing she wanted was for St. Aiden to awaken in the carriage. The house she was taking him to was the one she normally used for her liaisons. The staff there was discreet. And more importantly, she had Watson. He would be able to get the earl into the house and he would be able to guard him until the hour of the wedding had passed.

The plan, initially, was that after a few days, St. Aiden would be blindfolded, taken from the house, and then deposited in one of the city's many parks with another lump on his head and hopefully a very faulty memory. Watson would have instructions to eliminate any possibility of discovery.

But now, riding in the carriage with him, fearful that he might awaken at any moment, that plan was being replaced by another far more sinister one. It would be easier, she thought, and far less risky simply to kill him. But she wanted him to suffer, she wanted him to be utterly miserable. It was petty, but then she'd never aspired to be anything more than that. She would have to think on it for a bit before making her decision.

Chapter Twenty-Four

The not-so-gilded cage...

CALEB'S EYES OPENED abruptly. Instantly, he was aware of two things: the hard earth beneath him and the complete darkness that surrounded him. Still, he sat up, lifting his bound hands gingerly to his head. Dried blood was crusted on his skin and in his hair. The taste of it lingered in his mouth.

"Ah, you're awake. I wondered if perhaps they'd hit you a bit too hard."

The voice in the darkness was one he recognized, but it was not at all one he had expected. "Lady Crowden?"

"And now, when it is far too late, you've developed the ability to recognize me in the darkness." The words dripped with sarcasm and disdain.

Caleb moved his hands experimentally, testing the bonds that held him. "What is this about? I cannot imagine that even you would go to such lengths over the ridiculous misunderstanding between us."

"No. I wouldn't. Normally. But unfortunately, Mr. Stanford Williams has returned to town. Your former betrothed of your current betrothed, as it were. As I'm sure you are well aware, she jilted him on the day of their wedding causing an endless amount of embarrassment and ridicule to be heaped upon his head."

"Perhaps if he'd been a better man—and a faithful one—she would not have felt the need to 'jilt' him as you put it."

Her answering shrug was betrayed only by the sound of rustling fabric. "I suppose that is true enough. It does not change the fact that his reputation has suffered terribly after such a public rejection. In light of that, he's decided that he must restore his reputation before seeking another wife in society. Of course, now he's in even more dire straits because he had to marry outside his class in order to preserve his holdings—tainted with trade of all things. It's positively horrific."

Trade was so horrific, he thought, that Lady Crowden had been throwing herself at him despite the fact that he was more than simply tainted with an association to it. He'd been right in the thick of it. Regardless, Caleb remained silent and let her talk. The more she did so the more he could learn about his current situation and how the devil he might get out of it.

"Now, he wishes to marry again... and marry well. But he cannot do that without first taking the necessary steps to restore his own reputation, which Miss Ashton destroyed two years ago. That means, if you're keeping up with the plot thus far, my lord, that Miss Ashton's reputation must be destroyed. It's rather a fait accompli that the destruction will be wrought by being abandoned at the altar by you!"

"And where do you fit into all of this? Clearly you cannot marry him as you already have a husband... but he's been your lover before and I daresay is again?"

"Make no mistake, my lord. I might welcome him into my bed, but that doesn't mean that I love him... I detest him," she said. "But not as much as I loathe you."

Ah, there it was. They'd finally dug through the layers of nonsense to get to the real heart of it. "All this because of wounded vanity and pride?"

"And money, my lord, at least for him. Surely you understand how marriage can impact one's fortune. After all, weren't you in London to find a bride so you could secure your own inheritance?

While there is doubt amongst the matrons of society about *why* Miss Ashton elected to cry off, he will never be entertained as a serious suitor by any young woman of note until it is proven that she was the one at fault."

"What are you getting out of this? As you said yourself, Mr. Williams is hardly such a bosom companion to you that you would willingly engage in such high-risk activities as the abduction of a lord to aid him in his schemes!"

Another rustle of satin from the shadows as she shrugged yet again. "I have many reasons, not the least of which is my husband. While he doesn't mind that I enjoy carnal relations with other men, he does draw the line at being publicly embarrassed by my *appetites*. As for you, well, vengeance… spite, pettiness, scorn. You may call it anything you like," she teased. "I simply want to be a thorn in your side, my lord. And in hers, as you've made it abundantly clear that your feelings for her go far beyond simply finding her 'acceptable.' In short, my lord, my aim is to keep you from marrying Miss Ashton to make you both miserably unhappy and to keep Stanford Williams from revealing the truth to my husband lest I be banished to the countryside for daring to satisfy my desires when he cannot… I will certainly not suffer such a fate because you went calf-eyed at the very sight of a self-styled spinster!"

"I have never in my life encountered such selfish, self-serving people as I have in this city. It corrupts everyone," he said.

"And were you not self-serving when you delivered such a slight to me?" Lady Crowden snapped.

"Such a slight? You mean the fact that I had no wish to enter into an affair with a woman who was already wed? That is hardly a slight, madam!"

"No. Not that," she responded dryly. "The slight I refer to was done to me when I noted the expression on your face as you gazed upon the lovely and youthful form of Miss Ashton. You were not simply willing, by virtue of honor, to be linked in scandal with her. You were *pleased* to be trapped into a marriage with her. I had, much to my chagrin, given you exactly what you wanted when you would not give me a second look. Why is that, my lord? I've often wondered what is happening in the confounding minds of men that makes youth and innocence preferable to skill and experience? Or is it that so many gentlemen simply prefer a woman in their bed who hasn't the knowledge to recognize them as terrible lovers?"

"Your vanity is boundless! Has it never occurred to you, Lady Crowden, that it isn't age, experience, or even appearance, but rather it is your character, or lack thereof, that renders you undesirable?" It was likely not the most intelligent of actions—challenging the woman who, at least on the surface of things, held his very life in her hands.

She didn't pace the dimly lit room so much as she strolled the distance of it, back and forth, as if she hadn't a care in the world. "Very few men, Lord St. Aiden, ever pay enough attention to a woman beyond her figure and acquiescence to notice their character... or lack thereof. Indeed, frequently acquiescence isn't even deemed worthy of noting."

Caleb didn't bother to correct her. Firstly, because she wasn't entirely wrong. Secondly, the woman was completely irrational. There would be no reasoning with her.

Lady Crowden continued. "The worth of a woman is a fleeting thing, my lord, based entirely upon beauty and fertility—two things only ever associated with youth. And even as lovely as your Miss Ashton is, the windows of opportunity for her are closing. After all, she's past twenty, an unpardonable sin according to even the most aged roué. When you fail to turn up at the appointed time to wed your not-quite-fresh-faced beauty, it will leave her a pariah. With her reputation, she had limited prospects to start. Now she will have none. In short, she will suffer the same sort of embarrassment and insult that you have heaped upon me... being unwanted."

Her rambling was no longer even pertinent. She was simply pontificating on her own interpretation of the world around her, one which would always allow her to be the victim in the narrative rather than the villain—a fact that could not be further from the truth.

"Do you think she will weep and sob over her lost, last chance?" Lady Crowden asked, almost gleeful at the prospect.

Caleb gritted his teeth. "I should think not. She has more dignity than that. And I should hate to think that I, even against my own will, would ever have caused her tears."

Lady Crowden gaped at him in shock for a moment. Then she tossed her head back and laughed, almost maniacally. "Should I honestly believe that you are this much of a paragon?"

"I'm far from a paragon, but I do strive to never be the villain," he countered. "Clearly, that's an unfamiliar concept to you."

Chapter Twenty-Five

The ruse continues...

T HE NOTE HAD arrived that morning, informing them that the earl had obtained the license and that all was in readiness for the pair of them to be wed at St. George's Church the following morning. The note, addressed to Marina, had been given to Lord and Lady Deveril after. And it had raised concerns for Willa. It had been so perfunctory. Direct, to the point, and lacking any sort of emotion. But did that very dry note indicate that he lacked emotion? Still, Marina had insisted that he would come to call sometime that day. And given how attentive and present he'd been during the previous week Willa had no cause to doubt that. Except that teatime had already passed and still there was no sign of him.

"Stop worrying!"

Willa looked back at Lillian, and as she realized she'd been pacing the floor, sighed wearily. Returning to her seat, she said, "I'm afraid. I'm so terribly afraid. Though I suppose the time for that has passed. She deserves to be happy."

"And perhaps she will be, but that is no longer up to you," Lillian responded sagely. "She is an adult. A grown woman who is now responsible for her own happiness."

"I do not like this. I understand the need for it, but I do not like it," Willa said.

Lillian shook her head, her gaze locked on the screen behind which Marina was dressing. "Willa, Marina wants to marry this man. He clearly wants to marry her. Must it be some society event with orange blossoms and gathered guests whom we all secretly despise?"

Willa looked away. "What a wretched sister you are to point out my hypocrisy! I just had never imagined that, when Marina married, it would have to be some rushed and hurried affair. I wanted her to have the sort of wedding that young girls dream of."

Lillian laughed softly. "It isn't hypocrisy. You don't give a fig for how it all looks. Your concern is for her happiness, as it should be. My point in reminding you of our own hasty nuptials is to broach the possibility that, while this isn't how you pictured it, it may still prove to be precisely what she needs... Not being in love with him now does not preclude loving him in the future."

The hastiness of the wedding aside, Willa couldn't find one thing in Lord St. Aiden to which she could object. If she were to be entirely honest, her reluctance had little to do with him and more to do with the fact that Marina's coming absence from their home was plaguing her. "I know that. And I pray for that outcome. But I do not want her to regret this. I do not want her to feel that she has rushed headlong into this and made a mistake. Not after Stanford."

Lillian frowned. "Have you ever asked why, Willa?"

Willa frowned, her brows drawing together slightly. "It's terrible, Lillian. Completely awful. But it isn't my secret to tell."

Lillian was quiet for a moment, then nodded. "Willa, did you? When you married Devil in an equally hasty manner, did you regret it?"

Willa couldn't stop the sly smile that curved her lips. "You know I did not. Just as you never once regretted marrying Valentine."

"Well, momentarily perhaps," Lillian said with a smirk. "But he tends to redeem himself very well… I think, Willa, that you must accept that Marina is now a grown woman capable of making her own decisions. If she feels that marriage to the Earl of St. Aiden is the right course for her, then we must not disagree. And we must not drive a wedge between her and her family by haranguing her for that decision."

Willa said nothing more because the door to the drawing room had opened and Marina entered. Dressed in ivory silk embroidered with gold thread and pearls, she was a vision, despite the numerous pins that could be seen here and there. The dress had been made during her first Season when she'd been set to marry Mr. Stanford Williams, and her figure had become more womanly since that time. Still, looking at her in the gown, it was difficult to deny how much she had changed. Marina was not the terrified and silent child she had once soothed and cared for. She was now a woman grown. *She was a bride.*

Willa felt tears stinging her eyes as she looked at her niece— at the daughter of her heart. "Oh, Marina! You are exquisite. I declare that dress, once the alterations are complete, will be even more stunning on you now than when first commissioned."

Marina's answering smile was tight, reflecting her nervousness. "Let's hope it finally makes it down the aisle this time."

The gown was the one which had been commissioned for the wedding which had been called off more than two years prior. It had been packed away in a trunk along with much of her remaining trousseau.

"It will. If you wish it to. And if you do not… well, we'll cross that bridge when we come to it," Lillian insisted. "Now, you have something old, something borrowed, something blue?"

"Old, new, and blue… but I have nothing borrowed," Marina answered.

Lillian reached up and plucked a diamond pin from her elegant coiffure. She then tucked it into the mass of Marina's dark curls, just beneath her veil. "And I presume there is to be a sixpence tucked inside your slipper?"

"Naturally."

Willa stepped forward, hugging Marina tightly.

"The pins, Lady Deveril! Mind the pins," Stephens admonished them all.

Immediately, Willa stepped back. "Of course. Let us not be impractical and ruin all this hard work. Not when we still have other tasks to see to. Stephens, please help Marina out of the gown and then have a bit of tea sent up to her room for us. I think we shall need it."

A knowing look passed between Willa and Lillian, leaving Marina not as entirely in the dark as they no doubt wished to believe. Oh, she didn't know the particulars of the marriage bed, but she knew enough to understand that she would much rather gather that information through experience than embarrassing and stilted conversation.

Entering her chamber, Willa on her heels, Marina halted. "We do not need to do this. I've had enough friends who have gotten married off already that I'm not entirely ignorant."

With Stephens's assistance, she removed the gown that would be her wedding dress. Her cheeks flushed with embarrassment, the loyal retainer all but scurried away with the garment, leaving them alone with her pronouncement hanging between them.

After a moment, Willa cleared her throat lightly. "Well, that is a bit of relief. I confess to not knowing precisely where to begin with such a conversation. That does not mean, of course, that I do not have some sage wisdom to share with you."

Wearing her chemise and petticoats, Marina donned her wrapper and plopped down on the bench at the foot of her bed. Hugging her arms about her, she nodded to her aunt. "I'm listening."

"The physical aspect of your marriage is so much more important than most people, especially other ladies, will ever admit. It cannot be the basis of it, of course, but that doesn't mean it isn't one of the supports that will shore it up when times are tough.

And there will always be times that are tough, my dear. Perhaps not financially, but when your life becomes so entwined with another person's… well, complications are unavoidable. The intimacy of the marriage bed can often be the thing that will keep you—not together but connected. Because the trick is not falling in love with one's husband or even staying in love with one's husband. It's about developing the capacity for forgiveness that will allow you to fall in love with him over and over again even when he's been an absolute dolt."

"Has Uncle Devil been a dolt?"

Willa rolled her eyes heavenward. "Oh, countless times! Countless. But I adore him enough not to hold it against him. It helps that he's very, very handsome… as is the Earl of St. Aiden."

Marina felt a blush creeping over her cheeks. "He is quite handsome."

"And can I presume that there has been a stolen kiss or two?" Willa asked.

"I thought we weren't going to discuss this!"

Willa laughed. "It isn't easy for me, you know? I look at you and while I am perfectly aware that you are a woman grown, I still see the little girl who clung to me when she was terrified. To think that you will now be starting a life of your own, with your own children to tend to—I'm overcome by it all a bit."

"Understandably so," Marina conceded. "It's a bit over-whelming for me also. But exciting. I think this might be the first time that I have really felt like the future was full of possibilities. Not since… Well, since Stanford."

"Did you love him truly?"

"I thought I did," Marina admitted. It was time to tell the truth. "But after I discovered he had never loved me, I—The realization that the man I had thought myself in love with was simply a work of fiction helped me to understand that it had all been an elaborate illusion. A character he created and played with sublime skill."

Willa took her hand. "Why did you never say anything? You

were hurting so terribly and never asked for help, for support."

"It was too humiliating… Better to be thought a jilt than to be known for someone who was only sought for their fortune and stupid enough not to see it. I felt so foolish. So unbelievably idiotic. For believing his lies. And when I looked back, I could see all the little tell-tale signs of it that I hadn't wanted to see before. I couldn't bear for everyone—including him—to know what a fool I had been. So I ended our engagement, never letting on that I knew what he was about."

"You devious thing. You let him just think you didn't want him after all."

Marina ducked her head. "I did. And, in light of recent events, perhaps I ought to regret it, but I do not."

"On the contrary. I think it's divine. Worthy of Lillian, even."

Marina laughed then. "High praise!"

"It is. Now, I'm off to dress for an early dinner. We'll all need to seek our beds early tonight. We have a very big day tomorrow and one that will begin quite early… I'd advise you to do the same, lest you have shadows under your eyes."

Marina smiled in response. "Quite right."

Chapter Twenty-Six

Pride goeth before the fall...

"WHAT IN HEAVEN'S name are you talking about? How hard did those men hit you?" Lady Crowden laughed at that, a trilling sound that still rang cold.

Hard enough. "I can't imagine you're overly concerned for my well-being." He was fairly certain that she'd decided that he would not leave that hovel alive. Otherwise, she would have taken steps to conceal her identity. The longer he was conscious the more the cobwebs in his brain began to clear, and the more he realized just how dire his situation was.

"If Miss Ashton is dead then Stanford does not get the pleasure of her public humiliation," she explained. "If I had been unwilling to help him get you out of the way to make this happen, he would have exposed me. I would have had to face my husband's censure. I don't care enough about Marina Ashton to want her dead—only miserable. And she's of no use to Stanford in such a state."

It might be cold and calculating. Certainly it was self-serving. But it held a note of truth in it. So if it wasn't her and Stanford Williams trying to end Marina's life, then who? Miss Whitmore? Mr. Nutter? Jacob? And how would he be able to protect her while he was rotting in that hole? "She's in danger."

She clucked her tongue like a disapproving nanny. "I won't bother lying to you, my lord. So are you."

"I'd gathered," he replied sotto voce.

"It would be pointless to lie, I think. You are many things, Lord St. Aiden, but you are not stupid. I will say that I, initially, had thought simply to keep you here and have you released later… blindfolded naturally and possibly with a generous bit of laudanum in you to render your memories indistinct. But upon greater reflection, and considering the longing looks exchanged between you and Miss Ashton—an indication that there is much more to this marriage than simply avoiding scandal—I cannot trust that this would represent only a delay in your nuptials and not a complete cessation."

"Why? I cannot fathom that you could not have come up with a way to exact your petty vengeance that would not involve significantly less risk to yourself?"

"I need Williams on my side," she offered with a shrug. "He knows too much and could ruin me if he chooses. I need to keep him happy. So, the marriage will be delayed… long enough that it will be assumed you fled to parts unknown rather than go through with it. And, of course, I'd like you to suffer a bit for the insult you've dealt me."

If his head hadn't already been pounding, he would have banged it against the nearest hard surface. "You are a lunatic… fit for Bedlam."

She laughed. "I think you underestimate me," she crowed. "I'm not a lunatic, at all. I know precisely what I'm about and why. What I possess, Lord St. Aiden, is a well-developed sense of self preservation and a wealth of pride. You pose a threat to the former and have wounded the latter quite thoroughly. It is a matter of cause and effect."

There was a lengthy pause as she obviously was waiting for a reply. A reply which he was unwilling to give. The more he talked to her the more ammunition he was giving her.

With his stony silence, her temper spiked. "I will stop *her* from marrying you. From marrying anyone! After this, with the derision that will surely greet the very mention of her name, I doubt there will be any forgiveness to be had. Not when you've made her the same sort of laughingstock she made of poor Stanford. Will you beg her to give you one more chance? To accept you? Will you lay your pride and dignity at her feet to be trampled upon? Assuming you live to do so. That remains to be seen. A bit of humility could sway me."

"So that's your end goal," he mused. "You simply wish me to abase myself as you were so willing to do."

"Perhaps… or perhaps I just enjoy the chaos. Either way, you sparked my ire, and now you are paying the cost. Get comfortable, Lord St. Aiden. You're going to be here for some time. Long enough for Miss Ashton to flee the city and her current shame. Bath might be a good choice for her, though not far enough to outrun the gossip. The Continent might be nice. Fine weather and new vistas can do wonders for a broken heart, I'm told."

"And when Marina is gone, what is my fate to be?"

After a second's hesitation, Lady Crowden shrugged. "I suppose it doesn't really matter if you know the entire truth. After all, as you've no doubt guessed, you'll not leave this cellar alive… In a few days, perhaps a week, you will be found soaked in brandy, reeking of another woman's perfume, and with a knife in your back and an ace up your sleeve. It isn't as if Mr. Danvers would be your nearest and dearest friend if you didn't have something in common with him."

"You are banking on a great deal of assumptions," he informed her.

"Assumptions are what our society functions upon. What will happen to Miss Ashton when you do not arrive at the church on time, my lord? No one will think you might have been abducted or that you might have been prevented from being there against your will. The assumption will be that you came to your senses. You realized how inappropriate she would be as a countess—the bastard daughter of a woman of low morals and weak character and a father… well, who knows what he was? There are whispers and they are ugly enough that people will be only too eager to dig up those old rumors and bandy them about."

"And when my remains are discovered in the very unlikely scenario you painted previously?"

"You are a man. It will never be a stretch of the imagination to think you had gotten drunk and availed yourself of the cheaply bought companionship of some strumpet or other. Such behaviors are not only commonplace, they are practically encouraged."

The true hell of it, Caleb recognized, was that she spoke the absolute truth. That is exactly what would happen. Marina's life, at least as she knew it, would be forever altered. The other idea, that she might believe he'd willingly left her to face such humiliation alone, that was equally abhorrent to him. "You've considered all the angles, haven't you? You've crafted this scheme with the skill of a master." But she hadn't counted on one thing— the depth of his determination. He would get out of there and he would see Marina safe. But first, he had to determine if the madwoman before him had any information that was actually useful.

"So Miss Whitmore, despite her appearance of being quite viperous, has been mostly innocent in this fiasco. But what do you know of Mr. Nutter?" he asked. While she was feeling so free with information, he might as well make use of the opportunity.

"He's aptly named," she conceded with a sly smile. "There have been whispers for years about the unfortunate accident that befell the first poor girl to catch his eye. On the surface of it, most believed she had taken her own life, but there was just enough doubt… she'd been quite firm in her rejection of him, you see? Miss Ashton, at least to this point, had been careful of his feelings. As for Miss Whitmore, she's naught but a dupe—eating out of Stanford Williams's hand and swallowing his lies with a syrupy smile."

"Would he truly go to such insane lengths simply because she wounded his pride?"

"Of course, he would. Our situation is unique—because I've turned the tables. I've taken the power and the control. Men have always had it, and some are unable to let go of it. By virtue of being led by her own will, Miss Ashton has insulted his pride, his manhood, and indeed, his very understanding of what he is entitled to in this world... As for Miss Whitmore, she lacks the power to do any real harm to Miss Ashton. She lacks the gravitas and position in society, not to mention the connections, to ever truly ruin someone. Every ugly whisper that escapes her lips is viewed as sour grapes. If you wish to ruin someone, you must first give the appearance of being their ally. Then, when you turn on them, others will assume it's for just cause and will follow suit. Ask your Mr. Danvers about it... oh, no. I don't suppose you'll ever have that option."

Caleb didn't openly challenge her because he knew it would be a mistake to give away anything. Instead, he just glowered at her. Let her believe him to be impotent and mute with rage. It was to his benefit for her to underestimate him.

After a moment, she smiled smugly at him then turned to walk away. When she rapped on the door, it was opened by a beefy man who kept his eyes and a pistol trained on Caleb while she made her exit. He'd wondered if the place was guarded. Now he had an answer, even if it was the least desirable one available. Regardless, he intended to make his escape. She would not claim victory and she would not succeed in ruining Marina or his chance for happiness with her. The how of it all remained to be seen. He needed to clear the cobwebs from his brain; to strategize and execute the plan would require a steady hand and acuity of mind that he had not yet regained. The first step would be freeing his hands. Whoever had tied the knot in those ropes had done so with great enthusiasm. They were a tangled mass that would take ages to free.

Chapter Twenty-Seven

Unlikely allies...

THE DINNER HOUR came and went with no sign of Caleb. Marina couldn't quite dispel the feeling that something terrible was in the offing. His absence was surely not cause for such concern. Regardless, there was an uneasiness about her—an impending sense of doom. Surely she would have heard something from him beyond that simple to the point of terse note he'd sent earlier in the day that had only been part of their ruse.

"I'm certain everything is fine."

Marina looked over to see Willa eyeing her with concern. They were in the drawing room, Devil and her cousins having retreated to the billiard room. "Is my concern so obvious?"

"Well, you have decimated the book you've been reading."

Marina looked down at the book in her hands. She'd been gripping it so tightly that it had begun to warp. "I suppose I am a bit anxious."

"About the wedding or about the marriage?"

"About the fact that he has not come by today," she admitted. "It wasn't agreed upon, but it was... well, expected. I suppose that seems silly."

Willa shook her head. "Not at all. I find it worrisome as well. Likely not to the degree that you do, however. I'm certain he's simply making preparations for your journey after the ceremony. You will be departing immediately after, I take it?"

"I wish I could say," Marina mused. "We've not discussed it beyond him telling me the name of the estate and about the village where it is located. It is strange that he has not come to call today. If he didn't intend to call, surely he would have said."

"Are you certain?"

"What does that mean?" Marina asked sharply.

Willa sighed. "I only say that you do not know him well. Are you certain you know—not his character, because he seems to be of good character—but character and personality are very different things. Knowing he's a good man and knowing he's the right man? Those two things are worlds apart, my dear."

"He is the right man. I have no doubt about that. Perhaps I should," Marina mused. "Despite our acquaintance being so short... I've never known anyone else who makes me feel the way he does."

"And how is that?"

"As if I do not wish to be parted from him," she admitted. "As if he could be across the room and still I would know when he's looking at me without ever laying eyes on him. I could feel it. There's an awareness between us. I suppose that sounds silly, doesn't it?"

Willa sighed. "No, my dear. It sounds promising. Perhaps, at this stage, it's still only infatuation or attraction, but that is an excellent place to start."

Marina nodded. "I think I shall go up to bed. I'm certain everything is fine and this is naught but nerves."

"Get some rest, darling girl. Tomorrow is another busy day as we prepare for your wedding—hurried though it is. Stephens will have your dress ready. If she must stop time itself, her will shall not be denied. She's already stated that she intends to dress your hair."

At that, Marina shuddered. That brute of a woman would attack her head, arranging her hair into a way that defied all the laws of science and nature. There was no denying, of course, that Stephens was an excellent hairdresser. Anything she lacked in congeniality was certainly made up for with that enviable skill. But her results were not worth the pain of their execution.

Exiting the drawing room, Marina headed upstairs to her room. Stepping inside, she reached for the bell pull to call her maid, but something stopped her. Some sixth sense prevailed, and she knew instantly that she was not alone.

"Who's there?"

"I'm not here to harm you… I'm here to offer a warning, of sorts." The gas light overhead flickered to life and the man was instantly recognizable to her.

"Mr. Danvers," she acknowledged. "This is most irregular."

"I fear it will become more irregular still… I've not been a very good friend to Caleb," he admitted.

Friend. It was patently obvious to her that he could only be Caleb's relative—whether sibling or cousin she could not say. "Have you betrayed him in some way?"

"I've betrayed you both, I'm afraid. I owed a substantial gambling debt, and the markers were purchased by Mr. Stanford Williams. And he, in league with myself and Lady Crowden, have plotted to prevent Caleb from marrying you. My primary objective was simply to try and dissuade him, to make him doubt you. And I did that to the best of my ability but failed to shake him from his course. My failure prompted them to act more aggressively and in ways I had not imagined. You must believe me, Miss Ashton, when I say I never thought he would be harmed in any of this… alas, I have seen the error of my ways."

Her heart was in her throat. "Caleb is hurt?"

"He was knocked on the head and loaded into Lady Crowden's hired carriage. I followed as far as Bloomsbury but lost them there. I did, however, manage to locate the driver and he is to meet me tonight at a pub where I will pay him for the address."

"And that's why you're here. Because you can't pay him," she surmised.

"No. I cannot… I'll not deny that I've helped myself to Caleb's funds in the past, and he likely assumed that's why I was there this morning. The truth was even more nefarious—I was spying on behalf of Williams," he admitted. "I've made a terrible muddle of everything. But in this one instance, I'm at least trying to make it right."

Her heart was pounding painfully in her chest. Far more so than it should have for a man she merely liked. "How badly was he hurt?"

Jacob shrugged. "I wish I could say. He was unconscious when two hired thugs loaded him into the vehicle. Beyond that, it's anyone's guess. I could see him but was too far away to intervene… Mr. Williams, for his part, has not spoken of any intent to harm either of you physically. It is to his benefit for the pair of you not to wed and for everyone to see you living in disgrace. But Lady Crowden is another matter. She has quite a grudge against him for his 'rejection' of her. I fear her intent is not to let him go."

A shiver of fear raced through her. "No. No, she would not intend to let him go. But she will not risk Stanford becoming angry at her so nothing will happen to him until after the appointed time of our wedding. Which means we have less than twenty-four hours to save him."

"We?"

Marina squared her shoulders and faced him directly. "Yes, Mr. Danvers. We. You can go out the way you came in. I'll change into more appropriate attire for clandestine activities and meet you in the mews."

Chapter Twenty-Eight

The bell tolls...

SITTING IN THE darkness, Caleb continued patiently working at his restraints. The sad truth of it was that he was having more luck simply fraying the rough hemp than releasing the knots. In the distance, he heard the church bells as they chimed the hour which only heightened his sense of urgency. He had just under eighteen hours to free himself and get to the church. First, he had to somehow loosen his bonds. Without his hands free, he'd have no chance.

Now, with at least some knowledge of the timetable he was working with, Caleb rose to his feet and began scouring the darkened cellar. Inch by inch, he prowled that small, suffocating space. He'd all but given up hope when he found a single nail protruding from a beam overhead. Raising his arms high, he began using the sharp, protruding bit of metal to saw at the ropes around his wrists. When at last the twisted hemp gave way, his skin was bloody and raw from the efforts. But he was free. He let out a soft whoop of victory.

As if summoned by the sound of his voice, a scraping noise sounded beyond the door. Would it be Lady Crowden returned to gloat? Or would it be his guard for some reason? Retreating to the post he'd been leaning against during his earlier conversation with Lady Crowden, he concealed his freed wrists as best possible.

His question was answered quickly enough when the large, beefy figure of a man appeared in the doorway. Standing at his elbow was a cowed young woman, carrying a tray laden with crockery.

"Your supper has arrived, m'lord," he said with a sneering chortle.

"Is this typically the sort of work you do for her ladyship? Locking up men who have the audacity to refuse her?"

The man laughed. "I do what I'm paid to. Sometimes it's fetching and carrying a man to her. Sometimes it's carting 'em away."

"I suppose that makes you Lady Crowden's man of all work… so long as it's the dirty sort."

"It do. And I'll not be biting the hand that feeds, so you can just keep whatever you're about to offer. Me and the lady go way back. She weren't always so high in the instep, you know? Her mother and mine worked the same corner for many a year."

The man would never share such information with him if there were any chance of him leaving that room alive. "So will it be Lady Crowden who orders my death? Or do you work on the orders of Lord Crowden to clean up her messes?"

The man stepped aside, letting the young serving girl enter the room, but he kept his gaze locked on Caleb the entire time. "Lady Crowden is very careful about how she brings men here. But even careful folk make a mistake from time to time. You're a bit brighter than some of the others I've had to keep down here… but it won't help you none. Eat up. A humble last meal for a man such as yourself."

It would not be his last meal. Of that, Caleb was entirely certain. But bravado in informing the other man such would not be to his benefit. Instead, he remained quiet as the large, burly fellow exited the room, presumably to stand guard outside.

The moment the man was gone, Caleb grasped the wrist of

the serving girl and took note of the heavy tray she held. He had no interest in the crockery, or even the cutlery. His interest was in the tray itself. The heavy pewter might be his best chance of overpowering the brute and making his escape. Even from a distance, Caleb had seen the pistol clutched in the man's meaty fist.

"You must help me get out of here," he whispered.

"I can't, sir," she replied, her voice pitched just as low, even as she glanced furtively over her shoulder. Her fear was palpable. "But there's a chip in that bowl. Right sharp it is… and I reckon this tray is heavy enough to do some damage. Found the heaviest one I could for you, sir. It ain't right what she's doing."

That quick exchange offered him hope. It meant that not every servant in the house was so bound by loyalty to Lady Crowden that they would willingly aid her in committing such misdeeds. But the brute at the door was another matter. He poked his head in and shouted at the maid. "Quit your yapping and get back to work!"

The maid scurried out when the man barked at her and Caleb was once more alone in the darkness. He didn't dare eat or drink anything lest it be drugged. The maid was trustworthy, it seemed, but who knew about the cook? While Lady Crowden had said she wished to keep him alive for a bit, she never said she wished to keep him conscious. He couldn't afford to have his wits addled by whatever she might have slipped into the food.

Removing his coat, he laid it atop the bowl and then struck it with his fist, the fabric muffling any sound that would alert the guard. Shaking out any loose shards of porcelain, he put his coat back on, concealed the evidence of his preparation, and settled himself once more against the post. Then it was simply a matter of waiting. Whether the food had simply been drugged or poisoned, he would be unresponsive whenever anyone opened that door. So much so they'd be forced to come in and check to see if he still breathed. That would be his one singular chance of escape, and he could not falter.

FROM SOME LONG-AGO caper that had gotten the lot of them in trouble, Marina still had possession of a set of clothing that had belonged to Gervase. The trousers were more snug than they had been the last time she'd worn them, but they would do. With her hair pinned up and tucked into a hat, she could pass for a boy so long as no one looked too closely. She could only pray they would not. Given the darkness and the late hour, her chances were at least acceptable if not good.

Almost as an afterthought, she slipped into her uncle's study and retrieved the brace of pistols that he kept in a drawer there. She had no idea if Mr. Danvers was armed or not, but she did know he wasn't entirely trustworthy. Having access to her own weapon would make her feel safer. Thankfully, she'd been taught how to shoot. Willa, oddly enough, was the one who had insisted on the lessons.

With the guns tucked up inside her borrowed coat and her pin money in her pocket, she moved through the house much like a criminal would. When she finally reached the back door of the kitchen and could exit through the small garden into the mews, she breathed a sigh of relief. No one had called her out. No one had awakened and alerted the house to her current path of misadventure. And it was misadventure.

She and Caleb had not spoken at length regarding his friend, but he'd informed her that the man was not keen on their match. Was it any wonder she was curious about his motives? Be that as it may, it was a risk she had to take. If Caleb was in trouble, she would have to do whatever was necessary to help save him.

Making her way along the narrow space that abutted the stables, she found Jacob Danvers waiting for her. He was tense, his shoulders stiff and his jaw firm. "I'm ready," she told him.

"This could be dangerous," he informed her.

"I'm aware," she replied. "The potential danger is precisely why we must act. We cannot risk leaving Caleb to their whims."

He was quiet for a moment, then gave a jerky nod. "Agreed."

With that, the two of them departed, leaving the mews and making for the street beyond. A hansom cab waited there for them, his presence clearly having been prearranged. Climbing up into it, she tried to calm her nerves as Danvers climbed in beside her. She was in a vulnerable position, and he was not a man to trust. But what options did she have?

As the vehicle rumbled over the cobblestone streets, she hugged her arms about herself for warmth and to stave off her nervous trembling. Was she rescuing Caleb or was she sacrificing herself to assuage someone else's pettiness and greed?

"You have nothing to fear from me."

Marina glanced up. "Is it so obvious?"

"If you were sitting any farther away, you'd be outside the cab," he pointed out.

"You have made it abundantly clear that you do not want to see Caleb marry me. It would be very unwise if I simply put my blind faith in your current actions and motivations," she replied.

He nodded in concession. "For the record, my objections were rooted firmly in the fact that I didn't wish to see Caleb marry anyone. I was bitter, resentful, covetous, and—frankly—a bit of an arse."

"Only a bit?"

"More, perhaps. But while I allowed jealousy to cloud my judgment briefly, Caleb is my dearest friend and has stood by me when no one else would have or should have. And I've repaid him with betrayal… but I would not have seen him harmed."

"I'll take that under advisement," Marina replied. "But your sincerity will be demonstrated by deeds rather than words."

"Fair enough, Miss Ashton. Fair enough."

Chapter Twenty-Nine

The escape...

NEARLY HALF AN hour later, Marina was seated in a darkened corner of a pub—a place she had never anticipated that she would be. She was certainly in the company of someone she had not expected. Beside her, Jacob Danvers drummed his fingers nervously on the scarred tabletop. The tempo was erratic and nerve-wracking to the point that she reached out and slapped her hand atop his. "Pull yourself together," she instructed on a hiss.

"I'm fairly certain he won't show," the man admitted.

"We will cross that bridge when we come to it. How will we recognize this man when he arrives?"

"He wears a particularly bold top hat, accented with a dyed purple feather."

Marina blinked. "You are making that up. This entire thing is a farce, isn't it? Stanford Williams is going to walk through that door any minute. I've been lured to my untimely demise!"

"No, I am not making it up. I encountered two gentlemen near Caleb's home—Ollie and Harry, who aided in Caleb's abduction—and they provided those pertinent details and also what tavern the man frequented."

It was too bizarre to be made up, she reasoned. Even as that thought was crossing her mind, the door to the pub opened and an aging gentleman in a frayed topcoat and elaborate hat entered the establishment. The garishness of his feather adornment was such that even the dim light could not fully camouflage it. "Oh, and there he is."

"Wait here," Jacob told her.

Marina had no intention of getting up. Her boys' togs were far more convincing while she was seated in a darkened corner than parading about in breeches that fit in what could only be called an obscene manner. Still, she watched the exchange between the two men with rapt attention. When the driver's gaze landed on her, she gave a nod. A moment later, the pair of them moved toward their private corner.

"Good evening… sir," the driver said with an arched eyebrow, clearly having seen through or been informed of her disguise.

"And to you. I think you have some information we require… about a friend of ours whom you may have transported earlier today?" she asked.

"I might at that. But I like to be compensated for my time," he answered.

"And what sort of compensation do you require?"

"Five pound," he said.

"Two," she countered. Marina wasn't so foolish as to think just granting such an unreasonable sum without quibbling would not render her a target for heaven knew what.

He cocked his head to the side and eyed her with grudging respect. "Two pound… and you buy the ale."

"Agreed," Marina said, sliding the appropriate number of pound notes across the table to him, keeping them carefully concealed beneath her fingers. "Now, where did you take him?"

"Number eight on Greenwood Street," the driver said. "Fetch and carry the lady from there quite a bit… and more than a few gentlemen. Never had to carry one there unconscious though. That were new to be sure."

Marina slid a few coins across the table then to accompany

the notes. "Then enjoy your ale until your heart and belly are content. Thank you, sir."

Almost instantly, she and Jacob departed, heading back for the hansom cab that was waiting for them. Giving the driver the address, Marina prayed that whatever Lady Crowden might have had in store for Caleb, that they would arrive in time to put a stop to it. The alternative was unthinkable.

"You actually care for him, don't you?"

She glanced up to see Mr. Danvers watching her curiously. "It would be very difficult not to care for Caleb. He's kind, generous, intelligent, charming—and entirely himself. No matter who is around him or what setting he might find himself in, he is true to himself in a way that few people ever are."

"I think perhaps you share that trait," Jacob commented. "And perhaps that might be why I took an instant dislike to you, Miss Ashton. It is very difficult to look at someone who lacks the flaw you most despise in yourself."

❀

THE CLOCK TOWER struck eleven. Caleb still sat with the broken crockery concealed in his hand, waiting for an opportunity to escape. When at long last the door to the cellar opened, he remained where he was, slumped over, appearing either unconscious or dead.

"Is he dead?"

The voice belonged to Lady Crowden.

"I don't know, m'lady."

"Well check him, Watson!" she snapped. "He might simply be feigning his current state to lure me in there and do heaven knows what. There wasn't that much laudanum in his food. It should have only made him agreeable. Not unconscious."

There was some grumbling, and then the thump of heavy footfalls approaching. He waited until the man, Watson, was crouching over him, his weight on the balls of his feet, biding his time. When the man reached out to shake him, Caleb made his move. Taking the piece of broken pottery, he jammed it upward into the soft flesh beneath the man's chin, pushing him backward as he did so. He followed that up by lifting the heavy pewter tray the maid had left behind and slammed it against the man's head with as much force as he could muster.

Hands now sticky with blood, Caleb grabbed the pistol the man had tucked into his belt before jumping to his feet. He raced toward the door, leaving the man writhing in pain behind him. Lady Crowden had been too stunned to react initially, but as he neared the door, she tried to slam it closed—apparently having no concern at all for her loyal retainer. With one last surge of speed, he slammed his shoulder into the heavy wooden door, halting her from closing it entirely. When he shoved it open, she stumbled backward.

"Did you really think I would simply accept whatever fate you had planned for me?" he demanded.

She didn't answer, simply glared back at him in silence as he locked the cellar door behind him. Watson would simply have to wait until someone else came to free him. He wasn't about to leave Lady Crowden behind to do so.

"Up the stairs," he ordered her.

"Or what? You will shoot me?"

"If needs must," he replied. "I'll take no pleasure in it, but I will. Because I can't leave you here to continue meddling in my life to soothe your wounded vanity. You, madam, have made yourself a significant liability."

She looked at the gun in his hand. "What do you mean to do with me then?"

"I mean, Lady Crowden, to return you to your husband and share the whole sordid tale with him, come what may," Caleb stated. "I'd have been content enough to live and let live—to never mention our unfortunate meeting or misunderstanding again, but you've left me without options as—unchecked—you will not cease to torment us."

Her expression hardened into one of cold, deadly fury. "You are so smug. So self-righteous in your judgment and disapproval! I've been married to that impotent wretch for over two decades and had I not sought passion outside my marriage bed, my life would have been entirely devoid of it."

"That is between you and your husband, madam," he replied. "If you wanted passion then perhaps you should have married for love rather than wealth and position, as you once cautioned me to do."

She scoffed, the sound of disdain followed up with a bitter laugh. "And how long does love last if one is impoverished? No, thank you, my lord. If given the option to choose again, I would still take the security of an old and wealthy husband while enjoying the pleasure of a young, virile lover."

Caleb realized, not for the first time, that it was pointless to try and speak to her. The woman had such a sense of entitlement and such a puffed-up sense of her own importance and worth that she would never be reasonable. While he knew that in theory, seeing it an actual practice was always astounding. "That is a conversation that should be strictly between you and your husband, madam. Once I deliver you to him, I will be well out of it and glad of the fact... Now, please be so good as to precede me up the stairs. I won't make the mistake of turning my back to you again."

With great fanfare, her skirts swishing like the tail of an angry cat, she did just that. And through all of it, Caleb was wary. It had been too easy, and she was not to be trusted.

Chapter Thirty

Too late to rescue?

THEY REACHED THE house on Greenwood Street with little difficulty. The driver pulled up and they disembarked hurriedly. It all felt very urgent to Marina. She could not quite place the feeling of dread that had assailed her, but it was unrelenting. The fear that something would happen—or worse, that it already had—simply would not be denied.

But as they approached the house, those fears proved at least somewhat well-founded. The door burst open and Lady Crowden came stumbling out, Caleb behind her with a pistol in his hand.

"So much for rescuing him," Mr. Danvers murmured, sounding thoroughly unsurprised by it.

"Should he have waited for uncertain rescue instead of taking matters into his own hands?" Marina demanded.

"Not at all," he said. "It's just quite typical of Caleb to be inconveniently self-sufficient."

It was at that point that Lady Crowden caught sight of them. She let out a blood curdling shriek directed at Mr. Danvers. "And here he is to play the rescuing hero... if you worry about anyone stabbing you in the back, my lord, it should be your closest companion here. Are you aware, Miss Ashton, of Mr. Danvers's role in all of this?"

Marina looked at her flatly. "I am. But we came here to save Caleb because he saw the error of his ways. Pity the same could not be said for you."

"You are so smug and superior," the woman sneered. "You can afford to be with youth and beauty on your side. It will fade. It will fade and you will find yourself desperate for the adulation that was once laid at your feet. Then we will see how firmly you hold to your moral high ground."

Marina had stopped listening to her. Her attention instead was focused on Caleb. Even in the dim gaslight, it was apparent that he was wounded. "You're hurt!"

"Only a bit," he said. "I'll be fine once I wash the dirt off and get something to eat. It's helped tremendously just to see you."

Marina stepped forward, intending to go to him. What happened next was all a blur, a flurry of seething, feminine rage. Lady Crowden lunged at him, her dagger-like nails curled into claws. But she didn't go for his face. Instead, she wrapped her hands about the gun, trying to wrest it from his hands.

"You're going to shoot yourself, you fool!" Caleb shouted at her, clearly struggling to keep her from injuring herself or him.

"Better to die here than be exiled to the countryside to live in boredom and obscurity!" she all but shrieked back at him, when the door burst open behind them and a large man stumbled out, his neck covered with blood. Her attack had been naught but subterfuge—a distraction until her ruffian could intervene. "I get what I want, Lord St. Aiden! I always get what I want... and if I do not, then there are always—always—consequences."

"So what now?" he asked. "You mean to kill me? To kill us all here in the street with witnesses?"

She laughed then. "Oh, heavens no! What would be the enjoyment in that? No. I mean to simply keep you all here... until after the appointed time of your wedding has passed—a time, incidentally, that has already been reported to the local gossip rags. They'll be hovering before the church like vultures. The reality of it will matter far less than the tales they will spin," she stated, her expression smug. "Then your bride-to-be will have faced the very same humiliation she visited upon others. Abandoned at the altar. Any shred of respectability she had left will be naught but memory."

"You will not stop me from marrying her," Caleb said. "It might be delayed, but it will happen."

"I find that I care not at all. I need an ally, and Mr. Stanford Williams is one who is devious enough to be useful," Lady Crowden mused. "Now, move to where your lovely betrothed and your wastrel half-sibling are waiting for you. It's much easier to guard you with a single pistol when you are all in one place."

Reluctantly, Caleb crossed the uneven pavement to where Marina stood at Jacob's side. But as he approached her, he saw the glint of metal in her hand. *She was armed.* And no one was a better shot than Jacob. Glancing at his longtime friend, he saw the other man nod and then quickly grab the pistol from Marina.

The shot that rang out was deafening, but not nearly as ear splitting as the shriek that followed.

Looking over his shoulder, Caleb saw Lady Crowden on her knees, clutching one bloodied hand with the other. The shot, not fatal, had been true.

"Watson," she screamed, "get them!"

But Jacob had the other pistol then, raised and pointed directly at the large man. Watson looked down at her, holding her ruined hand to her chest, and made what could only be considered a wise decision. "No, m'lady. I don't think I will. You don't pay me enough to risk dying for it." With that, the brute sauntered off into the darkness leaving the woman who had been so certain of his devotion to stare after him in shock.

"I'll see her to her husband," Jacob offered. "And explain the whole sordid mess to him. You should see Miss Ashton home. After all, you do both have a wedding to attend."

Caleb watched him walk away, taking the protesting and caterwauling Lady Crowden with him. "I have many questions."

"I have a few of the answers," Marina replied. "Though not

all. I think some will have to come directly from the horse's mouth so to speak. First, let's get you home so that we can tend that rather nasty wound on your head. What in heaven's name did they do to you?"

"Not all that they wished," he admitted. "That is of a certain."

THE CAB PULLED up outside his Belgravia mansion at just past twelve, a fact underscored by the sounding of the clock as it rang out through the city. Alone in the darkened carriage, Marina had felt tears stinging her eyes. Now that it was all said and done, the idea of what might have happened—of all that could have gone wrong—left her feeling shaken and terribly frightened. Because it all mattered so much more to her than she might have imagined. *Because he meant more to her than she might have imagined.*

"I cannot simply send you home as upset as you are," he said.

"I hadn't planned to go home just yet anyway. You've refused to have a physician summoned and someone will need to deal with that cut on your forehead," she pointed out, wiping away her tears. "I simply cannot fathom why our marriage should be of so much interest and such an inconvenience for others that they would take such drastic measures to halt it."

Caleb sighed as he ushered her into the house and up the stairs. "It has nothing to do with them and everything to do with us, regardless of how it came to pass. But there are those in this world whose vanity is so boundless that they cannot conceive that every action of every single person around them is not somehow about them. That's the real issue—with Lady Crowden, with Stanford Williams, and even with Jacob, though he did redeem himself somewhat tonight."

"He cares for you," Marina insisted, as they stepped through the door Caleb had opened. "Very much. But jealousy is a truly terrible feeling. It can, if left unchecked, drive one to do awful things."

"I hope that is something neither of us will ever have cause to feel," he said.

"Why would we ever have cause for such a feeling?" Even as she asked the question, she was looking around, suddenly conscious of where they were. He'd shown her to his bedchamber. The awareness of that new level of intimacy was inescapable.

"We've not discussed it, but it needs to be said. Ours will not be a society marriage, Marina. Regardless of the circumstances under which we became betrothed, I intend for us to live fully as man and wife. I won't be keeping a mistress or consorting with other women. And even if you grow to despise the very sight of me, I'll not turn a blind eye. I'll fight for us every step of the way."

"I will fight for us too," she said.

He smiled at her. "Clearly. You proved that tonight. You were incredibly brave… Reckless, but brave."

"I couldn't let anything happen to you… I—you have become very important to me," she confessed, feeling terribly awkward and uncomfortable as she did so. Those words did not come close to describing what she felt for him, but the words that did describe it utterly terrified her.

"As you have become to me," he said softly. "I know that Stanford hurt you deeply—"

"He didn't actually. My pride? Certainly. My vanity? Beyond question… but I realized that, more than anything else, the ugliness with Stanford only made me feel foolish. I'm not certain my heart was ever truly engaged. I think I only accepted his suit because he had been the first man to court me before it became public knowledge that any man who married me would become ridiculously wealthy… And, as it turns out, he simply learned the truth of it before anyone else did."

Caleb was quiet for a moment, leaning back against the door, his arms crossed, but his expression revealing how clearly surprised he was by her admission. When he spoke, his voice was pitched soft and low. "And now, because you had the temerity to leave him rather than face whatever it was he had in store for you, he means to assassinate your character instead—to make himself appear less the villain and more the victim."

"I can only presume that is his aim. I don't think he has a heart to be hurt by my rejection… and if he does have a heart, I certainly never warmed it. Is it revenge? Possibly. But I tend to lean toward more mercenary motivations. There is, in retrospect, something innately cold and calculating about Stanford. I can see it clearly now though I was blind to it before," she admitted. Marina cast her gaze once more about the room, trying to look at everything but the bed which loomed so large in that chamber. "Casting me in a negative light will engender sympathy for him and thus improve his marital prospects."

"You mean being free of scandal, or as much as he can be, will allow him to ensnare some other young woman with an open heart and a large fortune."

A bitter smile twisted her lips. "Precisely."

"Regardless of recognizing that he was not the person you believed him to be, it still hurts you. *He still hurts you,*" Caleb stated.

Marina shook her head. "Not in the way that you might imagine. It isn't really about him at all… I do not pine for him. Not in any way. But I do miss the person I was before I learned of his perfidy. I miss being open and trusting and… hopeful, I suppose. I fear the entire experience left me very jaded and cynical."

Chapter Thirty-One

Jumping the gun...

A S IT SHOULD have, Caleb thought. Upon finding out that, on the eve of one's wedding, the marriage was simply a cash grab with no true feeling behind it at all, why wouldn't she feel cynical and jaded? Though he was relieved to hear that she had no unresolved feelings for Williams, more relieved than he cared to admit. In fact, one aspect of their arrangement still bothered him greatly. He was, after all, marrying her for money as well. It was his own rather than hers, but it still played a part in his decisions. Oh, it was not entirely the reason, of course. He had some time still and options had he wanted to continue his search for a bride... but she was the only woman he'd had any real interest in since his arrival in London. Indeed, the moment he'd first laid eyes on her, he'd simply known that she was different in some way. And that she was for him.

"I wish it didn't have to be this way," he offered. "I wish that we could take our time, get to know one another, and do this all in the more usual fashion."

Marina shook her head. "No. If things hadn't happened the way they did, we would not be here. I had made a decision, you see, to never marry. To never take that kind of risk ever again... I was only remaining on the marriage mart for appearances.

Choosing to be a spinster is somehow more of an embarrassment to a family than winding up that way due to lack of interest from others."

"Never? You truly had no inclination to wed?"

She made a sound of dismay. "Had we not been forced into this situation, I don't think we would ever have reached this point... and I should hate to think that we would not be on the cusp of saying our vows. When I think about how close you came to being killed—I told you that you had become important to me, Caleb, but it's more than that. I could not have anticipated feeling this way. I never imagined this might be the outcome."

His breath seized in his chest. "Are you saying that you love me?"

"No," she said, after the slightest hesitation. "Do you want me to say that?"

"Yes," he admitted. "Because I rather think that I've fallen in love with you... When I was locked in that cellar with everyone else attempting to meddle in our lives and halt our wedding, I wasn't thinking about the inheritance or even the scandal, truthfully. Beyond how it might impact you, of course. It was you I thought of, Marina. How hurt you might be, how embarrassed or disappointed—and the idea that I might ever be the cause of such feelings for you was completely abhorrent to me. I realized then just how much you had come to mean to me... that you are vital to me, even."

"I'm afraid to put a name to it," she admitted.

"Then we won't. Not yet. We'll tidy up this mess," he said, indicating the dried blood on his forehead, "and see what sort of damage has been done. Then we'll get you home."

Marina moved toward the washstand and poured water into the basin there. "Have you any bandages?"

"I have a stack of perfectly pressed cravats," he offered.

"Your valet would never forgive you... or me," she said.

"I don't care," he said. "If I never have to wear another one of these blasted things, I'll be quite happy. I much prefer the countryside where I can eschew such trappings… or the coalfields where I can discard the facade of gentleman altogether."

She smiled then, the corners of her lips turning up in such an enticing manner that he realized how truly risky their current situation was.

"I should send you home," he said. "I can rouse my valet to tend these wounds… this is a situation that—well, innocent as it may be, would certainly never appear that way to others."

She glanced over her shoulder at him, an unknowingly and unintentionally seductive pose. "Do you mean to shout it from the rooftops, then? To tell the world that I was alone with you in your bedchamber prior to our marriage? We've already, at least in the eyes of the *ton*, been caught in a terribly compromising position. I could hardly be worse off for it."

He chuckled softly. "No. Of course not, but if it were discovered, seduction would be assumed."

"Would that be so terrible? We are to be married later today, after all. Not every married couple says their vows first."

Caleb felt the blood rush from his head directly to other parts of his anatomy. Parts that had little to do with maintaining honor or doing the right thing. "Marina, that's a very bold statement."

"It is… but I meant it," she said. "Why should we wait? We are both determined on our course of action. Unless, of course, you are reconsidering. Given the degree of trouble that has been caused for you simply by virtue of deciding to marry me, of all people, one could hardly blame you."

"I'd do it all ten times over," he replied. And the degree of truth in that statement was staggering.

"Then let's tend your wound and see what happens after," she suggested softly. "I'm not so naive, Caleb, that I walked into your house with no notion of what might occur."

Chapter Thirty-Two

Moving forward...

MARINA WATCHED FROM beneath lowered lashes. Caleb had removed his soiled coat and shirt and was even now sluicing water over his skin as he stood at the wash basin in his chamber. With the blood and dirt washed away, the bruise on his forehead was still nasty but not nearly so severe as she might have imagined. In truth, she was finding it very difficult to concentrate on his injury at all. She was far too distracted by the breadth of his shoulders, by the smooth, bronze skin stretched taut over firm muscles. The crisp, dark hair curling over his chest intrigued her beyond reason and she had to wonder at its texture, what it would feel like beneath her fingers.

Recalling what it had felt like to be held against the firm wall of his chest, she felt her heart racing and her blood heating in her veins. Then she glanced up and in the mirror above his washstand, their gazes locked. Embarrassed, Marina looked away quickly.

"I want to kiss you again," he said. "And I want to touch you... but only if that is what you want. I can be as patient as you require."

Perhaps that was the problem, she thought. His patience wasn't what she needed, but rather his impatience. She needed some proof that he truly wanted her. "In all the time Stanford and I were betrothed, he never kissed me. I told you that. He never touched me with any sort of desire. I don't think, Caleb, that your patience will not offer me the sort of reassurance you are imagining... I'm less frightened of physical intimacy than I am of being married to a man who doesn't truly desire me."

"Is that what you think? That my reluctance represents a lack of desire?"

Marina nodded. "Perhaps think is too strong a word. Worry might be a better term. It's always in the back of my mind."

"Then let me thoroughly disabuse you of that notion."

There was no warning. He closed the distance between them so quickly his intent had barely registered before Marina found herself swept up in his embrace, his arms locked tightly about her and his lips moving seductively against her own. It was no different than any other kiss they had shared. The same languid heat stole through her, her mind went numb to everything but the sensations he stirred within her. And yet, despite those similarities there was one great difference. In this instance, the kiss was only the beginning.

Her hands lifted of their own volition, sliding over the smooth skin of his shoulders, and along the ridged muscles that flanked his spine. Everything about his form was so enticingly different from her own. Hard where she was soft, lean and firm where her own flesh was yielding. It stoked far more than just her curiosity.

Beneath his skilled and questing hands, her jacket dropped to the floor, followed by the boy's shirt she wore. The kiss broke long enough for him to tug the garment over her head and toss it aside, but that was the only quarter he offered her. His lips claimed hers again even as he walked her backward toward his waiting bed. When the backs of her knees bumped the edge of it, she sank down automatically. Then he was lifting her feet, tugging her boots off and discarding them carelessly to the floor.

She should have felt foolish, sitting there in her corset and a pair of borrowed trousers. But his gaze was locked on her, the heat of it unmistakable. She felt the weight of it like an actual caress. Then he stepped closer to her, his hands reaching for the buttons at her waist. Soon, her trousers had joined the rest of her clothing in a heap on the floor.

When he joined her on the bed, Marina couldn't stop the shudder that raced through her. It wasn't fear but anticipation.

"If you are uncertain—"

"I'm not," she said instantly. "I don't think I've ever been more certain of anything."

CALEB STARED DOWN at her. Not for the first time, he was awed by her beauty. But it was so much more than simply the symmetry of her features or that they met some sort of ideal that had been crafted by society as to what a beauty was. It was her spirit. It was the vitality in her and the courage. It was all the things about her that so many people deemed inconvenient or bothersome. Her face and form had drawn his interest, but the rest of her had captured it, making it impossible for him to look away. And yet she doubted her desirability, she doubted her worth at every turn. Stanford Williams hadn't created those doubts, but he'd cemented them firmly for her.

Reaching for her, Caleb tugged the pins from her hair, freeing the mass of dark tresses from its tight coronet. It spilled about her shoulders and across the pillow in a riot of curls that beckoned his touch. *But he didn't have to resist temptation.*

Delving his fingers into the silken strands, he dipped his head and kissed her again. But this was not like the relatively innocent kisses they'd shared previously. It was not about a slow seduction. It was a claiming—demanding, possessive, blatantly carnal. With that kiss, he demonstrated precisely how much he wanted her, and she simply gave herself up to it. Warm and pliant in his arms, she was also sweetly responsive and when he tugged the laces of her corset free, she offered no protest, but lifted herself slightly off the mattress to help him remove it.

His gaze raked over her, taking in every detail—every lush curve, every dimple and freckle on her satiny skin. "I'm not the sort of a man who can give you poems or lavish compliments… but I can tell you with complete certainty that I have never seen a woman more beautiful than you are, Marina. I have never known this kind of desire… this craving that I have for you."

"Then show me," she urged him.

Helpless to do anything else, Caleb kissed her again. But he was not content to simply taste her lips. Instead, he explored every inch of her as it was bared to him. With his hands, his lips, his tongue—he lavished attention on her, paying note to where she was most sensitive. And when he reached the tapes of her pantalettes, it was she who loosened them and tossed the garment aside, leaving her fully nude in his bed.

One day, he would be able to simply savor, to sit back and appreciate the sheer perfection of her at length. But this was not that day. Sliding one hand between her parted thighs, he touched her intimately, finding her flesh already slick with need. Her gasp of shock transformed into one of pleasure as he stroked the sensitive bud nestled between those delicate folds.

"Caleb!" she whispered brokenly as her body strained beneath his touch.

Claiming her mouth once more, he kissed her deeply, his tongue sweeping languidly against hers in a blatantly carnal dance that mimicked all the things he wanted to do with her. And when she came to a shuddering release, her body taut and quivering beneath him, he gloried in that moment. But not for long. Because his own need was too great.

Easing himself between her parted thighs, he opened his trousers, freeing his rigid flesh with a rush of relief. Then her hands were sliding around his waist, over his hips. Out of desperation, he caught them. "Not yet. If you touch me… I haven't the strength to resist right now, Marina. I'd prefer this not end before it can actually begin."

"I don't understand."

He smiled at her. "You will."

Hooking one hand behind her knee, he hitched her legs a bit higher on his hips. "I wish I could promise you that this would be perfect, but I can't."

"It's already been perfect," she whispered. "More than I could have dreamed."

"I hope you still feel that way."

Parting the tender folds, he began easing himself inside her. It was a kind of bliss he'd never known. The pleasure of it was unbearably intense and yet it offered no relief. Instead, it only spiked his need to greater heights.

Every muscle clenched tight as he fought for restraint, for some degree of control over his own desires, and it was all for naught. Marina's hands, pressed flat against his back, slid down to his hips urging him on. Unable to resist that silent invitation, he surged forward, her flesh yielding to his. And then they were both lost, clinging to one another as they climbed together toward release. When they tumbled over the edge, they held onto one another still.

Chapter Thirty-Three

No honor amongst thieves...

THE HANSOM CAB driver, the same one who'd been ferrying him about all night, was delivering them to the Crowdens' residence. With her hands bound with his cravat, Lady Crowden sat in stony silence.

"He used you… just as he used me," Jacob told her. "Perhaps you can't repay Caleb for his intolerably priggish nature—he didn't used to be that way, I swear—but you can repay Stanford Williams for exploiting both our weaknesses."

She looked away from him, but he could tell from the set of her jaw that she'd heard every word. But she was not entirely without interest. So he continued. "All you have to do is tell me the rest of his plan. I'll see to it that he's thwarted at every turn."

Her head whipped around, her eyes blazing as she glared at him. "Why?"

"Because I very nearly allowed him to turn me into precisely what he is… and now that I've returned to my senses, I mean to stop him from putting others through the same kind of torment. You could help me."

"And what's in it for me?"

"Your husband already knows about Stanford, doesn't he?"

She nodded.

Jacob smiled. "He need not know about Caleb. We will simp-ly tell him that Stanford has been blackmailing you, attempting to force you to interfere in Caleb's marriage to Miss Ashton... And in return, you will never bother either of them again. Not a single whisper of gossip or unkind word will be uttered about them by you. Or I will tell him everything. About Stanford. About Caleb. About how their compromising position was a work of fiction crafted by you. I hear the countryside is quite desolate this time of year... and every time of year for that matter. Cornwall, isn't it? Your husband's country estate is at the very edge of Britain."

Silence settled inside the cab, thick and heavy. Then in a rush, she said, "He means to marry Elizabeth Whitmore and will likely see her dead just as he did his first wife—the daughter of a wealthy merchant in the north."

Jacob's eyebrows lifted. "He killed her?"

"Perhaps. Or perhaps he simply made no effort to save her when she grew ill. It's much the same," she mused. "Miss Ashton would have faced a similar fate had she not had the good sense to heed the warning sent to her."

"What warning?"

Lady Crowden smiled coyly, the expression barely visible in the dim light streaking in through the windows of the cab. "A warning from 'a concerned acquaintance.'"

"You?"

"Indeed. She's never wronged me. Even now, she has been largely innocent in all of this—her only crime is being young and lovely... as I once was. But she possesses far greater wisdom than I ever had as she did not entangle herself with a controlling and cruel man."

"Your husband has tolerated your infidelity. That is hardly the mark of a cruel man," he observed.

"Cruelty comes in many forms, Mr. Danvers. Some are simp-ly more difficult to discern. They are no less damaging for it."

"And Miss Whitmore? What of her cruelty?"

Lady Crowden smirked. "Miss Whitmore plays a part but

does so out of fear. If you truly wish to see Stanford Williams pay for his misdeeds, that is where you should intervene… He's counting on her position in society, along with Miss Ashton's disgrace which likely will not occur now, to restore his. I have it on good authority that they are both to be in attendance at the Waldinghams' tonight."

Jacob said nothing. But he knew precisely where he was going as soon as Lady Crowden had been given over to the care of her husband.

"THE LADY'S LONDON Gazette had a most interesting tidbit about the pair of them this morning. Every indication is that she will likely leave him at the altar just as she did Mr. Williams! After all, she'd been betrothed to Williams for nearly a year and still she bolted!"

"It's true! What chance does he have after only a week? That girl will never make it to the altar… Just like her mother."

"I heard that if he does not marry, he will lose a significant inheritance from his late uncle! Surely with so much at stake he would have chosen a more likely option?"

Miss Elizabeth Whitmore stood on the edge of the ballroom, her dance card abysmally bare. It was largely her own fault, and she knew that. But being on the edge of the ballroom had allowed her to hear the gossip. The absence of the newly betrothed Earl of St. Aiden and his bride to be, Miss Marina Ashton was all anyone could talk about. Indeed, it seemed that people were laying wagers on whether or not she'd already given him the boot and he'd fled town in humiliation. Of course, Elizabeth knew that was in part because she herself had helped to spread the rumor that very thing had occurred.

And yet, she found no joy in it. It was one thing when her animosity for Miss Ashton had been prompted by her wounded vanity at having been passed over so completely by Stanford Williams their first Season out. He'd set his sights on Marina, and she might well have been invisible. Then, upon his return to town, he'd sought her out, apologizing profusely for having been so blind.

Initially, she'd been charmed by that, but the more she heard him say such things the more false they sounded to her ears. In truth, many things he said were ringing false for her. It had not escaped her notice that when he spoke of their future marriage, he would not look her directly in the eyes. That even when he kissed her—kisses that were as alarmingly chaste as they were few and far between—there was a decided lack of passion in his embrace. While she might have believed that he was merely being sensitive to her maidenly state, that explanation rang hollow even to her own ears.

His obsession with humiliating Marina Ashton publicly was the only thing that ever seemed to stir any passion in him. Oh, he insisted it was only to restore his own reputation, but as things continued on, she had to wonder about that. After all, Marina had done enough damage to her reputation on her own by continually refusing every reasonable suitor who crossed her path. He kept insisting that he needed to restore his reputation, but he didn't. Not if he intended to marry her. She was nearing the end of her third Season. Her father would happily accept any offer at this point, so long as she would go through with it.

As she peered around the ballroom, looking for any sign of him, she caught a glimpse of a familiar face. Mr. Jacob Danvers was present and he was making a beeline for her.

"Miss Whitmore, we need to have a word in private… about mutual acquaintances," he said when he reached her.

"Mr. Danvers, that would be highly inappropriate," she replied coolly.

"More or less inappropriate than your nightly meetings in the garden with Mr. Williams?" he asked with a single arched brow.

Elizabeth glanced about her, terrified someone might have heard. But everyone around them was engrossed in conversation and paying them not the least bit of mind. The benefit to being on the very cusp of spinsterhood, she thought somewhat bitterly. The closer she was to being firmly on the shelf the more invisible she became.

"Fine. Where?"

He looked pointedly toward the terrace doors. "You're quite fond of gardens, as it seems. That should suffice."

"Five minutes," she said. "I will meet you there."

After he left, Elizabeth began a circuitous route to the intended location. When she finally stepped outside, her cheeks were heated from her nervousness and the crisp night air was an immediate relief.

"I was beginning to think you wouldn't come."

Elizabeth glanced over at the sound of his voice, finding him concealed within the shadows. "What is it you wished to speak to me about?"

"In truth, it isn't what I wished to say to you. It's what I wished for you to hear Stanford Williams say to me... If you would be so good as to conceal yourself behind those potted trees yon, he should be here momentarily," Mr. Danvers stated.

Perhaps it was those ugly suspicions that she'd been having, but she found herself nodding and then seeking shelter behind the potted plants he'd indicated. It was only a matter of seconds before she heard Stanford's voice.

"What is it that you wanted, Danvers? I don't appreciate being summoned like some sort of errant servant!"

There was a hint of amusement in Danvers's voice as he replied, "I came to inform you that I am no longer willing to be a party to your schemes."

Stanford laughed. "As if it matters now! Lady Crowden has St. Aiden locked up nice and tight."

"Actually, she does not. I didn't simply have a change of heart, Williams. I had a change of allegiance... or rather, I remembered where my allegiance was actually due. I've surrendered her ladyship to the less-than-tender mercies of her husband while Caleb—and Miss Ashton—are all set to marry.

They are likely on the road to Scotland even now. Your schemes are at an end, as is our agreement."

Stanford's temper was obvious when he fired back. "You owe me!"

"I did," Mr. Danvers said. "But I made some inquiries… you're a known cheat, Williams. Always with an ace up your sleeve or a marked deck in your pocket. And you didn't purchase my markers—you won them. I can only presume that you cheated in order to get them and force my cooperation in your schemes. Well, no more… And the more I learn about you, the more I'm convinced that Miss Ashton must have had a very good reason to leave you at the altar. Infidelity? Fortune hunting? Or were you plotting to have her eliminated as soon as you'd secured her settlement? Isn't that what you did with that pitiable merchant's daughter?"

Elizabeth bit back a gasp. Was all that true?

"Of course, I had planned to eliminate her! Why would I want a wife who's the bastard offspring of a woman little better than a common doxy? Had it not been for her supremely generous fortune, I'd never have looked twice at her."

"And Miss Whitmore? What are your plans for her?" Danvers asked.

"She's convenient for the moment. Hardly wealthy enough to tempt me, but her animosity toward Miss Ashton is an asset. I'll string her along until I no longer need her then I'll end it. If she makes things difficult—well, it would hardly be shocking for a young woman on the cusp of spinsterhood to take her own life, would it?"

"No, I don't suppose it would be surprising," Mr. Danvers agreed. "But if something happens to her, you'll have me to contend with."

Stanford scoffed. "You're hardly the heroic type, Danvers. You're a wastrel through and through."

"I have been. I've made some truly terrible choices, and I have many things to atone for. This is how I begin. From this moment forward, you will leave Caleb and Miss Ashton alone… and Miss Whitmore, as well. I daresay you've done more than your share to drive the animosity between the two of them anyway as it has served your purpose."

"I think you're mistaken about which of us has the power here, Danvers. If I tell anyone what you've done—"

"The only people who matter already know. You think I care what these sycophants and liars think of me? I don't. You're the worst of the lot and for a moment, I forgot that I was better than this. I let jealousy and spite blind me to what actually mattered. Well, I'm done with that now and done with you."

Stanford stepped forward, leaning in and poking his finger into Mr. Danvers's chest. From her hiding place, Elizabeth stifled a gasp. Whatever was about to occur, she knew it would not be good.

As she'd predicted, it happened in a matter of seconds. Mr. Danvers drew back, his fist flying forward and connecting with Stanford's jaw, sending him sprawling. Unfortunately, he fell against a potted plant at the edge of the terrace and the vessel went careening over the edge and crashing onto the flagstones below. There was a rush of people emerging from the various rooms that faced that side of the house, drawn by the noise.

"Miss Whitmore!"

Elizabeth glanced over her shoulder to see their host and hostess staring at her aghast from the French doors that flanked her hiding place. There was no question of how it looked. She was alone on a terrace, entirely unchaperoned, with two disreputable gentlemen.

"Miss Whitmore and I had sought a moment's privacy," Mr. Danvers said. "I had a very particular question to ask her. Alas, we were interrupted by Mr. Williams before she could give me an answer… He has been attempting to woo her, as well, much to my dismay. And to hers."

"Indeed," Elizabeth replied, the lies falling easily from her lips. "He's been most insistent in his pursuit, despite my protests.

But do proceed with your question, Mr. Danvers, as I am most eager to hear it."

"It is my fondest wish, Miss Whitmore, to be granted the blessing of your hand in marriage. Will you do me the honor?"

Despite having anticipated the outcome, that he would propose in the face of such scandal, she was still shocked by the answer that simply fell from her lips. "Certainly, Mr. Danvers. I am most happy to graciously accept your proposal."

Chapter Thirty-Four

Interruptions...

THE SUN WAS barely up, but Marina was standing at her window, staring outside at the blue-gray light of an early morning—all of it diffused through a haze of coal smoke. It hadn't been dawn yet when Caleb had brought her home, helping her to slip inside with no one the wiser.

Now, as she looked out onto the fog shrouded city, she had to wonder if perhaps she would miss it. When they left London to live in the country, would she be filled with longing for dreary windowscapes such as the one before her? Or would the countryside offer green vistas and open fields that would soothe her spirit and wipe away the tension of the last several years?

She hadn't been entirely honest with her aunt about the things she'd heard Stanford saying about her. It hadn't merely been that he only wanted the money. No. It had been infinitely worse—disparaging her mother's memory and dredging up the ugly specter of her father's dishonor. The daughter of a fallen woman and a traitor, he'd jeered, uttering those words with such cold disdain. *Would Caleb hold her in such contempt if he knew the whole truth?*

Her musings were cut short as the maid entered the room to build up the fire.

"Oh, miss! I didn't expect you to be up so early," the girl said. "I'll go fetch your chocolate for breakfast."

"There's no need. I haven't much of an appetite."

"Some tea then and perhaps a scone! It wouldn't look the thing at all if you were to faint again, miss!"

The girl did make an excellent point. "Of course. You're quite right. Tea and scones would be delightful."

"Straight away, miss. Then I'll come back and help you with your hair."

Alone once more after the maid bustled out, Marina moved to her dressing table and began the arduous task of unplaiting the thick, curly locks that were both her greatest vanity and the bane of her existence. It was a mindless and tedious task, but it allowed her mind to simply wander, to consider all the implications of the day and what it might mean in the future.

The maid returned. They spoke very little as she took over the task of brushing Marina's hair. And when Stephens entered a short time later, holding the hastily but perfectly altered gown she would wear for her wedding, the enormity of the moment truly penetrated the fog that had settled over her. When her aunt's maid shooed hers away and assumed the task of dressing her hair, Marina braced herself for the torment. And it was. Her hair was tugged and pulled, coiled, pinned, curled, and beaten into submission. When it was done, she breathed a sigh of relief.

As she was being buttoned and laced into the beautiful silk, Willa entered. But there was a pinched and worried look on her face that did not at all match the hopeful expectation that she had displayed the night before.

Marina's stomach dipped nervously. "What is it?"

"Likely nothing," Willa said. To the servants she added, "Give us a moment, please."

When they were gone, Marina rose. "Caleb has cried off."

Willa's jaw dropped. "Good heavens, no! Why would you even think such a thing?"

Marina didn't answer. She was too consumed with relief. She

just shook her head and indicated that her aunt should continue.

"There was a bit of a scandal last night at the Waldinghams'. And while, in theory, another scandal should have taken attention away from you this—well, it's only drawn more."

"What is it?" Marina asked.

"Mr. Danvers and Miss Whitmore were caught alone on the terrace overlooking the garden... well, not precisely alone. Stanford was with them, lying flat on his back having apparently invoked Mr. Danvers's temper. Now, Mr. Danvers and Miss Whitmore are betrothed."

Marina blinked owlishly for a moment. But as the shock of it faded, she sighed with relief. "Oh, I thought you were going to tell me something horrid."

"It is a bit, don't you think? If they marry, you will never be able to avoid her!"

"I can't avoid her now," Marina said. "But as you said, perhaps with a husband and family of her own, Elizabeth will have less time to nurture her animosity toward me."

Willa stared at her for a moment, then nodded. "Why was Stanford with them?"

"I presume that Stanford has been courting Elizabeth in secret, though likely not with any real intent to wed her. The wager... well, it was his idea. He wanted to see me humiliated."

"And all these attacks?" Willa asked. "If not Stanford or Miss Whitmore, then who was behind them?"

It was the one remaining mystery. "I cannot say. It was not Lady Crowden. And do not ask how I know. Simply trust that I do. That leaves only Mr. Nutter. But save for the evening at the theater, I have not seen even a hint of him."

"It could be something else."

"You think this is about my father," Marina said.

"It could be. Devil thinks it possible."

"What did he do? Really. I do not need to be protected from the truth anymore. Ignorance is poor armor."

Willa took her hands. "His family business was the manufacturing of munitions. Munitions that were stolen by smugglers and then resold to the French. It was an elaborate scheme that took long to unravel as he was not alone in it. There were many players."

"I need to inform Caleb. I don't want him to find this out and think I have lied to him," she said.

"Devil has done so already," Willa stated. "And he does not care. Because you are not the man who sired you and you are not responsible for his sins. If there is one lesson to be taken away from all that I learned from Effie and the Darrow School, we are never responsible for the sins of our parents, whatever the world might try to make you believe."

He knew. He knew every terrible truth and still he wanted her. Perhaps he did truly love her, Marina thought. Even when he'd said those words, her doubts hadn't been assuaged. But she was inching ever closer to being able to believe them.

"Let's get to the church," she said. "I don't wish to be late."

Willa nodded. "Indeed. We shall depart immediately. The carriage is already waiting."

⇥⇤

CALEB WAS AT the church far earlier than he should have been. Certainly it was far earlier than was seemly. But he was eager to see her again, eager to recite their vows and make her his countess.

The church doors opened, and he looked up to see Jacob entering. "I did not think to see you here."

"Am I welcome?" Jacob asked.

Caleb nodded. "You are always welcome. And your be-trothed?"

"She is waiting in a coffee house across the street. Under the circumstances, she felt it best that she not attend… But we are to travel on the next train to Ashford and be married immediately in her parish church."

"With her family's approval?"

Jacob nodded. "Indeed. I was greeted with an eagerness that was truly shocking… I think, despite the unpleasantness she may have visited on others, that Miss Whitmore has been treated very poorly by her family."

Caleb nodded. "She is not the only one, I think. When the dust has settled, Jacob, we will revisit the matter of your involvement with the mines. I think perhaps our grandfather's fears were not as well founded as I once believed."

"Oh, no. They are. I've no head for business… and London has been a terrible influence on me. Miss Whitmore and I mean to remain at the small estate in Kent that is part of her marriage portion. I might not have a head for business but the notion of being a country gentleman has become quite tempting to me."

Their conversation was halted as the doors opened once more. Lady Deveril entered along with the Viscount and Viscountess Seaburn. In light of what had transpired the last time Marina had walked down the aisle, the guest list was limited to only family and a few select guests. It wasn't out of fear she would bolt or even faint. But she disliked being a spectacle and there had been enough of that already.

"I'll take my seat," Jacob said. "I wish you the best, Caleb."

As Caleb watched Jacob make his way toward the pews, he wished that for him as well.

Chapter Thirty-Five

An unlikely ally...

"ARE YOU READY?"

Marina looked at her uncle. "Much more so this time than last," she said with a rueful smile.

He let out a bark of laughter. "I should hope so." With that he opened the carriage door and climbed out, reaching in to offer her his hand.

Marina was reaching to take his hand, but her eye was drawn by motion. A screw lodged in her throat as she saw the heavy butt of a pistol come crashing down on her uncle's temple. As Devil collapsed to the ground, Mr. Reginald Nutter forced his way into the carriage and shoved her backward onto the seat. He knocked sharply on the roof of the carriage. "Drive on or I'll shoot her now!"

Immediately the carriage began rolling forward. The driver, Helmsley, had been with them since she was a small girl. He would have moved heaven and earth to keep her safe. "What are you doing?" she demanded.

"Getting even," he snapped. "What a fool you must have thought me! Following you about like a lost puppy while you laughed the whole while."

"No one laughed at you, Mr. Nutter," she said. And they had

not. They may have made every effort to avoid him, but they had not ridiculed him. "But what you are doing right now is complete madness!"

"I no longer care! I've toadied to you for three years. I watched you align yourself with that rat, Stanford Williams, and now I've watched you abase yourself with that ruffian who calls himself an earl. The man is little better than a laborer from the fields. That you'd prefer him to a true gentleman speaks volumes about your own character!"

Marina gaped at him. "You're kidnapping me, and you dare to question whether someone else is a gentleman?"

"This is what you've driven me to! With your indifference and derision," he insisted.

"And what is your plan, Mr. Nutter? To force me to marry you instead?"

He shook his head. "No. I no longer have any desire to marry you… but I'll be damned before I allow you to marry him. I vowed that I would see you dead before I saw you wed another."

He said it so dispassionately that it made her blood run cold. Attempting to appeal to any reason that he still possessed, Marina said, "You'd hang. Surely it isn't worth it."

"I won't live long enough for that," he said. "I fully intend to take my own life, as well. Better that than live with the humiliation you've heaped upon me."

"Mr. Nutter," she said, trying to keep her voice calm and steady despite the fact that she was trembling with fear, "We never thought poorly of you, and we certainly never derided you. I understood that you held a certain regard for me which I did not return. Perhaps I should have been more direct in informing you earlier, but it was only because I did not wish to insult you that I refrained from saying so."

"Do you think that makes it better? That you allowed me to fawn over you while you regarded me as an object of pity?" he snapped.

The coach stopped abruptly. Wild eyed, Mr. Nutter began

shouting. "Why have you stopped? I'll shoot her! I swear to you I will!"

"The road is blocked!" Helmsley called out. "There's a wagon with a broken wheel blocking the road. I can't go round!"

"I'll not wait here to be overtaken by whomever is foolish enough to attempt to rescue you," he said, grabbing her arm. He hauled her up and kicked open the carriage door, wood splintering.

Marina knew that if she got out of that carriage there would be no hope for her. As he tugged her forward, she began resisting, pulling back with all her might. He turned back to her and tugged viciously on her arm, her glove slipping from her hand. Thinking of all the games of tug of war she'd played with her cousins, Marina simply went dead weight, sinking to the floor, allowing the glove to pull completely free from her hand and for him to tumble backward out of the carriage and to the paving stones below.

Helmsley must have been watching. No sooner had Mr. Nutter hit the ground than did the carriage immediately shoot forward, the wheel rolling over Mr. Nutter's legs with a terrible thump that prompted Marina to cover her ears. Even then, she could still hear his cries of pain.

ELIZABETH SIPPED HER tea as she stared out the window of the small coffee house, her gaze locked on the carriage bearing the Ashton family crest. It goaded her now to think her animosity for Marina Ashton had been driven primarily by her feeling that she had somehow stolen Stanford Williams from her. In truth, they had both been spared a terrible fate at his hands. Of course, that hadn't been their only source of animosity. Elizabeth knew her behavior had often been seen as quite petty and even cruel. But she was only too well aware that often the sweetest of smiles hid the most vicious natures. All those insipid misses that she'd insulted and given the cut to had been the very ones who talked behind their backs and spread vicious gossip about others.

Movement caught Elizabeth's eye, and she glanced to the rear of that carriage. A familiar figure emerged from the shadowy alley beside the church.

"Mr. Nutter," she whispered. What on earth was he doing?

He approached the carriage but on the opposite side so that she couldn't see what was happening. Only a moment later, the carriage shot forward, into the street, revealing Lord Deveril unconscious on the pavement. Without hesitating, Elizabeth rushed from the coffee house and to the fallen man. A streak of blood marred his temple, but his eyes were beginning to open.

"Lord Deveril? How badly are you injured?"

"Get St. Aiden… go after her," he urged, then once more slipped into unconsciousness.

The implications of it all suddenly clicked into place, clearing the fog of confusion. Mr. Nutter had abducted Marina Ashton.

Getting to her feet, Elizabeth rushed to the doors of the church and burst inside. The small group of people assembled had turned expectantly toward the door, no doubt anticipating the entrance of the bride on her uncle's arm. "Lord Deveril is injured," she called out loudly, "and Mr. Nutter has driven off in the carriage with Miss Ashton."

Immediately, the Earl of St. Aiden, Mr. Danvers, and Viscount Seaburn were off, all of them charging past her as they made their way out of the church. Seaburn hoisted Lord Deveril up and aided him into the church. Once he was settled, the viscount took off once more in pursuit of the others.

"How did you happen to be here when this occurred, Miss Whitmore?" Lady Deveril demanded.

Elizabeth bit back a heated retort. The woman had no reason to trust her, after all. "I didn't wish to intrude today but Mr. Danvers wished to be here for the earl. I was waiting in a coffee house across the way when I saw Mr. Nutter approaching the carriage. I understand, Lady Deveril, that you have cause to doubt my motives, but in this instance, I am only trying to help. No one behaving as Mr. Nutter did today can be counted on to be reasonable."

Lady Deveril was seated next to her husband, her face etched with tenderness and concern for him. But when she turned to face Elizabeth once more, her expression shifted into something that could only be classified as dangerous. "If you are not being entirely truthful, Miss Whitmore, there will be the devil to pay. Is that clear?"

"Yes, ma'am," she replied with more meekness than she had displayed in a very long time.

Chapter Thirty-Six

Reaping what is sown...

CALEB COULD SEE the carriage up ahead. When it halted, his heart seized in his chest. Then Reginald Nutter appeared in the doorway, tumbling backward onto the paving stones. Even from a distance, his cries of agony were audible as the carriage rolled over his legs. But Nutter was not his concern. He only wanted to get to Marina.

With the crowd of people gathering around that side of the carriage and the injured—possibly gravely—man, Caleb went round to the other. Opening the door more forcefully than necessary, he saw Marina sitting on the floor of the vehicle, her arms wrapped about herself. When their eyes met, she simply flung herself into his arms.

Lifting her out of the carriage, he touched her face tenderly. "Are you hurt?"

"No. I'm unharmed. Terrified, but unharmed," she admitted breathlessly. "How is Uncle Devil?"

"Seaburn helped get him into the church... I took off in such a rush to get to you that I'm not entirely sure," he confessed. He finally felt as though he could draw a breath, as if the band squeezing his lungs had finally released.

"How did you know?"

Caleb shook his head, still confounded by it all. "You will not believe it when I tell you, but it was Miss Whitmore. She was waiting across the street for Jacob and saw the whole of it."

"You are quite right. I do not believe it."

"If we hurry, and if you wish to, we can still make it back to the church to see this done today—if you wish to wait, I understand," he told her. "But if we do wait, I cannot say how forgiving the gossips will be."

"No. I don't wish to wait. Let's go. Quickly."

As they walked around the carriage to the sidewalk, Caleb positioned himself to spare Marina the sight of Mr. Nutter. He dared a glance in Jacob's direction and the other man simply shook his head. Even if by some strange chance Nutter survived, he'd no longer be a threat to anyone.

"Will he live?" Marina asked softly.

"I don't think so," Caleb replied. "And I can't be sorry for it. Not really. Not when he very nearly killed you on multiple occasions… And I cannot help but think, if he were to live and be remotely capable, he'd likely try again."

She shuddered slightly. "I think you're right. I should have told him that I had no interest. In trying to spare his feelings, I gave him hope."

"No. No, you didn't. No rational man thinks a woman avoiding him for three years wants his pursuit… and further, if Lady Crowden was to be believed, you were not the first young woman whom he obsessed over to this degree. And that other young woman, if she was in fact the only one, suffered a terrible fate likely at his hands. We are both, in this moment, incredibly fortunate to be having this conversation. It could have gone very differently."

"It very nearly did," she said with a shudder.

They walked back to the church slowly. He kept her close to his side, not because he feared something would happen but because they both needed the reassurance of one another's nearness. Once they reached the entrance to St. George's and stepped inside, they were peppered with questions.

"What on earth is going on?" the Viscountess Seaburn demanded.

"Mr. Nutter apparently did not accept the fact that I had chosen to marry Caleb," Marina answered. "He attempted to abduct me… and injured Uncle Devil in the process. How is he?"

"He is fine," Lord Deveril pronounced as he sat up in one of the pews. "Now, let's get the pair of you married before someone else attempts to interfere."

"FOR AS MUCH as Caleb Halliwell and Marina Ashton have consented together in holy wedlock, and have witnessed the same before God and this company, and thereto have given and pledged their troth, each to the other, and have declared the same by giving and receiving a ring, and by joining hands; I pronounce that they are Man and Wife, In the Name of the Father, and of the Son, and of the Holy Ghost. Amen."

As the minister spoke the last word, Marina lifted her head and glanced over at Caleb. It was done. They were well and truly married. Despite everything and everyone that had attempted to come between them, they had managed to get it done.

"Thank heavens," she murmured.

The minister cleared his throat. How such a sound could ring with disapproval she didn't know, but that didn't alter the fact that he'd made his displeasure with her exclamation very clear.

"Indeed," Caleb seconded, ignoring the minister's disapproval altogether. "Thank heavens. Now, Countess St. Aiden, let us sign the register and make it entirely official."

They did so, with Lillian and Valentine acting as witnesses. Once it was done, it felt like such a burden had been lifted from her shoulders. It was finally, really done. She was married. No one had fainted. While she had been briefly absconded with, in the end it had not mattered. She was now Caleb's wife. And that was truthfully how she thought of it. Not as just being a wife, or a countess. She was *his* wife. And he was *her* husband.

As they all adjourned to the house on Park Lane for the wedding breakfast, the weight of it all began to dissipate and a kind of giddiness came in its wake. Happiness.

"What are you smiling about?" he asked her as the carriage halted before the house.

"We've actually done it. We are well and truly married. Despite the terrible best efforts of so many people, we've made it to the altar and signed our names on that book for all of posterity to see. It feels remarkable."

"Right. It feels right," he said. "And inevitable. I think from the moment I first laid eyes on you, this was the outcome that was simply destined to be. You and I, together forever... Starting a life far from London society and all its scheming inhabitants. Will you hate being apart from your family?"

Marina considered it for a moment. "I don't think I shall be fully apart from them. No doubt they will descend upon us quite regularly no matter where we go. But... I'm far more interested in building a family with you than in clinging to what I already have. Not that I don't love them and not that I am not eternally grateful for all they have given me both emotionally and financially—but this is how it's supposed to be, isn't it? Leaving the safety of what one has always known in order to embark on something new, something that is wholly one's own?"

"I suppose it is," he concurred. "I like the notion of starting a family of our own... of building something together that is the best parts of us both. I know I'm supposed to want sons to carry on the title. But I confess to hoping for daughters who will look like you, who will have your spirit and your bright-blue eyes, and who will surely wind me around their little fingers without any real effort at all."

Marina glanced through the carriage window. "I suppose we have to go in now, don't we?"

He reached for her, taking her hand and tugging her across the expanse of the vehicle until she was nestled in the circle of his arms. Not that she'd in any way resisted. Not when that was precisely where she longed to be. "What are you doing?"

"They can wait a moment or two," he said.

And then they didn't speak at all. He kissed her, his lips moving over hers in such a way that Marina simply didn't care who was waiting for them. She didn't care about anything at all except how to make that kiss last forever.

Epilogue

Happy endings...

One Year Later

MARINA FELT TEARS welling up in her eyes. Try as she might to dash them away, they fell regardless. Then a square of white linen was being tucked into her hand. Turning to glance up at her husband—a word she truly never tired of saying—she smiled at him through her very happy tears.

They'd returned to London for a joyous occasion. Her dear friend, Charlotte Hamilton, was no longer a Hamilton. Her wedding had been a beautiful ceremony. As was the current fashion, courtesy of their queen, she'd been radiant in an embroidered gown of white silk with a long veil trailing behind her. It had been magical, beautiful but it wasn't the beauty of the service itself that had made her so teary eyed, though it certainly had rendered others so. It had been the sparkle she'd seen in Charlotte's eyes.

She'd prayed for Charlotte to find the love she deserved and it seemed, very much, as though she had. By all rights, Mr. Atherton seemed to adore her. Perhaps he was a bit bookish with his spectacles, and perhaps he didn't cut quite the dashing figure that some gentlemen did, but Charlotte appeared to be blissfully happy and that was all that mattered.

As the service ended and the happy couple made their exit, Caleb noted quietly, "She appears very happy indeed."

"She does, indeed."

"Will you tell her?" Caleb asked.

Marina shook her head. "Not today... This is her day, after all. There will be time enough when she has returned from her honeymoon to share our happy news with her."

While she couldn't say exactly when their child would be born, she imagined it would be sometime in the summer, possibly late June or early July. And she would be counting down every single day until she would finally get to meet the child she knew would be a son. With Caleb's dark hair and the slight cleft in his chin.

"Girl," he said, as if reading her thoughts. "It will be a girl."

"How can you possibly be so sure? I'm the one carrying this child," she whispered softly. "Surely, I would have greater insight into that!"

He shrugged. "I just know. It will be a girl."

"It will be a boy," she insisted. "And when he is grown to manhood, he will marry the daughter that I know Charlotte will have in the next year or so. We've planned it that way since we were children!"

"The best-laid schemes o' mice an' men gang aft agley," Caleb quoted with a wicked grin.

Marina was stopped from replying as they had reached Charlotte and Mr. Atherton. With quick hugs and hasty congratulations, they made their way outside to gather with the other guests. A small silk bag filled with rice was pressed into her hand and Marina gleefully joined in showering the happy couple with it as they finally exited the church.

"You should have had a wedding like this," Caleb noted.

"I did," she said. "It simply wasn't our wedding."

He laughed at that. "Yes, but you didn't get married that day."

"And thank heaven for it. Otherwise, my dear husband, I never would have met you... and fallen hopelessly, head over heels in love with you."

Heedless of the crowd, he pressed a kiss to her lips. "All the scheming of others was well worth it for the sake of having you by my side... Now, let's make our appearance at the wedding breakfast and then go home."

"I'm not tired. The journey was not that taxing," she protested.

"Good. Because I have no inclination of letting you rest... I have other plans for you, Lady St. Aiden."

Marina sighed. "Would it be terrible if I said we should skip the wedding breakfast entirely and just go home? Charlotte, being a newly married woman herself, will no doubt understand."

"How very wicked you are!"

"Does that mean we must go?"

Caleb leveled a very heated stare in her direction. "I never said that. I simply said you were wicked... something I absolutely adore about you. But then I adore everything about you, don't I?"

He did. Adored. Cherished. Treasured. Not a day went by with him that she did not feel all these things from him and more. And she hoped that he felt them in turn, because she loved him more than she ever dreamed would be possible. "I love you. And I have no regrets about our marriage... not the marriage itself or the wedding that initiated it."

He lifted her hand and pressed a kiss there, just above the wedding ring he had placed there just over a year ago. "I would say it was the best day of my life... the day I married you. But every day that I spend with you is better than the last. I love you. I could say it a thousand times a day, and it would never fully express how much."

And at that, Marina's eyes began to tear up again. But once more, they were the happiest of tears.

The End

About the Author

Chasity Bowlin lives in central Kentucky with her husband and their menagerie of animals. She loves writing, loves traveling and enjoys incorporating tidbits of her actual vacations into her books. She is an avid Anglophile, loving all things British, but specifically all things Regency.

Growing up in Tennessee, spending as much time as possible with her doting grandparents, soap operas were a part of her daily existence, followed by back to back episodes of Scooby Doo. Her path to becoming a romance novelist was set when, rather than simply have her Barbie dolls cruise around in a pink convertible, they time traveled, hosted lavish dinner parties and one even had an evil twin locked in the attic.

Website: www.chasitybowlin.com

www.ingramcontent.com/pod-product-compliance
Lightning Source LLC
Chambersburg PA
CBHW060353310726
48976CB00003B/809